Praise for Michael Moorcock

MOTHER LONDON

'His is the grand, messy flux itself, in all its
unquenchable optimism. For Moorcock's Lond...
more magical than the real fabric of the city they love and ...
which it echoes' Angela Carter
**GUARDIAN**

'The towpaths, pubs, bombed churches and neglected marble angels.
Moorcock's descriptions of London are those of somebody who has
walked, looked and brooded on ways to make the obvious refreshingly
new'
**SUNDAY TIMES**

'From the material devastation of the Blitz to the moral devastation of the
present. It is rich, entertaining and anarchic'
**THE TIMES**

'Mother London is built solidly, confidently and on a generous scale. Its
richly depressed carnival atmosphere is reminiscent of Dickens ...
exhilarating and disturbing'
**OBSERVER**

KING OF THE CITY

'A great English novelist. King of the City is at once splenetic and hilarious
. . . yet affectionate about the many different, vital worlds of London and
its denizens'
**INDEPENDENT**

'The novel's energy is tremendous, the plot Victorian in its scope and
confidence'
**LITERARY REVIEW**

'Dazzlingly esoteric cultural rumpus'
**SPECTATOR**

'One unstoppable, spellbinding, brilliant voice'
**TLS**

'A blast of energy and pleasure'
**DAILY TELEGRAPH**

# London Bone

## Michael Moorcock

Scribner

First published in Great Britain by Scribner, 2001
An imprint of Simon & Schuster UK Ltd
A Viacom Company

1 3 5 7 9 10 8 6 4 2

Simon & Schuster UK Ltd
Africa House
64–78 Kingsway
London WC2B 6AH

Simon & Schuster Australia
Sydney

A CIP catalogue record for this book is available from the British Library

ISBN 0-684-86142-9

Typeset by SX Composing DTP, Rayleigh, Essex
Printed and bound in Great Britain by Bath Press, Bath

*For my Mother,*
*in loving memory*

# CONTENTS

# A WINTER ADMIRAL

After lunch she woke up, thinking the rustling from the pantry must be a foraging mouse brought out of hibernation by the unusual warmth. She smiled. She never minded a mouse or two for company and she had secured anything she would not want them to touch.

No, she really didn't mind the mice at all. Their forebears had been in these parts longer than hers and had quite as much right to the territory. More of them, after all, had bled and died for home and hearth. They had earned their tranquillity. Her London cats were perfectly happy to enjoy a life of peaceful coexistence.

"We're a family." She yawned and stretched. "We probably smell pretty much the same by now." She took up the brass poker and opened the fire door of the stove. "One big happy family, us and the mice and the spiders."

After a few moments the noise from the pantry

stopped. She was surprised it did not resume. She poked down the burning logs, added two more from her little pile, closed the door and adjusted the vents. That would keep in nicely.

As she leaned back in her chair she heard the sound again. She got up slowly to lift the latch and peer in. Through the outside pantry window, sunlight laced the bars of dust and brightened her shelves. She looked on the floor for droppings. Amongst her cat-litter bags, her indoor gardening tools, her electrical bits and pieces, there was nothing eaten and no sign of a mouse.

Today it was even warm in the pantry. She checked a couple of jars of pickles. It didn't do for them to heat up. They seemed all right. This particular pantry had mostly canned things. She only ever needed to shop once a week.

She closed the door again. She was vaguely ill at ease. She hated anything odd going on in her house. Sometimes she lost perspective. The best way to get rid of the feeling was to take a walk. Since the sun was so bright today, she would put on her coat and stroll up the lane for a bit.

It was one of those pleasant February days that deceives you into believing spring has arrived. *A cruel promise, really*, she thought. This weather would be gone soon enough. *Make the best of it*, she said to herself. She would leave the radio playing, put a light on in case it grew dark before she was back, and promise herself *The Charlie Chester Show*, a cup of tea and a scone when she got home. She lifted the heavy iron kettle, another part of her inheritance, and put it on the hob. She set her big, brown teapot on the brass trivet.

The scent of lavender struck her as she opened her coat cupboard. She had just relined the shelves and drawers. Lavender reminded her of her first childhood home.

"We're a long way from Mitcham now," she told the cats as she took her tweed overcoat off the hanger. Her Aunt Becky had lived here until her last months in the nursing home. Becky had inherited Crow Cottage from the famous Great-Aunt Begg. As far as Marjorie Begg could tell, the place had been inhabited by generations of retired single ladies, almost in trust, for centuries.

Mrs Begg would leave Crow Cottage to her own niece, Clare, who looked after Jessie, her half-sister. A chronic invalid, Jessie must soon die, she was so full of rancour.

A story in a Cotswold book said this had once been known as Crone's Cottage. She was amused by the idea of ending her days as the local crone. She would have to learn to cackle. The crone was a recognized figure in any English rural community, after all. She wondered if it were merely coincidence that made Rab, the village idiot, her handyman. He worshipped her. She would do anything for him. He was like a bewildered child since his wife had thrown him out: she could make more in benefits than he made in wages. He had seemed reconciled to the injustice: "I was never much of an earner." That apologetic grin was his response to most disappointment. It probably hadn't been fitting for a village idiot to be married, any more than a crone. Yet who had washed and embroidered the idiot's smocks in the old days?

She had been told Rab had lost his digs and was living wild in Wilson's abandoned farm buildings on the other side of the wood.

Before she opened her front door she thought she heard the rustling again. The sound was familiar, but not mice. Some folded cellophane unravelling as the cupboard warmed up? The cottage had never been cosier.

She closed the door behind her, walking up the stone path under her brown tangle of honeysuckle and through the gate to the rough farm lane. Between the tall, woven hedges she kept out of the shade as much as she could. She relished the air, the winter scents, the busy finches, sparrows, tits and yellowhammers. A chattering robin objected to her passing and a couple of wrens fussed at her. She clicked her tongue, imitating their angry little voices. The broad meadows lay across the brow of the hills like shawls, their dark-brown furrows laced with melting frost, bright as crystal. Birds flocked everywhere, to celebrate this unexpected ease in the winter's grey.

Her favourites were the crows and magpies. Such old, alien birds. So wise. Closer to the dinosaurs and inheriting an unfathomable memory. Was that why people took against them? She had learned early that intelligence was no better admired in a bird than in a woman.

The thought of her father made her shudder, even out here on this wide, unthreatening Cotswold hillside, and she felt suddenly lost, helpless, the cottage no longer her home. Even the steeple on the village church, rising beyond the elms, seemed completely inaccessible. She hated the fear more than she hated the man who had infected her with it – as thoroughly as if he had infected her with a disease. She blamed herself. What good was hatred? He had died wretchedly, of exposure, in

Hammersmith, between his pub and his flat, a few
hundred yards away.

Crow Cottage, with its slender evergreens and lattice
of willow boughs, was as safe and welcoming as always
when she turned back into her lane. As the sun fell it
was growing colder, but she paused for a moment. The
cottage, with its thatch and its chimney, its walls and its
hedges, was a picture. She loved it. It welcomed her –
even now, with so little colour in the garden.

She returned slowly, enjoying the day, and stepped
back over her hearth, into her dream of security, her
stove and her cats and her rattling kettle. She was in
good time for *Sing Something Simple* and would be
eating her scones by the time Charlie Chester came on.
She had never felt the need for a television here, though
she had been a slave to it in Streatham. Jack had liked
his sport.

He had been doing his pools when he died.

When she came back to the flat that night, Jack was
in the hall, stretched out with his head on his arm. She
knew he was dead, but she gave him what she hoped
was the kiss of life, repeatedly blowing her warm breath
through his cold lips until she got up to phone for the
ambulance. She kept kissing him, kept pouring her
breath into him, but was weeping almost uncontrollably
when they arrived.

He wouldn't have known anything, love, they con-
soled her.

No consolation at all to Jack! He had hated not
knowing things.

She had never anticipated the anguish that came with
the loss of him, which had lasted until she moved to
Crow Cottage. She had written to Clare. By some

miracle, the cottage had cured her of her painful grief and brought unexpected reconciliation.

It was almost dark.

Against the sprawling black branches of the old elms, the starlings curled in ranks towards the horizon, while out of sight in the tall wood the crows began to call, bird to bird, family to family. The setting sun had given the few clouds a powdering of terracotta and the air was suddenly a Mediterranean blue behind them. Everything was so vivid and hurrying so fast, as if to greet the end of the world.

She went to draw the back curtains and saw the sunset over the flooded fields fifteen miles away, spreading its bloody light into the water. She almost gasped at the sudden beauty of it.

Then she heard the rustling again. Before the light failed altogether, she was determined to discover the cause. It would be awful to start getting fancies after dark.

As she unlatched the pantry door something rose from the floor and settled against the window. She shivered, but did not retreat.

She looked carefully. Then, to her surprise: "Oh, it's a butterfly!"

The butterfly began to beat again upon the window. She reached to cup it in her hands, to calm it. "Poor thing."

It was a newborn Red Admiral, its orange, red and black markings vibrant as summer. "Poor thing." It had no others of its kind.

For a few seconds the butterfly continued to flutter, and then was still. She widened her hands to look in.

She watched its perfect, questing antennae, its extra-ordinary legs, she could almost smell it. *A small miracle*, she thought, *to make a glorious day complete.*

An unexpected sadness filled her as she stared at the butterfly. She carried it to the door, pushed the latch with her cupped hands, and walked into the twilight. When she reached the gate she opened her hands again, gently, to relish the vivacious delicacy of the creature. Mrs Begg sighed, and with a sudden, graceful movement lifted her open palms to let the Admiral taste the air.

In two or three wing-beats the butterfly was up, a spot of busy, brilliant colour streaming towards the east and the cold horizon.

As it gained height, it veered, its wings courageous against the freshening wind.

Shielding her eyes, Mrs Begg watched the Admiral turn and fly over the thatch, to be absorbed in the setting sun.

It was far too cold now to be standing there. She went inside and shut the door. The cats still slept in front of the stove. With the pot-holder she picked up the kettle, pouring lively water over the tea. Then she went to close her pantry door.

"I really couldn't bear it," she said. "I couldn't bear to watch it die."

# LONDON BLOOD

There are certain memories that never really reach your brain. They stay in your blood like a dormant virus. Then something triggers them and you don't remember the moment; instead, you relive every detail. It's the reliving, not the original experience, that your brain registers. I think this happens to you more as you get older. And you don't always welcome it, either, however ordinary. Last week I was just looking out of the window and suddenly I was back at Gloria's funeral, with all the family there and Mum still alive. It's when it stays on as a memory that it hurts. Nine of us survived childhood out of thirteen. Three boys and six girls. Little Jimmy, named after Dad, Freddy, Ellie, Sammy, Nora, Lilly, Nellie, me and Gloria. Everyone but Mum and Gloria is still with us. We're a bit too crotchety to travel much; but we stay in touch on the phone.

I had a flashback the other day of what we called Mum's grieving chair. It was a funny name for such a big, comfortable bit of furniture, but usually she only sat there when somebody had died. An old-fashioned Victorian easy with dark flower patterns and enclosing wings. You could divide a chair like that into flats, these days. Of course, there'd be nowhere to put it in a place this size. The chair survived the Blitz but not the Fifties. Mum's buildings were knocked down as part of the Battersea project and we sold everything to a dealer. Ellie, who was staying at Mum's then, didn't want it. She was moving to Australia to live with her son.

Gloria died of cancer in Bournemouth within a year of her husband. It was a real shock. We'd never had anyone with cancer before. It was just before Mum moved to Lilly's, so it was probably the last time she used her chair.

We were all sorry Ellie missed the Coronation and the Festival of Britain. Mum visited the South Bank eventually, though she blamed it for knocking down her flats. She really enjoyed herself when she got there, especially at the funfair. Outside the Skylon she helped an old man. He'd collapsed with heatstroke and she looked after him till the St John's Ambulance Brigade turned up. She took care of everything. She did all the right things. They said she probably saved his life. We couldn't help feeling proud of her, even though we were a bit embarrassed by all the attention. And then, of course, it was too late to do anything else. We never did get to the Dome of Discovery.

Lilly's kids adored Mum. She was a perfect grandma. She couldn't have done better than Lilly who was married to a GP. They made her a lovely little flat of her own in their really posh old house looking out over the common. But she still missed her chair.

It's one of my first memories, that chair. I couldn't have been more than six, 1924 at the latest, when our little Gus went down with TB. After Gus's final illness, when all the funeral arrangements had been made and the rest of the formalities were over, Mum sat in that chair for five days. Hardly spoke a word. Most of us were still at home. We knew what to expect. We were all old enough by then to look after ourselves.

Of course, she didn't sit for five days solid. She ate a bit and slept a bit and so on. She was very sweet to us when we had to speak. But distant. She sat there nights, too, with her favourite cat on her lap.

Tizer was a massive green-eyed African orange brindle Mr Simpson the missionary gave Mum when he had to go into Sunnydales. Tizer loved her as much as she loved him. He'd mope when she was away and he'd shake with a deep vibrant purr whenever she came back. He was the boss cat but he had a kind, dignified nature.

Half our cats were from other homes, not always with their owners' knowledge. Mum would send us out to find them; then she'd pick the best and make us put the others back. It was the only crime she'd condone. Of course, she didn't see it as crime. She knew she could look after cats better than anyone. She could double their lifespans. She understood them. Everything about them. She'd always talk to them in her ordinary voice and you had the feeling they answered back the same. She could tell you if a cat was going to get sick or leave or pine. And she wouldn't have it she was psychic.

Another ordinary memory. A family story, really.

One frosty Boxing Day we were out on Tooting Common with Sammy's new roller skates and we found this skinny dog we took home. Mum was horrified. "Look at his poor ribcage!" She offered him a huge plate of goose and chicken scraps. He wolfed them down, grinning and wagging and panting for more. So, while Tizer twitched his tail in outrage, she gave the dog seconds. Eventually the owner was found and arrived glad to see his dog again, if a bit glum.

Mum was relieved. He seemed a decent sort of bloke. The animal clearly liked him. "He was so hungry when he got here." Looking fondly down at the contented dog, Mum folded her arms in a gesture of self-satisfaction. Mum was tall, with a nose that could cut concrete, thick raven hair and blue X-ray eyes. People didn't often argue with her. "He must have been lost for days. I bet you're glad to have him back. You keep him well. Greyhound, is he?

"Yes," the man replied sadly. "He was due to run at Summerstown this afternoon. We rather fancied he'd win."

Mum didn't say anything then but after she closed the door on him she said she thought it was wicked to starve animals for sport. Let the skinny little bugger have a good sleep instead. It was Christmas, wasn't it? Nobody should have to work over Christmas. She offered me a secret wink. God, I loved my mum.

She could pick horses, too, even though she had a feeling steeple-chasing might be cruel. When she got the chance she'd have a couple of bob each way on the National and she'd always win. She'd never put too much on, and she never told Dad. I often took her bets to Mr Phelps in the greengrocers, there being no betting

11

shops in those days. He was what they used to call a bookie's runner. But only a couple of bob. Always each way. She felt it would break her luck otherwise. Dad used to try to get her to pick a name off his card, but she wouldn't.

Mum's room was the long narrow one at the back. It was the noisiest but that didn't matter too much to her since she was going a bit deaf and she had the wireless by then. She'd made the room her own after Jim married. Nellie, Gloria and me all got her big bedroom to share. Me and Nellie were best friends. We loved it. But Gloria thought we were horrible tomboys and kept her little bed neatly to herself in the corner. Nellie got prissy like that. Lives in Hove. Won't relax and have a laugh. All health food and perms, these days. Disapproves when I have a gin.

People thought we were Irish because we had red hair and green eyes like Nellie or black hair and blue eyes, like me. They always described us as vivacious or full of life. They'd have called us slappers if we'd been ugly. But we were the famous Lee girls. We were never short of mashers. And Mum saw to it we didn't fall in love with anyone unsuitable. My first husband was a civil engineer. More engineer than civil, I must say. While I was entertaining the troops, he was entertaining the girls they'd left behind.

After our Gus died I was the youngest but one. I was born at Stone Cottages, Mitcham, when there was a village green and one pump, and the tram link with Streatham went across lavender fields. That was at the end of the first German war. But I was brought up in Tooting, which we thought of as proper South London. You could take the tram direct to Vauxhall.

Ours was a big flat. We had the first and second floors above a furniture showroom. Their warehouse was over in Figges Marsh, so most of the flat was never too noisy. We were at the pointed end of a parade of shops, handy for the market. Our building was wedge-shaped because it was on the corner where the trams turned down towards Mitcham Cricketers. "The prow", Dad called it. "Ahoy, ahoy, I'm captain of the clipper," he'd sing when in a good mood. Then Mum would tell him off when he mumbled the rest of the words and he'd laugh that infectious, dirty laugh of his. He drew you in to stuff like that, even if you didn't like it much.

When I lay in bed I could see the spider web of tram-lines reflecting the light of the shops sparkling through our net curtains. I thought those lines were roads through fairyland. On the whole we weren't very imaginative as a family. Probably that's why almost everyone but me went into politics. I used to lie there, hearing Mum and Dad in hissing argument. I'd actually teach myself to go somewhere else – into a fantasy so vivid I almost remembered it as real. I kept it all to myself, even from Nellie. Dad would have laughed himself silly if he'd have guessed. Especially if he'd had a few of his "noggins".

Even early on Mum would sometimes lock Dad out until his pleading and oaths threatened to involve the neighbours. Then she'd let him back in on promises to stop drinking and playing the horses. He'd cheer up for a few days and stay around the house. "Bai Jove, bai jove," he'd sing, "Our Jimmy's a jolly old cove!" But sooner or later the kids would drive him out to the pub or the racecourse. He complained she didn't discipline us.

13

Mum kept us in order all right. I don't remember her ever raising her hand. And when she was grieving you didn't feel you had to behave any differently. You only heard her going to the lavatory or having a wash, but you were always aware of her, there in her room, sitting in her chair. Doing nothing but staring and thinking. I think it was her way of praying. And the respect we automatically gave her was our way of joining in.

She wasn't a religious woman. Though she'd been a suffragette her hero was still Lloyd George, whom she saw as the people's prime minister. She believed fiercely – and fierce was the word if she heard you putting down some underdog – in equality, liberty and all that other stuff. With a couple of exceptions, she bred a family of men and women who could stand rock-solid on their own feet and look anyone in the eye as an equal. But natural arguers. We had the lot, from Tories to Trots.

Tooting's changed since our day, naturally, because of the bombing. What you see now that isn't concrete is a collection of ancient and modern: the old blood-red brick of South London or that new hard-fired pale brick which they used so much in the Fifties, when they thought it looked clean and contemporary. There's no warmth to it, except what you can write with a spray-can. The people who painted messages on walls in my day were communists and fascists. This new stuff's prettier and wittier.

We're now in our nineties, except for Ellie and Nora who are 104 and 105 respectively. That's London blood for you. You can't find a gene pool like that any more. Antibiotics is what I blame. Wiping out the cheap and natural and replacing it with the pricey and artificial. You see it everywhere, don't you? The only time you looked for bottled water when I was a kid was when there was a cholera scare. And a scare was all it was.

I've had two penicillin shots in my life and benefited from both of them. And apart from the junior aspirin I take every day, that's all I've ever needed or wanted. I've got kids, grandkids and great-grand-kids and we're all the same in the main: healthy as horses. Four of them are actors now, all doing well. Better than me. I still do some radio stuff and get good offers, and I'm in that new red-grapefruit commercial. Apart from the home help once a week I'm as completely self-sufficient as ever. At this rate our family will survive a nuclear holocaust. It's survived most other kinds.

Anyone the gypsies admired they'd say had gypsy blood. It was their way of praising you. My mother used to say that you had to give *yourself* deep roots. If you didn't know what your original roots were, if they were lost somehow, you made up a set of rules and a history to go with them. Find them in a book. A novel. Anything. The best you could be. The best your people could have been. People you admired. You invented your ancestors if you didn't have any. And those were the roots you kept alive and they kept you alive. It was nothing to do with staying in the same place, she said, though that helped. It was to do with being the same, whatever else changed. Listening to your blood, Mum called it. Being yourself and as good as you could be. It sounded like gypsy lore to us, so we took it seriously. You stuck to your word for your own sake, she said. You didn't let anyone tell your story for you. You trusted yourself because your private behaviour matched your public conversation. She told us never to lie knowingly, except sometimes to authority, and

15

never to give too much away either. Sometimes a little
white lie was all right because it wasn't so much the lie
in that case as who you told it to.

By the time Jim came back from the War, Mum had
four lots of money coming in. Jim's, Freddy's, Ellie's
and Sammy's. Ellie was a bookkeeper at the Home and
Colonial. The boys went into the civil service and all
did very well. The Depression was looming. They kept
jobs that were certain and steady and unaffected by lay-
offs and bankruptcies. They could give Mum money
regularly. And she was still manageress at the Sunlight
Laundry.

For a while she must have taken over Dad's money,
too, when he earned at all. He was a master tailor, but
he couldn't hold a job. She'd told him enough times
about his drinking and gambling. You could say she
waited until she was no longer in any way financially
dependent on him before exerting her power. The boys
were leaving home, getting married, and she'd come to
rely on them. She was probably a bit scared of what
might happen. Though my brothers all worshipped her,
they knew she wouldn't have wanted them to stay.
They had their own lives.

She worked late on Mondays and sometimes Fridays
to pay for her pleasures. She liked the pictures but
would never go in seats any more expensive than the
one-and-threes. She also went to the music hall once a
month, in the evening. She complained about the new
acts but loved Max Miller, of all people. She thought it
was narrow-minded of the BBC to keep banning him.
She'd always insisted on her nights out. Which meant
sometimes only Dad was home when we got back from
school.

Dad said I was his favourite, and I think it was true.
I couldn't easily resist his crooked charm any more than
Mum had been able to. He could make me squirm, half
embarrassed, half delighted. Like her I was a bit unsure
of him. There was something aggressive and needy
under the jokes. He said I was the only one who understood him. I knew he wasn't really misunderstood. I'd
noticed the difference betweeen him and ordinary
people. And when he was away life became more
secure, more predictable. The house cheered up quietly.

Mum never seemed to miss him. To be honest, I
missed his attention, the flattery. I knew he was a
drunkard, a gambler and a conman, and nasty sometimes, too. As Mum grimly said to me around the time
Gloria died, it wasn't his charm that gave her thirteen
kids.

When they were courting, my dad promised her the
earth. Jimmy Lee was considered a catch. He was
finishing his tailoring apprenticeship. Nothing safer
than the rag trade, he said. He'd told her he was well
connected. Marks and Spencer's, I think. Of course, all
he was really attached to was the track and the saloon
bar.

Dad had inherited half a gent's outfitters in
Streatham Hill. The family he sold it to kept the name.
You could see it for years. *Lee and Green, Bespoke
Tailor*. Green was his cousin who went to America. My
brother Jimmy, who wound up in the Foreign Office,
met him out there.

Mum saved what she could from the sale. She had
three boys to educate into good jobs and six girls who
had to be properly schooled so as to be married to
professional men. That was six weddings just there.

17

And six dowries. She hid the money from Dad, of course. He never knew, as he worried how to pay his bookie, that he was sleeping over a chest of sovereigns.

There's a story how later, when Dad had gone and Nellie was thinking of getting married, there was some dispute between the families. Someone had suggested Nellie was marrying for money. Mum dragged her box out and showed it to the intended in-laws to prove we weren't poor just because we didn't live in a road with trees. "That's my Jewish side," she said. "Romany, too, I suppose."

Mum had an insurance policy to pay for her funeral, small endowments for us when we were twenty-one, but nothing else. She nurtured a deep suspicion of 'paper promises'. She and her family had been through what they called the Great Depression which had lasted well into the 1890s. When she'd met my dad she was reluctantly going into service.

She was too much of an egalitarian to show respect for authority just for the sake of it, and she defied respectability, too. From the first year she was married, she regularly took the tram up to the Corinthians in New Jewry. Mostly to see Marie Lloyd, whom she adored. She always went on her own. I suspect she reckoned it wasn't right to bring kids. They had a Ladies Only bar by then. And she'd always have a pint of Guinness in the course of the evening, coming home a little jolly. Otherwise she generally drank half a pint, but no more, at suppertime. To keep up her strength, she said.

We ate well. Most of our stuff was home-made. Mum was a dedicated putter-up of pickles, pies and preserves. She had routines. We always knew when the times came round for beetroot jars or salt beef or apple butter or plum puddings. And we had a huge pantry, which she tended to keep locked, to stop us pinching the pickles and crystallized fruit. She refused to use the butcher two doors down because she'd seen rats in their yard. The same went for the baker's. She wouldn't accept that most yards had rats. Ours didn't, she said, because she kept enough cats.

Really she just had a passion for moggies. When Tizer died of kidney failure, she sat in her chair with him in her lap for over twenty-four hours, then took him to the pet cemetery at Streatham and had him buried. It wasn't cheap. His stone said *TIZER: Born Nairobi, 1909. Died Tooting, 1930.* You can go and see it. It's still there, if it hasn't been vandalized. He was a wonderful old cat, that Tizer.

One day I came home and Dad was sitting in Mum's room, on his own, drunk. It was probably Monday. Everyone else was out doing something, including Nellie who was round at Aunty Rachel's getting her piano lesson. The worst thing was, he was sitting in Mum's grieving chair.

"And how's my little princess?" he said. He knew he shouldn't be in that chair. I was alarmed, but fascinated by his effrontery, what might be his courage. He told me to come and give my old dad a peck on the cheek. Then he sat me up on his knee and bounced me and kissed me and I was a bit startled, because I was too old for it and he'd never done it much before. I wanted to go to the lavatory. I was praying I wouldn't pee on his leg. Then Mum bustled into the hall with Nellie, shouting for me, saw him and he turned very funny. Very placatory. Put me down with his hands round my waist. It hurt. I stood there for a moment in the silence.

Then I was sent out with Nellie to get some butter Mum had forgotten.

Next day Dad was gone for good. Almost without trace. I don't think it had anything to do with me. I knew he'd overstepped the mark at last, sitting in her special chair. She had the locks changed right away. I heard her talking to her sister, who had come up from Brighton. "I sometimes think I prefer the company of the dead," she said. "It's the peace. They stop struggling." I didn't understand her. I probably heard wrong. But she'd sat out her share of death, one way or another.

Not many remember the big tram crash of 1929, partly because of the City news. The tram came off the rails on the corner and almost smashed through our front windows. It was a terrible accident. Mum had been on her way home. She was one of the first there. She helped a dozen people until the ambulances started turning up. This old lady died in her arms, blood running down her head. Mum said she couldn't get the stench of death out of her nostrils for months, though Freddy said it was probably the butcher's she was smelling.

Mum wouldn't let us come near. There were two dead little boys whose heads had been crushed. Twins. Nobody in Tooting saw worse in the war. It was pretty gruesome. Sammy told me the details later. It made me queasy. I nearly passed out. I've always had a weak stomach. I can't watch the news. I won't let people tell me things like that any more. Why fill your head with horror you can't do anything about? You just worry all the time. Mum sat through her personal storms in her chair, I suppose. I'd need a drink at that point. But

Mum didn't drink, except for her usual Guinness. Nora said Dad had done enough boozing for all of us.

I was the only one who occasionally missed Dad. Mum joked that I was always flirting, but I don't think I really was. I just didn't like to offend anyone. Everyone said I was highly strung. It wasn't attention I needed, it was approval, security to be left alone. So I don't think I loved him. I just trusted him in a way. It was as if I could make a deal with him. I've tried to explain it in the past. As if I could buy privacy by giving in to him for a little while. He wanted to know the old smile worked for him. I wanted to be daydreaming in my own world. But the reality was nasty.

When Dad left we were all upset. Mum told us under no circumstances to let him in if he came round to the flat. And he did come round. Usually in the evening when he'd had a few. She instructed us not to answer the door and went into her room. Can you imagine? Not answering the door to your own dad? But Mum wouldn't have it different, and we cared a lot more for her approval than his.

Do you know how hard it is to disobey your dad? Particularly back in those days. I remember shivering on the other side of the big, curtained door and crying. "I can't, Dad. I can't. Don't, Dad. Don't." I didn't dare shout at him to go away and leave me in peace.

"Come on, darling, open it for me. It's just your daddy."

My stomach turned over and I continued to cry silently as he cajoled me through the letter box. "Come on, princess. Come on, little 'un." I used to dread it and would try to be somewhere else in the house at any time he was likely to arrive, just so I wouldn't have to say no

21

to him. Mum would let Nellie off, but I was part of her anti-Dad guard. I never blamed her. I was always on her side. But I just hated doing it.

I was congratulating myself that I'd got avoiding him down to a fine art when I came out of school one day after gym, and there he was, all glittering false teeth and cosmetic dash. He was wearing that cream suit of his with a straw hat. His new moustache gave him a bit of a Ronald Colman look from a distance. He said he was passing and did I mind if he joined me on the tram home. What could I say? Apart from his face, which close up was a map of Mars, he looked dapper and genial as ever. He always wore a fresh pink rosebud in his lapel. On Armistice Day he wore a poppy. "Call me old-fashioned," he'd say, "but I'm a bit of a patriot."

When the tram came Dad bowed me aboard like a lady. He knew the tram conductor by name. He paid my fare. I was already in profit. He made a friendly enquiry about the conductor's wife. I loved those trams, rattling, bouncing, sparking and swaying, with their scarlet and brass, their reversible wooden seats varnished almost orange. There was always a chance they'd go somewhere new. When the tram reached the terminus you ran along the grooved wooden floors, thumping the seats back on their big oiled brass hinges. All the metal was worn and golden, and everything had that strange metallic smell of electricity.

I got off at the usual stop and he went on. And that was all. Of course, he told me not to tell Mum, but that suited me. I'd rather have felt a bit guilty and still been able to see them both. I cheered up. He started taking the tram with me a couple of times a week.

Once he bought me a quarter of toffees, which I had

to stuff down before I got home. Then I couldn't eat my
tea and was sick, and Mum was cautious and let me
have the next morning off. Dad had that way of "not
wanting to worry people" with too much information.
Soon he'd meet me almost every day. I had to make up
delayed trams and late chats with teachers at school to
explain the odd half-hour. Once or twice Mum noticed
chocolate on me, and I said another kid had given me
some. I remember telling my first conscious lie to her
and how easy it was and how she believed me and there
were no consequences. It worked. Life became easier.

One Monday Dad said he was going to show me
where he lived. Would I like that? I was really curious.
It might put the picture together for me, I thought.
Maybe explain why he'd left. He said he'd have me
home in an hour, long before Mum got back. My knees
were knocking, but I felt excited, too. I'd know something even Mum didn't know about him.

So we stayed on the tram for another two stops and
got off at Mitcham Road. His road was called Undine
Street and he was about halfway down on the left. A
nice road, I thought, with trees in it. I was impressed
when we went into a proper garden but then wondered
why we had to go up so many stairs to the top of the
house. "My little hideaway," Dad laughed. "Bai Jove,
bai Jove, Ai'm a comical cove!"

I think it was what they used to call a bed-dinette. All
one room, with a kitchen area curtained off. It had a
cold feel and stank of grease, tobacco and beer. There
was a big wardrobe, a single bed covered with a green
silk counterpane, a table and chair and an old horsehair
sofa. A bit of faded carpet on cracked lino. Mum
wouldn't have tolerated it. She set high store by appear-

ances. Sporting papers and race cards were everywhere. And empty bottles. I didn't want to stay, but he said I'd hurt his feelings if I didn't accept his hospitality. So I sat on the edge of his bed and drank some tea I didn't like and ate a piece of stale buttered bun that looked as if he'd brought it home from a Lyons tea shop in his pocket.

Dad was in a very sentimental mood. I knew from the familiar smell that his cup didn't have tea in it. That smell made me feel sick, and it was so close and nasty in there. I got a headache. I think I must have fainted. My weak stomach was always my worst enemy. I probably threw up. The next thing is I'm going out his door and I'm in Garratt Lane, still feeling weak, while he tells me I need some fresh air. Maybe a glass of lemonade? I say I want Mum. He thinks there must be a gas-leak in his room. "Just say I met you from school," he keeps telling me. "Say you were sick before I saw you."

I remember him delivering me back home and Mum not talking much to him. He didn't seem to want to come in.

I'm not sure what she said, because she went out onto the landing to say it, but I never saw him at my school or on the tram again. I think I caught a glimpse of him once or twice in the street. I waved but he never said hello.

The next day there was a funny question about my clothes. Mum'd found a spot of blood and wanted to know if I'd been scratching myself. I couldn't remember, I said. I really couldn't. She started asking more questions. And then I lied. I don't know why. I said, oh, yes, I'd been climbing a tree. I'd put some iodine on a graze. But this time Mum didn't seem reassured. I said

I had to go to the toilet. I used a pin to scrape my leg in case she wanted to see it. But I never really knew why she'd mentioned the blood.

Funnily enough, Mum sat in her chair for a day or two after that, even though nobody was dead. It was more like she was thinking, as well as praying. Something about Dad, maybe? She was nice to me, so it couldn't have been about the lies. Later she talked to me a bit. How telling the truth sometimes was harder than not. And the difference between pretending and deceiving. For instance, she said, Dad didn't know the difference between a game and reality. It meant nothing much to me, although it probably helped me get the idea of going into the theatre.

By then I'd started reading those *Playgoer* magazines Lilly gave me, and it was dreamland for years and years. I got in with a crowd Nellie knew. They did local theatricals and things. I told them all sorts of stuff and they believed me. I told them I'd been schooled by nuns in Portugal. That my father was an exiled Spanish count. I fell out with Nellie for a while, because she wouldn't back me up. It was only for fun. Just white lies. They didn't do anyone any harm.

I was married and twenty when I got my first real job in Dicky Diamond's Pierrots. At first Mum wasn't sure about it, but she spoke to Dicky himself who offered all sorts of guarantees and contracts. No mixed accommodation or facilities, I heard him tell her. Entertainers were in demand. It paid to stay wholesome. I'd hear him say that a few times in the coming years. Les was all right about it, too. Of course, I didn't know why. Then I got into films and was offered the Jessie Matthews parts she didn't want, because I looked quite a lot like her apparently, though I could only see it when dressers posed me in her style. I could dance like her, that sort of slinky stepping and kicking that went out when American dancing came in.

Like Jessie, I didn't have luck with men. I expected too much of them, I suppose. All I've wanted for years is my cats and my little garden. A comfortable easy chair. Something decent on the telly. I think it's really all Mum ever wanted, too. Most of my career, though, there was something in me that really craved a chap's approval, even when I was starring in the West End. Well, obviously that kind of approval's the easiest thing in the world to get. So you wind up never valuing it for long. Chaps aren't a lot different, are they?

We were touring the South Coast that wonderful summer of 1939 and I was still married to Les Andrews when I heard that Dad had died. It was a stroke, apparently. They found him on the steps of the Horse and Groom. We were finishing the season, so I was able to pop up from Worthing to see Mum and help with the arrangements. I stayed two or three nights in my old room. What surprised me was that while she was withdrawn and briskly sad, she never once sat in her chair. It was as if she was avoiding it.

After we buried him in Streatham Cemetery with the other Lees, Mum didn't want to go home. We were with her, all nine of us. Jimmy was over from Washington. Ellie came on the boat train from Paris, where she was living with an Italian count who couldn't get a divorce. Everyone else still lived nearby, then, in Norbury and Streatham. Sammy was furthest in West Kensington. We had a brief reception at Auntie Rachel's in Khartoum Road. Then Mum took us up to

Streatham Hill on the tram. Her treat, she said. We were going to the pictures. Not the old ABC or the State, but the new Astoria. These days they'd call it a luxury cinema. They charged top prices because the posh films were first shown there after they left the West End. Mum had a big white five-pound note. She paid for everything, including ice creams. It was like being kids again, only better. This time we sat in the half-crown seats, which were wonderful, almost like sitting at home. We watched *Dark Victory* with Bette Davis, George Brent and Humphrey Bogart.

Mum cried all the way through.

# DOVES IN THE CIRCLE

Situated between Church Street and Broadway, several blocks from Houston Street, just below Canal Street, *Houston Circle* is entered via Houston Alley from the North, and *Lispenard, Walker* and *Franklin* Streets from the West. The only approach from the South and East is via *Courtland Alley*. Houston Circle was known as *Indian Circle* or *South Green* until about 1820. It was populated predominantly by Irish, English and, later, Jewish people and today has a poor reputation. The circle itself, forming a green, now an open market, has some claims to antiquity. Aboriginal settlements have occupied the spot for about five hundred years and early travelers report finding non-indigenous standing stones, remarkably like those erected by the Ancient Britons. The *Kakatanawas*, whom early explorers first

encountered, spoke a distinctive Iroquois dialect and were of a high standard of civilisation. Captain Adriaen Block reported encountering the tribe in 1612. Their village was built around a stone circle 'whych is their *Kirke.*' When, under the Dutch, Fort Amsterdam was established nearby, there was no attempt to move the tribe which seems to have become so quickly absorbed into the dominant culture that it took no part in the bloody Indian War of 1643–5 and had completely disappeared by 1680. Although of considerable architectural and historical interest, because of its location and reputation Houston Circle has not attracted redevelopment and its buildings, some of which date from the 18th century, are in poor repair. Today the Circle is best known for 'The Three Sisters', which comprise the Catholic Church of *St Mary the Widow* (one of Huntingdon Begg's earliest commissions), the Greek Orthodox Church of *St Sophia* and the Orthodox Jewish Synagogue which stand side by side at the East end, close to *Doyle's Ale House,* built in 1780 and still in the same family. Next door to this is *Doyle's Hotel* (1879), whose tariff reflects its standards. Crossed by the Elevated Railway, which destroys the old village atmosphere, and generally neglected now, the Circle should be visited in daylight hours and in the company of other visitors. *Subway:* White Street IRT. *Elevated:* 6thAve.El. at Church Street, *Streetcar:* B&7thAve,B'way & Church.
NEW YORK: A TRAVELER'S GUIDE. R.P. Downes, Charles Kelly, London, 1924.

## 1.

If there is such a thing as unearned innocence, then America has it, said Barry Quinn mysteriously, lifting his straight glass to the flag and downing the last of Corny Doyle's passable porter. Oh, there you go again, says Corny, turning to a less contentious customer and grinning to show he saw several viewpoints. Brown as a tinker, he stood behind his glaring pumps in his white shirtsleeves, his skin glowing with the bar work, polishing up some silverware with all the habitual concentration of the rosary.

Everyone in the pub had an idea that Corny was out of sorts. They thought, perhaps, he would rather not have seen Father McQueeny there in his regular spot. These days the old priest carried an aura of desolation with him so that even when he joined a toast he seemed to address the dead. He had never been popular and his church had always chilled you but he had once enjoyed a certain authority in the parish. Now the Bishop had sent a new man down and McQueeny was evidently retired but wasn't admitting it. There'd always been more faith and Christian charity in Doyle's, Barry Quinn said, than could ever be found in that damned church. Apart from a few impenetrable writers in the architectural journals, no one had ever liked it. It was altogether too modern and Spanish-looking.

Sometimes, said Barry Quinn putting down his glass in the copper stand for a refill, there was so much goodwill in Doyle's Ale House he felt like he was taking his pleasure at the benign heart of the world. And who was to say that Houston Circle, with its profound history, the site of the oldest settlement on Manhattan, was not a centre of conscious grace and mystery like Camelot or Holy Island or Dublin, or possibly London? You could find all the inspiration you needed here. And you got an excellent confessional. Why freeze your bones talking to McQueeny in the box when you might as well talk to him over in that booth? Should you want to.

The fact was that nobody wanted anything at all to do with the old horror. There were a few funny rumours about him. Nobody was exactly sure what Father McQueeny had been caught doing, but it must have been bad enough for the Church to step in. And he'd had some sort of nasty secretive surgery. Mavis Byrne and her friends believed the Bishop made him have it. A popular rumour was that the Church had castrated him for diddling little boys. He would not answer if you asked him. He was rarely asked. Most of the time people tended to forget he was there. Sometimes they talked about him in his hearing. He never objected.

She's crossed the road now, look. Corny pointed through the big, gold-lettered green window of the pub to where his daughter walked purposefully between the wrought-iron gates of what was nowadays called Houston Park on the maps and Houston Green by the realtors.

She's walking up the path. Straight as an arrow. He was proud of her. Her character was so different from his own. She had all her mother's virtues. But he was more afraid of Kate than he had ever been of his absconded spouse.

Will you look at that? Father McQueeny's bloody eyes stared with cold reminiscence over the rim of his glass. She is about to ask Mr Terry a direct question.

He's bending an ear, says Barry Quinn, bothered by the priest's commentary, as if a fly interrupted him. He seems to be almost smiling. Look at her coaxing a bit of warmth out of that grim old mug. And at the same time she's getting the info she needs, like a bee taking pollen.

Father McQueeny runs his odd-coloured tongue around his lips and says, shrouded safe in his inaudibility, his invisibility: What a practical and down-to-earth little creature she is. She was always that. What a proper little madam, eh? She must have the truth, however dull. She will not allow us our speculations. She is going to ruin all our fancies!

His almost formless body undulates to the bar, settles over a stool and seems to coagulate on it. Without much hope of a quick response, he signals for a short and a pint. Unobserved by them, he consoles himself in the possession of some pathetic and unwholesome secret. He marvels at the depths of his own depravity, but now he believes it is his self-loathing that keeps him alive. And while he is alive, he cannot go to hell.

## 2.

"Well," says Kate Doyle to Mr Terry McLear, "I've been sent out and I beg your pardon but I am a kind of deputation from the whole Circle, or at least that part of it represented by my dad's customers, come to ask if what you're putting up is a platform on which you intend to sit, to make, it's supposed, a political statement of some kind? Or is it religious? Like a pole?"

And when she has finished her speech, she takes one

step back from him. She folds her dark expectant hands before her on the apron of her uniform. There is a silence, emphasized by the distant, constant noise of the surrounding city. Framed by her bobbed black hair, her little pink oval face has that expression of sardonic good humour, that hint of self-mockery, that attracted his affection many years ago. She is the picture of determined patience, and she makes Mr Terry smile.

"Is that what people are saying these days, is it? And they think I would sit up there in this weather?" He speaks the musical, old-fashioned, precisely pronounced English he learned in Dublin. He'd rather die than make a contraction or split an infinitive. He glares up at the grey Atlantic sky. Laughing helplessly at the image of himself on a pole, he stretches hard-worn fingers towards her to show he means no mockery or rudeness to herself. His white hair rises in a halo. His big old head grows redder, his mouth rapidly opening and closing as his mirth engulfs him. He gasps. His pale blue eyes, too weak for such powerful emotions, water joyfully. Kate Doyle suspects a hint of senile dementia. She'll be sorry to see him lose his mind, it is such a good one, and so kind. He never really understood how often his company had saved her from despair.

Mr Terry lifts the long thick dowel onto his sweat-shirted shoulder. "Would you care to give me a hand, Katey?"

She helps him steady it upright in the special hole he had prepared. The seasoned pine dowel is some four inches in diameter and eight feet tall. The hole is about two feet deep. Yesterday, from the big bar, they had all watched him pour in the concrete.

The shrubbery, trees and turf of the Circle nowadays

wind neatly up to a little grass-grown central hillock. On this the City has placed two ornamental benches. Popular legend has it that an Indian chief rests underneath, together with his treasure.

When Mr Terry was first seen measuring up the mound, they thought of the ancient redman. They had been certain, when he had started to dig, that McLear had wind of gold.

All Doyle's regulars had seized enthusiastically on this new topic. Corny Doyle was especially glad of it. Sales rose considerably when there was a bit of speculative stimulus amongst the customers, like a sensational murder or a political scandal or a sporting occasion.

Katey knew they would all be standing looking out now, watching her and waiting. They had promised to rescue her if he became unpleasant. Not that she expected anything like that. She was the only one local that Mr Terry would have anything to do with. He never would talk to most people. After his wife died he was barely civil if you wished him 'good morning'. His argument was that he had never enjoyed company much, until he had met her, and now precious little other company satisfied him in comparison. Neither did he have anything to do with the Church. He'd distanced himself a bit from Katey when she started working with the Poor Clares. This was the first time she'd approached him in two years. She's grateful to them for making her come but sorry that it took the insistence of a bunch of feckless boozers to get her here.

"So," she says, "I'm glad I've cheered you up. And if that's all I've achieved, that's good enough for today, I'm sure. Can you tell me nothing about your pole?"

"I have a permit for it," he says. "All square and official." He pauses and watches the Sears delivery truck that has been droning round the Circle for the last fifteen minutes, seeking an exit. Slumped over his wheel, peering about for signs, the driver looks desperate.

"Nothing else?"

"Only that the pole is the start of it." He's enjoying himself. That heartens her.

"And you won't be doing some sort of black magic with the poor old Indian's bones?"

"Magic, maybe," he says, "but not a bit black, Katey. Just the opposite, you will see."

"Well, then," she says, "then I'll go back and tell them you're putting up a radio aerial."

"Tell them what you like," he says. "Whatever you like."

"If I don't tell them something, they'll be on at me to come out again," she says.

"You would not be unwelcome," he says. "Or averse, I am sure, to a cup of tea." And gravely he tips that big head homeward, towards his brownstone basement on the far side of the Circle.

"Fine," she says, "but I'll come on my own when I do and not as a messenger. Good afternoon to you, Mr Terry."

He lifts an invisible hat. "It was a great pleasure to talk with you again, Katey."

She's forgotten how that little smile of his so frequently cheers her up.

## 3.

"Okay, Katey, so what's the story?" says Father McQueeny, wearing his professional cheer like an old shroud, as ill-smelling and threadbare as his clerical black. The only life on him is his sweat, his winking veins. The best the regulars have for him these days is their pity, the occasional drink. He has no standing at all with the Church or the community. But, since Father Walsh died, that secret little smirk of his always chills her. Knowing that he can still frighten her is probably all that keeps the old shit alive. And since this knowledge actually informs the expression that causes her fear, she is directly feeding him what he wants. She has yet to work out a way to break the cycle. Years before, in her best attempt, she almost succeeded.

To the others, the priest remains inaudible, invisible. "Did he come out with it, Katey?" says Corny Doyle, his black eyes and hair glinting like pitch, his near-fleshless body and head looking as artificially weathered as those shiny smoked hams in Belladonna's. "Come on, Kate. There's real money riding on this now."

"He did not tell me," she says. She turns her back on Father McQueeny but she cannot control a shudder as she smiles from behind the bar where she has been helping out since Christmas, because of Bridget's pneumonia. She takes hold of the decorated china pump-handle and turns to her patient customer. "Two pints of Murphy's was it, Mr Gold?"

"You're an angel," says Mr Gold. "Well, Corny, the book, now how's it running?" He is such a plump, jolly man. You would never take him for a pawnbroker. And it must be admitted he is not a natural profiteer. Mr

Gold carries his pints carefully to the little table in the alcove, where Becky, his secretary, waits for him. Ageless, she is her own work of art. He dotes on her. If it wasn't for her he would be a ruined man. They'll be going out this evening. You can smell her perm and her *Chantilly* from here. A little less noise and you could probably hear her mascara flake.

"Radio aerial's still number one, Mr Gold," says Katey. Her father's attention has gone elsewhere, to some fine moment of sport on the box. He shares his rowdy triumph with his fellow aficionados. He turns back to her, panting. "That was amazing," he says.

Kate Doyle calls him over with her finger. He knows better than to hesitate. "What?" he blusters. "What? There's nothing wrong with those glasses. I told you it's the dishwasher."

Her whisper is sharp as a needle in his wincing ear. She asks him why, after all she's spoken perfectly plainly to him, he is still letting that nasty old man into the pub?

"Oh, come on, Katey," he says, "where else can the poor devil go? He's a stranger in his own church these days."

"He deserves nothing less," she says. "And I'll remind you, Dad, of my original terms. I'm off for a walk now and you can run the bloody pub yourself."

"Oh, no!" He is mortified. He casts yearning eyes back towards the television. He looks like some benighted sinner in the picture books who has lost the salvation of Christ. "Don't do this to me, Kate."

"I might be back when he's gone," she says. "But I'm not making any promises."

Every so often she has to let him know he is going too

far. Getting her father to work was a full-time job for her mother but she's not going to waste her own life on that non-starter. He's already lost the hotel next door to his debts. Most of the money Kate allows him goes in some form of gambling. Those customers who lend him money soon discover how she refuses to honor his IOUs. He's lucky these days to be able to coax an extra dollar or two out of the till, usually by short-changing a stranger.

"We'll lose business if you go, Kate," he hisses. "Why cut off your nose to spite your face?"

"I'll cut off *your* nose, you old fool, if you don't set it to that grindstone right now," she says. She hates sounding like her mother. Furiously, she snatches on her coat and scarf. "I'll be back when you get him out of here." She knows Father McQueeny's horrible eyes are still feeding off her through the pub's cultivated gloom.

"See you later, Katey, dear," her father trills as he places professional fingers on his bar and a smile falls across his face. "Now, then, Mrs Byrne, a half of Guinness, is it, darling?"

## 4.

The Circle was going up. There were all kinds of well-heeled people coming in. You could tell by the brass door-knockers and the window boxes, the dark green paint. With the odd *boutique* and *croissanterie*, these were the traditional signs of gentrification. Taking down the last pylons of the ugly elevated had helped, along with the hippies who in the Sixties and Seventies had made such a success of the little park, which now had a playground and somewhere for the dogs to go. It was lovely in the summer.

It was quiet, too, since they had put in the one-way system. Now the only strange vehicles were those that thought they could still make a short cut and wound up whining round until, defeated, they left the way they had entered. You had to go up to Canal Street to get a cab. They wouldn't come any further than that. There were legends of drivers who had never returned.

This recent development had increased the sense of the Circle's uniqueness, a zone of relative tranquillity in one of the noisiest parts of New York City. Up to now they had been protected from a full-scale yuppie invasion by the nearby federal housing. Yet nobody from the projects had ever bothered the Circle. They thought of the place as their own, something they aspired to, something to protect. It was astonishing the affection local people felt for the place, especially the park, which was the best-kept in the city.

She was on her brisk way, of course, to take Mr Terry McLear up on his invitation but she was not going there directly for all to see. Neither was she sure what she'd have to say to him when she saw him. She simply felt it was time they had one of their old chats.

Under a chilly sky, she walked quickly along the central path of the park. Eight paths led to the middle these days, like the arms of a compass, and there had been some talk of putting a sundial on the knoll, where Mr Terry had now laid his discreet foundations. She paused to look at the smooth concrete of his deep, narrow hole. A flag, perhaps? Something that simple? But this was not a man to fly a flag at the best of times.

39

And even the heaviest banner did not need so sturdy a pole. However, she was beginning to get a notion. A bit of a memory from a conversation of theirs a good few years ago now. *Ah*, she thought, *it's about birds, I bet.*

Certain some of her customers would still be watching her, she took the northern path and left the park to cross directly over to Houston Alley, where her uncle had his little toy-soldier shop where he painted everything himself and where, next door, the Italian shoe-repairer worked in his window. They would not be there much longer now that the real-estate people had christened the neighborhood 'Houston Village'. Already the bar had had a sniff from Starbuck's. Up at the far end of the alley the street looked busy. She thought about going back, but told herself she was a fool.

The traffic in Canal Street was unusually dense and a crew-cut girl in big boots had to help her when she almost fell into the street, shoved aside by some thrusting Wall Street stockman in a vast raincoat that might have sheltered half the Australian outback. She thought she recognized him as the boy who had moved into Number 91 a few weeks ago and she had been about to say hello.

She was glad to get back into the quietness of the Circle, going round into Church Street and then through Walker Street, which would bring her out only a couple of houses from Mr Terry's place.

She was still a little shaken but had collected herself by the time she reached the row of brownstones. Number 27 was in the middle and his flat was in the basement. She went carefully down the iron steps to his area. It was as smartly kept up as always, with the flower baskets properly stocked and his miniature greenhouse raising tomatoes in their gro-bags. And he was still neat and clean. No obvious slipping of standards, no signs of senile decay. She took hold of the old black-lion knocker and rapped twice against the dented plate. That same vast echo came back, as if she stood at the door to infinity.

He was slow as Christmas unbolting it all and opening up. Then everything happened at once. Pulling back the door, he embraced her and kicked it shut at the same time. The apartment was suddenly very silent. "Well," he said, "it has been such a long time. All my fault, too. I have had a chance to pull myself together and here I am."

"That sounds like a point for God for a change." She knew all the teachers had been anarchists or pagans or something equally silly in that school of his. She stared around at the familiar things, the copper and the oak and the big ornamental iron stove that once heated the whole building. "You're still dusting better than a woman. And polishing."

"She had high standards," he says. "I could not rise to them when she was alive, but now it seems only fair to try to live up to them. You would not believe what a slob I used to be."

"You never told me," she says.

"That is right. There is quite a bit I have not told you," he says.

"And us so close once," she says.

"We were good friends," he agreed. "The best of company. I am an idiot, Kate. But I do not think either of us realized I was in a sort of shock for years. I was afraid of our closeness, do you see? In the end."

41

"I believe I might have mentioned that." She went to put the kettle on. Filling it from his deep old-fashioned stone sink with its great brass faucets, she carried it with both hands to the stove while he got out the teacakes and the toasting forks. He must have bought them only today from Van Beek's Bakery on Canal, the knowing old devil, and put them in the icebox. They were still almost warm. She fitted one to the fork. "It doesn't exactly take Sigmund Freud to work that out. But you made your decisions, Mr Terry. And it is my general rule to abide by such decisions until the party involved decides to change. Which in my experience generally happens at the proper time."

"Oh, so you have had lots of these relationships, have you, Kate?"

She laughed.

## 5.

"I was sixteen when I first saw her. In the Circle there she was, coming out of Number 10, where the dry-cleaner's is now. I said to myself, that is whom I am going to marry. And that was what I did. We used to sing quite a bit, duets together. She was a much better and sweeter singer than I, and she was smarter, as well." Mr Terry looks into the fire and slowly turns his teacake against the glare. "What a little old snob I was in those days, thinking myself better than anyone, coming back from Dublin with an education. But she liked me anyway and was what I needed to take me down a peg or two. My father thought she was an angel. He spoke often of the grandchildren he would care for. But both he and she died before that event could become any sort of reality. And I grew very sorry for myself, Kate. In those first days, when we were having our chats, I was selfish."

"Oh, yes," she says, "but you were more than that. You couldn't help being more than that. That's one of the things hardest to realize about ourselves sometimes. Even in your morbid moments you often showed me how to get a grip on things. By example, you might say. You cannot help but be a good man, Mr Terry. A protector, I think, rather than a predator."

"I do not know about that."

"But I do," she says.

"Anyway." He flips a teacake on to the warming plate. "We had no children and so the McLears have no heirs."

"It's a shame," she says, "but not a tragedy, surely?" For an instant it flashes through her head, *Oh, no, he doesn't want me to have his bloody babies, does he*?

"Not in any ordinary sense, I quite agree. But you see there is an inheritance that goes along with that. Something that must be remembered accurately and passed down by word of mouth. It is our family tradition and has been so for quite a time."

"My goodness," she says. "You're Brian Boru's rightful successor to the high throne of Erin, is that it?" With deft economy she butters their teacakes.

He takes some jam from the dish and lays it lightly on top. "Oh, these are good, eh?"

When they are drinking their last possible cup of Assam he says, very soberly, "Would you let me share this secret, Kate? I have no one else."

43

"Not a crime, is it, or something nasty?" she begs.

"Certainly not!" He falls silent. She can sense him withdrawing and laughs at his response. He sighs.

"Then get on with it," she says. "Give me a taste of it, for I'm a busy woman."

"The story does not involve the Irish much," he says. "Most of the Celts involved were from Southern England, which was called Britannia in those days, by the Romans."

"Ancient history!" she cries. "How long, Mr Terry, is your story?"

"Not very long," he says.

"Well," she says, "I will come back another time to hear it." She glances at her watch. "If I don't go now I'll miss my programme."

As he helps her on with her coat she says: "I have a very low tolerance for history. It is hard for me to see how most of it relates to the here and now."

"This will mean something to you, I think, Kate."

They exchange light kisses upon the cheek. There is a new warmth between them that she welcomes.

"Make it scones tomorrow," she says. "Those big juicy ones they do, with the raisins in them, and I will hear your secret. We'll have Darjeeling, too. I'll bring some if you don't have any."

"I have plenty," he says.

"Bye-bye for now," she says.


## 6.

"All the goodness is in the marrow!" declares Mrs Byrne, waving her bones at the other customers. "But these days the young people all turn their noses up at it."

"That's not the problem at all, Mavis. The plain truth is, you're a bloody noisy eater," says Corny Doyle, backing up the other diners' complaints. "And you've had one too many now. You had better go home."

With her toothless mouth she sucks at her mutton.

"They don't know what they're missing, do they, Mavis?" says Father McQueeny from where he sits panting in a booth.

"And you can fuck off, you old pervert." Mavis rises with dignity and sails towards the ladies'. She has her standards.

"Well, Kate, how's the weather out there?" says Father McQueeny.

"Oh, you are here at last, Kate. It seems Father McQueeny's been locked out of his digs." In other circumstances Corny's expression of pleading anxiety would be funny.

"That doesn't concern me," she says, coming down the stairs. "I just popped in for something. I have told you what I want, Dad." She is carrying her little bag.

He rushes after her, whispering and pleading. "What can I do?"

"I have told you what you can do."

She looks back into the shadows. She knows he is staring at her. Often she thinks it is not exactly him that she fears, only what is in him. What sense does that make? Does she fear his memories and secrets? Of course Father Walsh, her confessor, had heard what had happened and what she had done and she had been absolved. What was more, the Church, by some means of its own, had discovered at least part of the truth and taken steps to curb him. They had sent Father Declan down to St Mary's. He was a tough old bugger but wholesome as they come. McQueeny was supposed to assist Declan who had found no use for him. However, since Father Walsh died, McQueeny revelled in their hideous secret, constantly hanging around the pub even before she started working there, haunting her, threatening to tell the world how he had come by his horrid surgery.

She is not particularly desperate about it. Sooner or later, she knows, her father will knuckle down and ban the old devil. It must be only a matter of time before the priest's liver kills him. She's never wished anyone dead in her life save him, and her hatred of him is such that she fears for her own soul over it.

This time she goes directly across the park to Mr Terry McLear's. It might look as if she plans to spend the night there but she does not care. Her true intention is to return eventually to her own flat in Delaware Court and wait until her father calls. She gives it twenty-four hours from the moment she stepped out of the pub.

But when she lifts the lion's head and lets it fall there is no reply. She waits. She climbs back up the steps. She looks into the park. She is about to go down again when an old chequer cab pulls up and out of its yellow-and-black depths comes Mr Terry McLear with various bags and bundles. "Oh what luck!" he declares. "Just when I needed you, Kate."

She helps him get the stuff out of the cab and down into his den. He removes his coat. He opens the door into his workshop and switches on a light. "I was not expecting you back today."

"Circumstances gave me the opportunity." She squints at the bags. "Who is Happy the Hammer?"

"Look on the other side. It is Stadtler's Hardware. Their mascot. Just the last bits I needed."

"Is it a bird-house of some kind that you are building?" she asks.

"And so you are adding telepathy to your list of extraordinary qualities, are you, Katey?" He grins. "Did I ever mention this to you?"

"You might have done. Is it pigeons?"

"God bless you, Katey." He pulls a bunch of small dowels out of a bag and puts it on top of some bits of plywood. "I must have told you the story."

"Not much of a secret, then," she says.

"This is not the secret, though I suppose it has something to do with it. There used to be dovecotes here, Katey, years ago. And that is all I am building. Have you not noticed the little doves about?"

"I can't say I have."

"Little mourning doves," he says. "Brown and cream. Like a kind of delicate pigeon."

"Well," she says, "I suppose for the non-expert they'd be lost in the crowd."

"Maybe, but I think you would know them when I pointed them out. The city believes me, anyhow, and is anxious to have them back. And it is not costing them a penny. The whole thing is a matter of fifty dollars and a bit of time. An old-fashioned dovecote, Katey. There are lots of accounts of the dovecotes, when this was more or less an independent village."

"So you're building a little house for the doves," she says. "That will be nice for them."

"A little house, is it? More a bloody great hotel." Mr Terry erupts with sudden pride. "Come on, Kate. I will take you back to look."

47

## 7.

She admires him, turning the wood this way and that against the whirling lathe he controls with a foot pedal.

"It is a wonderful smell," she says, "the smell of shavings." She peers with casual curiosity at his small, tightly organized workshop. Tools, timber, electrical bits and pieces, nails, screws and hooks are neatly stowed on racks and narrow shelves. She inspects the white-painted sides of the near-completed bird house. In the room, it seems massive, almost large enough to hold a child. She runs her fingers over the neatly ridged openings, the perfect joints. Everything has been finished to the highest standard, as if for the most demanding human occupation. "When did they first put up the dovecotes?"

"Nobody knows. The Indians had them when the first explorers arrived from Holland and France. There are sketches of them in old books. Some accounts call the tribe that lived here 'the Dove Keepers'. The Iroquois respected them as equals and called them the Ga-geh-ta-o-no, the People of the Circle. But the phrase also means People of the Belt.

"The Talking Belts, the 'wampum' records of the Six Nations, are invested with mystical meanings. Perhaps our tribe were the Federation's record keepers. They were a handsome, wealthy, civilized people, apparently, who were happy to meet and trade with the new-comers. The famous Captain Block was their admirer and spoke of a large stone circle surrounding their dovecotes. He believed that these standing stones, which were remarkably like early European examples, enclosed their holy place and that the doves represented the spirit they worshipped.

"Other accounts mention the stones, but there is some suspicion that the writers simply repeated Block's observations. Occasionally modern construction work reveals some of the granite, alien rock driven into the native limestone like a knife, and there is a suspicion the rock was used as part of a later stockade. The only Jesuit records make no mention of the stones but concentrate on the remarkable similarity of Kakatanawa (as the Europeans called them) myths to early forms of Christianity."

"I have heard as much myself," she agrees, more interested than she expected. "What happened to the Indians?"

"Nothing dramatic. They were simply and painlessly absorbed, mainly through intermarriage and mostly with the Irish. It would not have been difficult for them, since they still had a considerable amount of blood in common. By 1720 this was a thriving little township, built around the green. It still had its dovecotes. The stones were gone, reused in walls of all kinds. The Kakatanawa were living in ordinary houses and inter-marrying. In those days it was not fashionable to claim native ancestry. But, you see, the Kakatanawa were hardly natives. They resembled many of the more advanced Iroquois peoples and spoke an Iroquois dialect, but their tradition had it that their ancestors came from the other side of the Atlantic."

"Where did you read all this?" she asks in some bewilderment.

"It is not conventionally recorded," he says. "But this is my secret."

And he told her of Trinovante Celts, part of the Boudicca uprising of AD 69, who had used all their wealth to buy an old Roman trading ship with the intention of escaping the Emperor's cruel justice and sailing to Ireland. They were not navigators but good fortune eventually took them to these shores where they built a settlement. They chose Manhattan for the same reason as everyone else, because it commanded an excellent position on the river, had good harbours and could be easily defended.

They built their village inland and put a stockade around it, pretty much the same as the villages they had left behind. Then they sent the ship back with news and to fetch more settlers and supplies. They never heard of it again. The ship was, in fact, wrecked off Cornwall, probably somewhere near St Ives, but there were survivors and the story remained alive amongst the Celts, even as they succumbed to Roman civilization.

When, some hundreds of years later, the Roman legions were withdrawn and the Saxon pirates started bringing their families over, further bands of desperate Celts fled for Ireland and the land beyond, which they had named Hy-Brasil. One other galley reached Manhattan and discovered a people more Senecan than Celtic.

This second wave of Celtic immigrants were the educated Christian stone-raisers, Romanized astronomers and mystics, who brought new wisdom to their distant cousins and were doubtless not generally welcomed for it. For whatever reasons, however, they were never attacked by other tribes. Even the stern Iroquois, the Romans of these parts, never threatened them, although they were nominally subject to Hiawatha's Federation. By the time the Dutch arrived, the dominant Iroquois culture had again absorbed the Celts, but they retained certain traditions, stories and a few artefacts. Most of these appear to have been sold amongst the Indians and travelled widely through the North-East. They gave rise to certain rumours of Celtic civilizations (notably the Welsh) established in America.

"But the Kakatanawa spoke with the same eloquence and wore the finery and fashions of the Federation. Their particular origin-legend was not remarkable. Other tribes had far more dramatic conceptions, involving spectacular miracles and wildly original plots. So nobody took much notice of us and so we have survived."

"Us?" says Kate Doyle. "We?"

"You," he says, "represent the third wave of Celtic settlement of the Circle, during the nineteenth and twentieth centuries. And I represent the first and second. I am genuinely, Katey, and it is embarrassing to say so, the Last of the Kakatanawas. That was why my father looked forward to an heir, as did I. I suppose I was not up to the burden, or I would have married again."

"You'd be a fool to marry just for the sake of some old legend," she says. "A woman deserves more respect than that."

"I agree." He returns to his work. Now he's putting the fine little touches to the dowels, the decorations. It's a wonder to watch him.

"Do you have a feathered headdress and everything? A peace pipe and a tomahawk?" Her mockery has hardly any scepticism in it.

"Go over to that box just there and take out what is in it," he says, concentrating on the wood.

51

She obeys him.

It is a little modern copper box with a Celtic motif in the lid. Inside is an old dull coin. She picks it up between wary fingers and fishes it out, turning it to try to read the faint letters of the inscription. "It's Constantine," she says. "A Roman coin."

"The first Christian Emperor. That coin has been in New York, in our family, Katey, since the sixth century. It is pure gold. It is what is left of our treasure."

"It must be worth a fortune," she says.

"Not much of one. The condition is poor, you see. And I am sworn never to reveal its provenance. But it is certainly worth a bit more than the gold alone. Anyway, that is it. It is yours, together with the secret."

"I don't want it," she says. "Can't we bury it?"

"Secrets should not be buried," he says, "but kept."

"Well, speak for yourself," she says. "There are some secrets best buried."

While he worked on, she told him about Father McQueeny. He turned the wood more and more slowly as he listened. The priest's favourite joke that always made him laugh was "Little girls should be screwed and not heard." With her father's half-hearted compliance, the old wretch had enjoyed all his pleasures on her until one day, when she was seventeen, she had taken his penis in her mouth and, as she had planned, bitten down like a terrier. He had torn her hair out and almost broken her arm before he fainted.

"And I did not get all the way through. You would not believe how horrible it feels – like the worst sort of gristle in your mouth and all the blood and nasty crunching, slippery stuff. At first, at least, everything in you makes you want to stop. I was very sick afterwards, as you can imagine, and just able to dial 911 before I left him there. He almost died of losing so much blood. I hadn't expected it to spurt so hard. I almost drowned. I suppose if I had thought about it I should have anticipated that. And had a piece of string ready, or something. Anyway, it stopped his business. I was never reported. And I don't know how confessors get the news out, but the Church isn't taking any chances with him, so all he has now are his memories."

"Oh, dear," says Mr Terry gravely. "Now there is a secret to share."

"It's the only one I have," she said. "It seemed fair to reciprocate."

## 8.

Two days later, side by side, they stand looking up at his magnificent bird-house, complete at last. He's studied romantic old plans from the turn of the century, so it has a Charles Rennie Mackintosh touch or two about it in its white austerity, its sweeping gables. There are seven fretworked entrances and eight beautifully turned perches, black as ebony, following the lines of the park's paths. He's positioned and prepared the cote exactly as instructed in Tiffany's *Modern Gardens* of 1892 and has laid his seed and corn carefully. At her request, and without much reluctance, he's buried the Roman coin in the pole's foundation. "Now we must be patient," he says. "And wait." As he speaks, a whickering comes from above and a small dove, fawn and pale grey, settles for a moment upon the gleaming roof, then takes fright when she sees them.

"What a pretty thing. I will soon have to get back to my flat," she says. "My father will be going frantic by now. I put the machine on, but if I know him he'll be too proud to leave a message."

"Of course." He stoops to pick up a delicately coloured wing feather. It has a thousand shades of rose, beige, pink and grey. "I will be glad to come with you if you want anything done."

"I'll be all right," she says. But he falls in beside her.

As they turn their backs on the great bird-house three noisy mourning doves land on the perches as if they have been anticipating this moment for a hundred and fifty years. The sense of celebration, of relief, is so tangible it suffuses Kate Doyle and Mr Terry McLear even as they walk away.

"This calls for a cup of coffee," says Mr Terry McLear. "Shall we go to Belladonna's?"

They are smiling when Father McQueeny, evicted at last, comes labouring towards them along the path from the pub and pauses, suddenly gasping for his familiar fix, as if she has turned up in the nick of time to save his life.

"Good morning, Katey, dear," His eyes begin to fill with powerful memories. He speaks lovingly to her. "And Terry McLear, how are you?"

"Not bad, thanks, Father," says Mr Terry, looking him over.

"And when shall we be seeing you in church, Terry?" The priest is used to people coming back to the faith as their options begin to disappear.

"Oh, soon enough, Father, I hope. By the way, how is Mary's last supper doing? How is the little hot dog?" And he points.

It is a direct and fierce attack. Father McQueeny folds before it. "Oh, you swore!" he says to her.

She tries to speak but she cannot. Instead she finds herself laughing in the old wretch's face, watching him die, his secret, his sustenance lost for ever. He knows at once, of course, that his final power has gone. His cold eyes stare furiously into inevitable reality as his soul goes at last to the devil. It will be no more than a day or two before they bury him.

"Well," says Katey, "we must be getting on."

"Goodbye, Father," says Mr Terry McLear, putting his feather in his white hair and grinning like a fool.

When they look back the priest has disappeared, doubtless scuttling after some mirage of salvation. But the dovecote is alive with birds. It must have a dozen on it already, bobbing in the little doorways, pecking up the seed. They glance around with equanimity. You would think they had always been here. The distant noise of New York's traffic is muffled by their excited voices, as of old friends meeting after years. There is an air of approving recognition about their tone.

"They like the house. Now we must see if, when they have eaten the food, they will stay." Mr Terry McLear links a proud arm with his companion. "I never expected it to happen so quickly. It was as if they were waiting to come home. It is a positive miracle."

Amused, she looks up at him. "Come on now, a grown man like you with tears in his eyes!

"After all, Mr Terry." She takes his arm as they continue down the path towards Houston Alley. "You must never forget your honour as the Last of the Kakatanawas."

"You do not believe a word of it, do you, Kate?" he says.

"I do," she says. "Every word, in fact. It's just that I cannot fathom why you people went to so much trouble to keep it dark."

"Oh, you know all right, Kate," says Mr Terry McLear, pausing to look back at the flocking doves. "Sometimes secrecy is our only means of holding on to what we value."

Whistling, she escorts him out of the Circle.

# THE CLAPHAM
# ANTICHRIST

Begg Mansions,
Sporting Club Square

The Editor,
Fulham & Hammersmith *Telegraph*
Bishops Palace Avenue,
London W14

13th October 1992

Sir,

## *SPIRIT OF THE BLITZ*

It is heartening to note, as our economy collapses
perhaps for the last time, a return to the langauge
and sentiments of mutual self-interest. London
was never the kindest of English cities but of late
her cold, self-referential greed has been a

57

watchword around the world. Everything we value is threatened in the name of profit.

I say nothing original when I mourn the fact that it took the Blitz to make Londoners achieve a humanity and heroism they never thought to claim for themselves and that no one expected or demanded of them!

Could we not again aspire to achieve that spirit, without the threat of Hitler but with the same optimistic courage? Can we not, in what is surely an hour of need, marshall what is best in us and find new means of achieving that justice, equity and security for which we all long? The existing methods appear to create as many victims as they save.

Yours faithfully, Edwin Begg,
former vicar of St Odhran's, Balham.

HEAR! HEAR! says the *Telegraph*. This week's Book Token to our Letter of the Week! Remember, your opinions are important to us and we want to see them! A £5.00 Book Token for the best!

## ONE

*My First Encounter With the Clapham Antichrist;*
*His Visions & His Public Career; His Expulsion*
*from the Church & Subsequent Notoriety; His*
*Return To Society & Celebrity as a Sage; His*
*Mysterious & Abrupt Departure Into Hermitage;*
*His Skills in the Kitchen.*

"SPIRIT OF THE BLITZ" (a sub-editor's caption) was the last public statement of the Clapham Antichrist.

Until I read the letter at a friend's I believed Edwin Begg dead some twenty years ago. The beloved TV eccentric had retired in the 1950s to live as a recluse in Sporting Club Square, West Kensington. I had known him intimately in the 1960s and 1970s and was shocked to learn he was still alive. I felt a conflicting mixture of emotions, including guilt. Why had I so readily accepted the hearsay of his death? I wrote to him at once. Unless he replied to the contrary I would visit him on the following Wednesday afternoon.

I had met Begg first in 1966 when, as a young journalist, I interviewed him for a series in the *Star* about London's picturesque obscurities. Then too I had contacted him after reading one of his letters to the *Telegraph*. The paper, still a substantial local voice, was his only source of news, delivered to him weekly. He refused to have a telephone and communicated mostly through the post.

I had hoped to do a few paragraphs on the Antichrist's career, check a couple of facts with him and obtain a short, preferably amusing, comment on our

Fab Sixties. I was delighted when, with cheerful courtesy, Edwin Begg had agreed by return to my request. In a barely legible old-fashioned hand he invited me to lunch.

My story was mostly drafted before I set off to see him. Research had been easy. We had half a filing drawer on Edwin Begg's years of notoriety, first before the War, then afterwards as a radio and early TV personality. He had lived in at least a dozen foreign cities. His arguments were discussed in every medium and he became a disputed symbol. Many articles about him were merely sensational, gloating over alleged black-magic rites, sexual deviation, miracle-working, blasphemy and sorcery. There were the usual photographs and also drawings, some pretending to realism and others cruel cartoons: the Clapham Antichrist as a monster with blazing eyes and glittering fangs, architect of the doom to come. One showed Hitler, Stalin and Mussolini as his progeny.

The facts were pretty prosaic. In 1931, at the age of twenty-four, Begg was vicar of St Odhran's, Balham, a shabby North London living where few parishioners considered themselves respectable enough to visit a church and were darkly suspicious of those who did. The Depression years had almost as many homeless and hungry people on the streets as today. Mosley was gathering a more militant flock than Jesus and those who opposed the Fascists looked to Oxford or the secular left for their moral leadership. Nonetheless, the Reverend Begg conscientiously performed his duty, offering the uncertain comforts of his calling to his flock.

Then quite suddenly in 1933 the ordinary hard-
working cleric became an urgent proselytizer, an
orator. From his late-Victorian pulpit he began preaching a shocking message, urging Christians to act
according to their principles and sacrifice their own
material ambitions to the common good, to 'take a risk
on God being right', as he put it. This Tolstoyan
exhortation eventually received enough public attention to make his sermons one of London's most popular
free attractions, from Southwark to Putney – which, of
course, brought him the attention of the famous
Bermondsey barrackers, the disapproval of his
establishment and the closer interests of the press.

The investigators the Church sent down heard a
sermon touching mainly on the current state of the
Spanish Republic, how anarchists often acted more like
ideal Christians than the priests, how people seemed
more willing to give their lives to the anarchists than to
the cause of Christ. This was reported in *Reynolds
News*, tipped off that the investigators would be there,
as Begg's urging his congregation to support the coming
Antichrist. The report was more or less approving. The
disapproving Church investigators, happy for a lead to
follow, confirmed the reports. Overnight, the Reverend
Edwin Begg, preaching his honest Christian message of
brotherly love and equity under the law, became the
Clapham Antichrist, Arch-Enemy of British Decency,
Proud Mocker of All Religion and Hitler's Right Hand,
a creature to be driven from our midst.

In the course of a notoriously hasty hearing Edwin
Begg was unfrocked, effectively by public demand. In
his famous defence Begg confirmed the general opinion
of his guilt by challenging the commission to strip itself

61

naked and follow Christ, if they were indeed
Christians! He made a disastrous joke: and if they were
an example of modern Christians, he said, then after all
he probably *was* the Antichrist!

Begg never returned to his vicarage. He went
immediately to Sporting Club Square. Relatives took
him in, eventually giving him his own three-roomed flat
where it was rumoured he kept a harem of devil-
worshipping harlots. The subsequent Siege of Sporting
Club Square in which the *News of the World* provoked
a riot causing one near-fatality and thousands of
pounds' worth of damage was overshadowed by the
news of Hitler's massacre of his storm troopers, the SA.
Goebbels's propaganda became more interesting and
rather more in the line of an authentic harbinger of evil,
and at last Edwin Begg was left in peace.

Usually attached to a circus or a fair and always
billed as *"Reverend" Begg, The Famous Clapham
Antichrist!*, he began to travel the country with his
message of universal love. After his first tours he was
never a great draw since he disappointed audiences
with urgent pleas for sanity and the common good and
never rose to the jokes or demands for miracles. But at
least he had discovered a way of making a living from
his vocation. He spent short periods in prison and there
were rumours of a woman in his life, someone he had
mentioned early on, though not even the worst of the
Sundays found evidence to suggest he was anything but
confirmed in his chastity.

When the War came Edwin Begg distinguished
himself in the ambulance service, was wounded and
decorated. Then he again disappeared from public life.
This was his first long period of seclusion in Begg

Mansions until suddenly, on 1 May 1949, encouraged by his cousin Robert in BBC Talks, he gave at 9:45 p.m. on the Home Service the first of his Fireside Observer chats.

No longer the Old Testament boom of the pulpit or the side-show, the Fireside Observer's voice was level, reassuring, humorous, a little sardonic sometimes when referring to authority. He reflected on our continuing hardships and what we might gain through them if we kept trying – what we might expect to see for our children. He offered my parents a vision of a wholesome future worth working for, worth making a few sacrifices for, and they loved him.

He seemed the moral spirit of the Festival of Britain, the best we hoped to become, everything that was decent about being British. An entire book was published proving him the object of a plot in 1934 by a Tory bishop, a Fascist sympathizer, and there were dozens of articles, newsreels and talks describing him as the victim of a vicious hoax or showing how Mosley had needed a scapegoat.

Begg snubbed the Church's willingness to review his case in the light of his new public approval and continued to broadcast the reassuring ironies that lightened our 1950s darkness and helped us create the golden years of the 1960s and 1970s. He did not believe his dream to be illusory.

By 1950 he was on television, part of the *Thinkers' Club* with Gilbert Harding and Professor Joad, which every week discussed an important contemporary issue. The programme received the accolade of being lampooned in *Radio Fun* as *The Stinkers' Club* with

Headwind Legg, which happened to be one of my own childhood favourites. He appeared, an amiable sage, on panel games, quiz shows, programmes called *A Crisis of Faith* or *Turning Point* and at religious conferences eagerly displaying their tolerance by soliciting the opinion of a redeemed Antichrist.

Suddenly, in 1955, Begg refused to renew all broadcasting contracts and retired from public life, first to travel and finally to settle back in Begg Mansions with his books and his journals. He never explained his decision and then the public lost interest. New men with brisker messages were bustling in to build utopia for us in our lifetime.

Contenting himself with a few letters, mostly on parochial matters, to the Hammersmith *Telegraph*, Edwin Begg lived undisturbed for a decade. His works of popular philosophy sold steadily until British fashion changed. Writing nothing after 1955, he encouraged his books to go out of print. He kept his disciples, of course, who sought his material in increasingly obscure places and wrote to him concerning his uncanny understanding of their deepest feelings, the ways in which he had dramatically changed their lives, and to whom, it was reported, he never replied.

That first Wednesday I took the 28 from Notting Hill Gate down North Star Road to Greyhound Gardens. I had brought my *A-Z*. I had never been to Sporting Club Square before and was baffled by the surrounding network of tiny twisting streets, none of which seemed to go in the same direction for more than a few blocks, the result of frenzied rival building work during the speculative 1880s when developers had failed to follow the plans agreed between themselves, the freeholder, the architect and the authorities. The consequent recession ensured that nothing was ever done to remedy the mess. Half-finished crescents and abrupt culs-de-sac, odd patches of wasteland, complicated rights of way involving narrow alleys, walls, gates and ancient pathways were interrupted, where bomb damage allowed, by the new council estates, totems of clean enlightenment geometry whose erection would automatically cause all surrounding social evils to wither away. I had not expected to find anything quite so depressing and began to feel sorry for Begg ending his days in such circumstances. But turning out of Margrave Passage I came suddenly upon a cluster of big, unkempt oaks and cedars gathered about beautiful wrought-iron gates in the baroque oriental regency style of Old Cogges, that riot of unnatural ruin, the rural seat of the Beggs that William the Goth remodelled in 1798 to rival Strawberry Hill. They were miraculous in the early afternoon sun: the gates to paradise.

The square now has a preservation order and appears in international books of architecture as the finest example of its kind. Sir Hubert Begg, its architect, is mentioned in the same breath as Gaudi and Norman Shaw, which will give you some notion of his peculiar talent. Inspired by the fluid aesthetics of the *fin-de-siècle* he was loyal to his native brick and fired almost every fancy from Buckingham clay to give his vast array of disparate styles an inexplicable coherence. The tennis courts bear the motifs of some Mucha-influenced smith, their floral metalwork garlanded with living roses and honeysuckle from spring until autumn: even the benches are on record as one of the loveliest expressions of public *art nouveau*.

Until 1960 there had been a black chain across the Square's entrance and a porter on duty day and night. Residents' cars were never seen in the road but were garaged in the little William Morris cottages originally designed as studios and running behind the eccentrically magnificent palaces, which had been Begg's Folly until they survived the Blitz to become part of our heritage. When I walked up to the gates in 1966 a few cars had appeared in the gravel road running around gardens enclosed by other leafy ironwork after Charles Rennie Mackintosh, and the Square had a bit of a shamefaced seedy appearance.

There were only a few uniformed porters on part-time duty by then and they too had a slightly hangdog air. The Square was weathering one of its periodic declines, having again failed to connect with South Kensington during a decade of prosperity. Only the bohemian middle classes were actually proud to live there, so the place had filled with actors, music-hall performers, musicians, singers, writers, cheque-kiters and artists of every kind, together with journalists, designers and retired dance instructresses, hairdressers and disappointed legatees muttering bitterly about any blood not their own, for the Square had taken refugees and immigrants. Others came to be near the tennis courts maintained by the SCS Club affiliated to nearby Queen's.

Several professionals had taken apartments in Wratislaw Villas, so the courts never went down and neither did the gardens, which were preserved by an endowment from Gordon Begg, Lord Mauleverer, the botanist and explorer, whose elegant vivarium still pushed its flaking white girders and steamy glass above exotic shrubbery near the Mandrake Road entrance. Other examples of his botanical treasures, the rival of Holland's, flourished here and there about the Square and now feathery exotics mingled with the oaks and hawthorn of the original Saxon meadow.

Arriving in this unexpected tranquillity on a warm September afternoon when the dramatic red sun gave vivid contrast to the terracotta, the deep greens of trees, lawns and shrubbery, I paused in astonished delight. Dreamily I continued around the Square in the direction shown me by the gatehouse porter. I was of a generation that enthused over pre-Raphaelite paint and made Beardsley its own again, who had bought the five-shilling Mackintosh chairs and sixpenny Muchas and ten-bob Lalique glass in Portobello Road to decorate Liberty-oriental pads whose fragrant patchouli never disguised the pungent dope. They were the best examples we could find in this world to remind us of what we had seen on our acid voyages.

To my father's generation the Square would be unspeakably old-fashioned, redolent of the worst sub-urban pretension, but I had come upon a gorgeous secret. I understood why so few people mentioned it, how almost everyone was either enchanted or repelled. My contemporaries, who thought "Georgian" the absolute height of excellence and imposed their stern developments upon Kensington's levelled memory, found Sporting Club Square hideously "Victorian" – a gigantic, grubby whatnot. Others dreamed of the day when they would have the power to be free of Sporting Club Square, the power to raze her and raise their fake

Le Corbusier mile-high concrete in triumph above the West London brick.

I did not know, as I made my way past great mansions of Caligari Tudor and Kremlin De Mille, that I was privileged to find the Square in the final years of her glory. In those days I enjoyed a wonderful innocence and could no more visualize this lovely old place changing for the worse than I could imagine the destruction of Dubrovnik.

Obscured, sometimes, by her trees, the mansion apartments of Sporting Club Square revealed a thousand surprises. I was in danger of being late as I stared at Rossettian gargoyles and Blakean caryatids, copings, gables, corbels of every possible stamp yet all bearing the distinctive style of their time. I was filled with an obscure sense of epiphany.

In 1886, asymmetrical Begg Mansions was the boldest expression of modernism, built by the architect for his own family use, for his offices and studios, his living quarters, a suite to entertain clients, and to display his designs, accommodation for his draughts- and crafts-people whose studios in attics and basements produced the prototype glass, metal, furniture and fabrics that nowadays form the basis of the V&A's extraordinary collection. By the 1920s, after Hubert Begg's death, the Square became unfashionable. Lady Begg moved to Holland Park and Begg Mansions filled up with the poorer Beggs who paid only the communal fee for general upkeep and agreed to maintain their own flats in good condition. Their acknowledged patron was old Squire Begg, who had the penthouse. By 1966 the building was a labyrinth of oddly twisting corridors and stairways, unexpected landings reached by two old oak-and-copper cage elevators served by their own generator, which worked on an eccentric system devised by the architect and was always going wrong. Later I learned that it was more prudent to walk the six flights to Edwin Begg's rooms but on that first visit I got into the lift, pressed the stud for the sixth floor and was taken up without incident in a shower of sparks and rattling brass to the ill-lit landing where the Antichrist himself awaited me.

I recognized him, of course, but was surprised that he seemed healthier than I had expected. He was a little plumper and his bone-white hair was cropped in a self-administered pudding-basin cut. He was clean-shaven, pink and bright as a mouse, with startling blue eyes, a firm, rather feminine mouth and the long sharp nose of his mother's Lowland Presbyterian forefathers. His high voice had an old-fashioned Edwardian elegance and was habitually rather measured. He reminded me of a Wildean *grande dame*, tiny but imposing. I was dressed like most of my Ladbroke Grove peers and he seemed pleased by my appearance, offering me his delicate hand, introducing himself and muttering about my good luck with the lift. He had agreed to this interview, he said, because he'd been feeling unusually optimistic after playing the new Beatles album. We shared our enthusiasm.

He guided me back through those almost organic passages until we approached his flat and a smell so heady, so delicious that I did not at first identify it as food. His front door let directly on to his study which led to a sitting room and bedroom. Only the dining room seemed unchanged since 1900 and still had the original Voysey wallpaper and furniture, a Henry dresser and Benson copperware. Like many reclusive people he enjoyed talking. As he continued to cook he sat me on a sturdy Wilson stool with a glass of wine and asked me about my career, showing keen interest in my answers.

"I hope you don't mind home cooking," he said. "It's a habit I cultivated when I lived on the road. Is there anything you find disagreeable to eat?"

I would have eaten strychnine if it had tasted as that first meal tasted. We had mysterious sauces whose nuances I can still recall, wines of exquisite delicacy, a dessert that contained an entire orchestra of flavours, all prepared in his tiny perfect 1920s "modern" kitchenette to one side of the dining room.

After we had eaten he suggested we take our coffee into the bedroom to sit in big wicker chairs and enjoy another wonderful revelation. He drew the curtains back from his great bay window to reveal over two miles of almost unbroken landscape all the way to the river, with the spires and roofs of Old Putney beyond. In the far distance was a familiar London skyline but immediately before us were the Square's half-wild communal gardens and cottage gardens, then the ivy-covered walls of St Mary's Convent, the Convent School sports field and that great forest of shrubs, trees and memorial sculptures, the West London Necropolis, whose Victorian angels raised hopeful swords against the ever-changing sky. Beyond the cemetery was the steeple of St Swithold's and her churchyard, then a nurtured patchwork of allotments, some old alms cottages and finally the sturdy topiary of the Bishop's Gardens surrounding a distant palace whose Tudor dignity did much to inspire Hubert Begg. The formal hedges marched all the way to the bird sanctuary on a broad, marshy curve where the Thames approached Hammersmith Bridge, a medieval fantasy.

It was the pastoral and monumental in perfect harmony that some cities spontaneously create. Edwin Begg said the landscape was an unfailing inspiration. He could dream of Roman galleys beating up the river, cautiously alert for Celtic war-parties, or Vikings striking at the Bishop's Palace, leaving flames and murder behind. He liked to think of other more contemplative eyes looking on a landscape scarcely changed in centuries. "Hogarth, Turner and Whistler amongst them. Wheldrake, writing *Harry Wharton*, looked out from this site when staying at the Sporting Club Tavern and earlier Augusta Begg conceived the whole of *The Bravo of Bohemia* and most of *Yamboo; or, The North American Slave* while seated more or less where I am now! Before he went off to become an orientalist and London's leading painter of discreet seraglios James Lewis Porter painted several large land-scapes that show market gardens where the allotments are, a few more cottages, but not much else has changed. I can walk downstairs, out of the back door, through that gate, cross the convent field into the grave-yard, take the path through the church down to the allotments all the way to the Bishop's Gardens and be at the bird sanctuary within half an hour, even cross the bridge into Putney and the Heath if I feel like it and hardly see a house, a car or another human being!" He would always stop for a bun, he said, at the old Palace Tea Rooms and usually strolled back via Margrave Avenue's interesting junkyards. Mrs White, who kept the best used-book shop there, told me he came in at least twice a week.

He loved to wake up before dawn with his curtains drawn open and watch the sun gradually reveal familiar sights. "No small miracle, these days, dear! I'm always afraid that one morning it won't be there." At the time I thought this no more than a mildly philosophical remark.

For me he still had the aura of a mythic figure from my childhood, someone my parents had revered. I was prepared to dislike him but was immediately charmed by his gentle eccentricity, his rather loud plaid shirts and corduroys, his amiable vagueness. The quality of the lunch alone would have convinced me of his virtue!

I was of the 1960s, typically idealistic and opinionated and probably pretty obnoxious to him but he saw something he liked about me and I fell in love with him. He was my ideal father.

I returned home to rewrite my piece. A figure of enormous wisdom, Edwin Begg offered practical common sense, I said, in a world ruled by the abstract sophistries and empty reassurances heralding the new spirit of competition into British society. It was the only piece of mine the *Star* never used, but on that first afternoon Begg invited me back for lunch and on almost every Wednesday for the next eight years, even after I married, I would take the 28 from the Odeon, Westbourne Grove to Greyhound Gardens and walk through alleys of stained concrete, past shabby red terraces and doorways stinking of rot until I turned that corner and stood again before the magnificent gates of Sporting Club Square.

My friend kept his curiosity about me and I remained

flattered by his interest. He was always fascinating company, whether expanding on some moral theme or telling a funny story. One of his closest chums had been Harry Lupino Begg, the music-hall star, and he had also known Al Bowlly. He was a superb and infectious mimic and could reproduce Lupino's patter by heart, making it as topical and fresh as the moment. His imitation of Bowlly singing 'Buddy, Can You Spare a Dime' was uncanny. When carried away by some amusing story or conceit his voice would rise and fall in rapid and entertaining profusion, sometimes taking on a birdlike quality difficult to follow. In the main, however, he spoke with the deliberate air of one who respected the effect of words upon the world.

By his own admission the Clapham Antichrist was not a great original thinker but he spoke from original experience. He helped me look again at the roots of my beliefs. Through him I came to understand the innocent intellectual excitement of the years before political experiments turned one by one into tyrannical orthodoxies. He loaned me my first Kropotkin, the touching *Memoirs of an Anarchist*, and helped me understand the difference between moral outrage and social effect. He loved works of popular intellectualism. He was as great an enthusiast for Huxley's *The Perennial Philosophy* as he was for Winwood Reade's boisterously secular *Martyrdom of Man*. He introduced me to the interesting late work of H.G. Wells and to Elizabeth Bowen. He led me to an enjoyment of Jane Austen I had never known. He infected me with his enthusiasm for the more obscure Victorians who remained part of his own living library and he was generous with his books. But, no matter how magical our afternoons, he insisted

I must always be gone before the BBC broadcast Choral Evensong. Only in the dead of winter did I ever leave Sporting Club Square in darkness.

Naturally I was curious to know why he had retired so abruptly from public life. Had he told the church of his visions? Why had he felt such an urgent need to preach? To risk so much public disapproval? Eventually I asked him how badly it had hurt him to be branded as the premier agent of the Great Antagonist, the yapping dog, as it were, at the heels of the Son of the Morning. He said he had retreated from the insults before they had grown unbearable. "But it wasn't difficult to snub people who asked you questions like 'Tell me, Mr. Begg, what does human blood taste like?' Besides, I had my Rose to sustain me, my vision . . ."

I hoped he would expand on this but he only chuckled over some association he had made with an obscure temptation of St Anthony and then asked me if I had been to see his cousin Orlando Begg's *Flaming Venus*, now on permanent display at the Tate.

Though I was soon addicted to Edwin Begg's company, I always saw him on the same day and at the same time every week. As he grew more comfortable with me he recounted the history of his family and Sporting Club Square. He spoke of his experiences as a young curate, as a circus entertainer, as a television personality, and he always cooked. This was, he said, the one time he indulged his gourmet instincts. In the summer we would stroll in the gardens or look at the tennis matches. Sitting on benches we would watch the birds or the children playing. When I asked him questions about his own life his answers became fuller, though

74

never completely unguarded.

It was easy to see how in his determined naivety he was once in such frequent conflict with authority.

"I remember saying, my dear, to the magistrate – Who does not admire the free-running, intelligent fox? And few, no matter how inconvenienced, begrudge him his prey, which is won by daring raiding and quick wits, risking all. A bandit, your honour, one can admire and prepare against. There is even a stirring or two of romance for the brigand chief. But once the brigand becomes a baron that's where the balance goes wrong, eh, your honour? It gets unfair, I said to him. Our sympathies recognize these differences so why can't our laws? Our courts make us performers in pieces of simplistic fiction! Why do we continue to waste so much time? The magistrate said he found my last remark amusing and gave me the maximum sentence."

Part of Edwin Begg's authority came from his vivacity. As he sat across from me at the table, putting little pieces of chicken into his mouth, pausing to enjoy them, then launching off on to a quite different subject, he seemed determined to relish every experience, every moment. His manner offered a clue to his past. Could he be so entertaining because he might otherwise have to confront an unpleasant truth? Anyone raised in a post-Freudian world could make that guess. But it was not necessarily correct.

Sometimes his bright eyes would dart away to a picture or glance through a window and I learned to interpret this fleeting expression as one of pain or sadness. He admitted readily that he had retreated into his inner life, feeling he had failed in both his public and private missions. I frequently reassured him of his value, the esteem in which he was still held, but he was unconvinced.

"Life isn't a matter of linear consequences," he said. "We only try to make it look like that. Our job is not to force grids upon the world but to achieve harmony with nature."

At that time in my life such phrases made me reach for my hat, if not my revolver, but because I loved him so much I tried to understand what he meant. He believed that in our terror we imposed perverse linearity upon a naturally turbulent universe, that our perceptions of time were at fault since we saw the swirling cosmos as still or slow-moving just as a gnat doubtless sees us. He thought that those who overcame their brute terror of the truth soon attained the state of the angels.

The Clapham Antichrist was disappointed that I was not more sympathetic to the mystical aspects of the alternative society but because of my familiarity with its ideas was glad to have me for a devil's advocate. I was looking for a fast road to utopia and he had almost given up finding any road at all. Our solutions were wrong because our analysis was wrong, he said. We needed to rethink our fundamental principles and find better means of applying them. I argued that this would take too long. Social problems required urgent action. His attitude was an excuse for inaction. In the right hands there was nothing wrong with the existing tools.

"And what are the right hands, dear?" he asked. "Who makes the rules? Who keeps them, my dear?" He ran his thin fingers through hair that became a milky halo around his earnest face. "And how is it possible to make them and keep them when our logic insists on such oppressive linearity? We took opium into China and bled them of their silver. Now they send heroin to us to lay hands upon our currency! Am I the only one enjoying the irony? The Indians are reclaiming the south-western United States in a massive migration back into the old French and Spanish lands. The world is never still, is it, my dear?"

Edwin Begg's alert features were full of tiny signals, humorous and anxious, inquiring and defiant, as he expanded on his philosophy one autumn afternoon. We strolled around the outer path, enjoying the late roses and early chrysanthemums forming an archway roofed with fading honeysuckle. He wore his green raglan, his yellow scarf, his hideous turf accountant's trilby, and gestured with the blackthorn he always carried but hardly used. "The world is never still and yet we continue to live as if turbulence were not the natural order of things. We have no more attained our ultimate state than has our own star! We have scarcely glimpsed any more of the multiverse than a toad under a stone! We are part of the turbulence and it is in turbulence we thrive. Once that's understood, my dear, the rest is surely easy? Brute warfare is our crudest expression of natural turbulence, our least productive. What's the finest? Surely there's no evil in aspiring to be our best? What do we gain by tolerating or even justifying the worst?"

I sat down on the bench looking the length of a bower whose pale golds and browns were given a tawny burnish by the sun. Beyond the hedges was the sound of a tennis game. "And those were the ideas that so offended the Church?" I asked.

He chuckled, his face sharp with self-mockery. "Not really. They had certain grounds, I suppose. I don't know. I merely suggested to my congregation after the newspapers had begun the debate, that perhaps only through Chaos and Anarchy could the Millennium be achieved. There were, after all, certain clues to that effect in the Bible. I scarcely think I'm to blame if this was interpreted as calling for bloody revolution, or heralding Armageddon and the Age of the Antichrist!"

I was diplomatic. "Perhaps you made the mistake of overestimating your audiences?"

Smiling, he turned where he sat to offer me a reproving eye. "I did not overestimate them, my dear. They underestimated themselves. They didn't appreciate that I was trying to help them become one with the angels. I have experienced such miracles, my dear! Such wonderful visions!"

And then, quite suddenly, he had risen and taken me by the arm to the Duke's Elm, the ancient tree that marked the border of the larger square in what was really a cruciform. Beyond the elm were lawns and well-stocked beds of the cross's western bar laid out exactly as Begg had planned. Various residents had brought their deckchairs here to enjoy the last of the summer. There was a leisurely good-humoured holiday air to the day. It was then, quite casually and careless of passers-by, that the Clapham Antichrist described to me the vision that converted him from a mild-mannered Anglican cleric into a national myth.

"It was on a similar evening to this in 1933. Hitler had just taken power. I was staying with my Aunt Constance Cunningham, the actress, who had a flat in D'Yss Mansions and refused to associate with the other Beggs.

I had come out here for a stroll to smoke my pipe and think over a few ideas for the next Sunday's sermon, which I would deliver, my dear, to a congregation consisting mostly of the miserably senile and the irredeemably small-minded who came to church primarily as a signal to neighbours they believed beneath them . . .

"It was a bloody miserable prospect. I have since played better audiences on a wet Thursday night in a ploughed field outside Leeds. No matter what happened to me I never regretted leaving those dour, ungiving faces behind. I did my best. My sermons were intended to discover the smallest flame of charity and aspiration burning in their tight little chests. I say all this in sad retrospect. At the time I was wrestling with my refusal to recognize certain truths and find a faith not threatened by them.

"I really was doing my best, my dear." He sighed and looked upward through the lattice of branches at the jackdaw nests just visible amongst the fading leaves. "I was quite agitated about my failure to discover a theme appropriate to their lives. I wouldn't give in to temptation and concentrate on the few decent parishioners at the expense of the rest." He turned to look across the lawns at the romantic rococo splendour of Moreau Mansions. "It was a misty evening in the Square with the sun setting through those big trees over there, a hint of pale gold in the haze and bold comforting shadows on the grass. I stood here, my dear, by the Duke's Elm. There was nobody else around. My vision stepped forward, out of the mist, and smiled at me.

"At first I thought that in my tiredness I was hallucinating. I'd been trained to doubt any ecstatic experience. The scent of roses was intense, like a drug!

Could this be Carterton's ghost, said to haunt the spot where he fell to his death, fighting a duel in the branches after a drunken night at Begg's? But this was no young duke. The woman was about my own height, with graceful beauty and the air of peace I associated with the Virgin. My unconventional madonna stood in a mannish confident way, a hand on her hip, clearly amused by me. She appeared to have emerged from the earth or from the tree. Shadows of bark and leaves still clung to her. There was something plant-like about the set of her limbs, the subtle colours of her flesh, as if a rose had become human and yet remained thoroughly a rose. I was rather frightened at first, my dear.

"I'd grown up with an Anglicanism permitting hardly a hint of the Pit, so I didn't perceive her as a temptress. I was thoroughly aware of her sexuality and in no way threatened by it or by her vitality. After a moment the fear dissipated. Then, after a few minutes more, she vanished and I was left with what I could only describe as her inspiration, which led me to write my first real sermon that evening and present it on the following Sunday."

"She gave you a message?" I thought of Jeanne D'Arc.

"Oh, no. Our exchange was wordless on that occasion."

"And you spoke of her in church?"

"Never. That would have been a sort of betrayal. No, I based my message simply on the emotion she had aroused in me. A vision of Christ might have done the same. I don't know."

"So it was a Christian message? Not anti-Christian?"

"Not anti-religious, at any rate. Perhaps, as the

bishop suggested, a little pagan."

"What brought you so much attention?"

"In the church that Sunday were two young chaps escorting their recently widowed aunt, Mrs Nye. They told their friends about me. To my delight, when I gave my second sermon I found myself with a very receptive congregation. I thanked God for the miracle. It seemed nothing else, my dear. You can't imagine the joy of it! For any chap in my position. I'd received a gift of divine communication, perhaps a small one, but it seemed pretty authentic. And the people began to pack St Odhran's. We had money for repairs. They seemed suddenly so willing to give themselves to their faith!"

I was mildly disappointed. This Rose did not seem much of a vision. Under the influence of drugs or when overtired I had experienced hallucinations quite as elaborate and inspiring. I asked him if he had seen her again.

"Oh, yes. Of course. Many times. In the end we fell in love. She taught me so much. Later there was a child."

He stood up, adjusted his overcoat and scarf and gave his stick a little flourish. He pointed out how the light fell through the parade of black gnarled maples leading to the tennis courts. "An army of old giants ready to march," he said. "But their roots won't let them."

The next Wednesday when I came to lunch he said no more about his vision.

# TWO

## *A Brief History of the Begg Family & of Sporting Club Square*

In the course of my first four hundred lunches with the Clapham Antichrist I never did discover why he abandoned his career but I learned a great deal about the Begg family, its origins, its connections and its property, especially the Square. I became something of an expert and planned a monograph until the recent publication of two excellent Hubert Begg books made my work only useful as an appendix to real scholarship.

Today the Square, on several tourist itineraries, has lost most traces of its old unselfconscious integrity. Only Begg Mansions remains gated and fenced from casual view, a defiantly private museum of human curiosities. The rest of the Square has been encouraged to maximize its profitability. Bakunin Villas is now the Hotel Romanoff. Ralph Lauren for some time sponsored D'Yss Mansions as a fashion gallery. Beardsley Villas is let as company flats to United Foods, while the council (which invested heavily in BBIC) took another building, the Moorish fantasy of Flecker Mansions, as offices. There is still some talk of an international company "theme-parking" Sporting Club Square, running commercial tennis matches and linking it to a television soap. Following the financial scandals involving Begg Belgravia International and its associate companies, the Residents' Association has had some recent success in reversing this progress.

When I visited Edwin Begg in 1992, he welcomed me

as if our routine had never been broken. He mourned his home's decline into a mere fashion, an exploitable commodity instead of a respected eccentricity, and felt it had gone the way of the Chateau Pantin or Derry & Toms famous Roof Garden, with every feature displayed as an emphatic curiosity, a sensation, a mode, and all her old charm a wistful memory. He had early on warned them about these likely consequences of his nephew's eager speculations. "Barbican wasn't the first to discover what you could do in a boom economy with a lick of paint, but I thought his soiling of his own nest a remote chance, not one of his first moves! The plans of such people are generally far advanced before they achieve power. When they strike you are almost always taken unawares, aren't you, dear? What cold, patient dreams they must have."

He derived no satisfaction from Barbican Begg's somewhat ignoble ruin but felt deep sympathy for his fellow residents hopelessly trying to recover their stolen past.

"It's too late for us now and soon it won't matter much, but it's hard to imagine the kind of appetite that feeds upon souls like locusts on corn. We might yet drive the locust from our field, my dear, but he has already eaten his fill. He has taken what we cannot replace."

Sometimes he was a little difficult to follow and his similes grew increasingly bucolic.

"The world's changing physically, dear. Can't you feel it?" His eyes were as bright a blue and clear as always, his pink cheeks a little more drawn, his white halo thinner, but he still pecked at the middle distance when he got excited, as if he could tear the truth from the air with his nose. He was clearly delighted that we had resumed our meetings. He apologized that the snacks were things he could make and microwave. They were still delicious. On our first meeting I was close to tears, wondering why on earth I had simply assumed him dead and deprived myself of his company for so long. He suggested a stroll if I could stand it.

I admitted that the Square was not improving. I had been appalled at the gaudy golds and purples of the Hotel Romanoff. It was, he said, currently in receivership, and he shrugged. "What is it, my dear, that allows us to become the victims of such villains, time after time! Time after time they take what is best in us and turn it to our disadvantage. It's like being a conspirator in one's own rape."

We had come up to the Duke's Elm again in the winter twilight and he spoke fondly of familiar ancestors.

Cornelius van Beek, a Dutch cousin of the Saxon von Beks, had settled in London in 1689, shortly after William and Mary. For many Europeans in those days England was a haven of relative enlightenment. A daring merchant banker, van Beek financed exploratory trading expeditions, accompanying several of them himself, and amassed the honourable fortune enabling him to retire at sixty to Cogges Hall, Sussex. Amongst his properties when he died were the North Star Farm and tavern, west of Kensington, bought on the mistaken assumption that the area was growing more respectable and where he had at one time planned to build a house. This notorious stretch of heath was left to van Beek's nephew, George Arthur Begg, who had Anglicized his name upon marriage to Harriet Vernon, his second cousin, in 1738. Their only surviving grandson was Robert Vernon Begg, famous as Dandy Bob Begg and ennobled under the Prince Regent.

As financially impecunious as his patron, Dandy Bob raised money from co-members of the Hell-Fire, took over the old tavern at North Star Farm, increased its size and magnificence, entertained the picaro captains so they would go elsewhere for their prizes, ran bare-knuckle fights, bear-baitings and other brutal spectacles, and founded the most notorious sporting establishment of its day. Fortunes were commonly lost and won at Begg's; suicides, scandals and duels no rarity. A dozen of our oldest families spilled their blood in the meadow beneath the black elm, and perhaps a score of men and women drowned in the brook now covered and serving as a modern sewer.

Begg's Sporting Club grew so infamous, the activities of its members and their concubines such a public outrage, that when the next William ascended, Begg rapidly declined. By Victoria's crowning the great dandy whom all had courted had become a souse married into the Wadhams for their money, got his wife Charlotte pregnant with male twins and died, whereupon she somewhat boldly married his nephew Captain Russell Begg and had three more children before he died a hero and a colonel in the Crimea. The twins were Ernest Dumara and Louis Palmate Begg, her two girls were Adriana Circe and Julianna Aphrodite and her youngest boy, her favourite child, was Hubert Alhambra, born on 18 January 1855 after his father's fatal fall at Balaclava.

A youthful disciple of Eastlake, by the late 1870s Hubert Begg was a practising architect whose largest single commission was Castle Bothwell on the shores of Loch Ness (his sister had married James Bothwell), which became a victim of the Glasgow blitz. "But it was little more than a bit of quasi-Eastlake and no rival to, for instance, the V&A," Edwin Begg had told me. He did not share my admiration for his great-uncle's achievement. "Quite frankly, his best work was always his furniture." He was proud of his complete bedroom suite in Begg's rather spare late style but he did not delight in living in "an art nouveau wedding cake". He claimed the Square's buildings cost up to ten times as much to clean as Oakwood Mansions, for instance, at the western end of Kensington High Street. "Because of the crannies and fancy mouldings, those flowing fauns and smirking sylphs the late Victorians found so delicious sexy. Dust traps all. It's certainly unique, my dear, but so was Quasimodo."

Hubert Begg never struggled for a living. He had married the beautiful Carinthia Hughes, an American heiress, during his two years in Baltimore and it was she who suggested he use family land for his own creation, tearing down that ramshackle old firetrap. The Sporting Club Tavern, which together with a small-holding was rented to a family called Foulsham whom Begg generously resettled on prime land, complete with their children, their cow, their pig and various other domestic animals, near Old Cogges.

The North Star land was cleared. North Star Square was named but lasted briefly as that. It was designed as a true square with four other smaller squares around it to form a sturdy box cross, thus allowing a more flexible way of arranging the buildings, ensuring residents plenty of light, good views and more tennis. Originally there were plans for seven tennis courts. By the 1880s tennis was a social madness rather than a vogue and everybody was playing. Nearby Queens Club was founded in Begg's shadow. Begg's plans were altogether more magnificent and soon the projected settlement blossomed into Sporting Club Square. The name had a slightly raffish, romantic resonance and attracted the more daring young people, the financiers who still saw themselves as athletic privateers and who were already patrons to an artist or two as a matter of form.

Clients were encouraged to commission favourite styles for Begg to adapt. He had already turned his back on earlier influences, so Gothic did not predominate, but was well represented in Lohengrin Villas which was almost an homage to Eastlake, commissioned by the Church to house retired clergy who felt comfortable with its soaring arches and mighty buttresses. Encouraged by the enthusiasm for his scheme, the architect was able to indulge every fantasy, rather in the manner of a precocious Elgar offering adaptations of what Greaves called, in *The British Architect*, "Mediterranean, Oriental, Historical and Modern styles representing the quintessence of contemporary taste." But there were some who even then found it fussy and decadent. When the Queen praised it as an example to the world Begg was knighted. Lady Carinthia, who survived him by many years, always credited herself as the Square's real procreator and it must be said that it was she who nudged her husband away from the past to embrace a more plastic future.

Work on Sporting Club Square began in 1885 but was not entirely completed until 1901. The slump of the 1890s destroyed the aspirations of the rising bourgeoisie, who were to have been the likely renters; Gibbs and Flew had bankrupted themselves building the Olympia Bridge, and nobody who still had money felt secure enough to cross into the new suburbs. Their dreams of elevation now frustrated, the failed and dispossessed took their new bitter poverty with them into the depths of a North Star development doomed never to rise and to become almost at once a watchword for social decrepitude, populated by loafers, psychopaths, unstable landladies, exploited seamstresses, drunkards, forgers, beaten wives, braggarts, embezzlers, rat-faced children, petty officials and prostitutes who had grown accustomed to the easy prosperity of the previous decade and were now deeply resentful of anyone more fortunate. They swiftly turned the district into everything it remained until the next tide of prosperity lifted it for a while, only to let it fall back almost in relief as another generation lost its hold upon life's ambitions. The terraces were occupied by casual labourers and petty thieves while the impoverished petite bourgeoisie sought the mews and parades. North Star became a synonym for wretchedness and miserable criminality and was usually avoided even by the police.

By 1935 the area was a warren to rival Notting Dale, but Sporting Club Square, the adjoining St Mary's Convent and the churchyard retained a rather dreamy, innocent air, untouched by the prevailing mood. Indeed, locals almost revered and protected the Square's tranquillity as if it were the only thing they had ever held holy and were proud of it. During the last war the Square was untouched by incendiaries roaring all around, but some of the flats were already abandoned and then taken over by the government to house mostly Jewish political exiles: these added to the cosmopolitan atmosphere. For years a Polish delicatessen stood on the corner of North Star Road; it was possible to buy all kinds of kosher food at Mrs Green's grocery, Mandrake Terrace, and the Foulsham Road French patisserie remained popular until 1980 when Madame Stejns retired. According to Edwin Begg, the war and the years of austerity were their best, with a marvellous spirit of cooperation everywhere. During the war and until 1954 open-air concerts were regularly performed by local musicians and an excellent theatrical group was eventually absorbed into the Lyric until that was rationalized. A song, 'The Rose of Sporting Club Square', was popular in the 1930s and the musical play it was written for was the basis of a Hollywood musical in 1940. The David Glazier Ensemble, perhaps the most innovative modern dance troupe of its day, occupied all the lower flats in Le Gallienne Chambers.

Edwin Begg was not the only resident to become famous with the general public. Wheldrake's association with the old tavern, where he spent two years of exile, is well known. Audrey Vernon lived most of her short life in Dowson Mansions. Her lover, Warwick Harden, took a flat in Ibsen Studios next door and had a door built directly through to her bedroom. John Angus Gilchrist, the mass murderer, lived here but dispatched his nearest victim three miles away in Shepherd's Bush. Others associated with the Square, sometimes briefly, included Pett Ridge, George Robey, Gustav Klimt, Rebecca West, Constance Cummings, Jessie Matthews, Sonny Hale, Jack Parker, Gerald Kersh, Laura Riding, Joseph Kiss,

John Lodwick, Edith Sitwell, Lord George Creech, Angela Thirkell, G.K. Chesterton, Max Miller, Sir Compton Mackenzie, Margery Allingham, Ralph Richardson, Eudora Welty, Donald Peers, Max Wall, Dame Fay Westbrook, Graham Greene, Eduardo Paolozzi, Gore Vidal, Bill Butler, Jimi Hendrix, Jack Trevor Story, Laura Ashley, Mario Amayo, Angela Carter, Simon Russell Beale, Ian Dury, Jonathan Carroll and a variety of sports and media personalities. As its preserves were stripped, repackaged and sold off during the feeding frenzy of the 1980s only the most stubborn residents refused to be driven from the little holdings they had once believed their birthright, but it was not until Edwin Begg led me back to his bedroom and raised the newly installed blind that I understood the full effect of his nephew's speculations. "We do not rest, do we," he said, "from mortal toil? But I'm not sure this is my idea of the new Jerusalem. What do you think, dear?"

They had taken his view. I was consumed with a sense of unspeakable outrage! They had turned that beautiful harmony into a muddy wasteland in which it seemed some monstrous, petulant child had scattered at random its filthy Tonka trucks and Corgi cranes, Portakabins, bulldozers in crazed abandon, then in tantrum stepped on everything. That perfect balance was destroyed and the tranquillity of Sporting Club Square was now forever under siege. The convent was gone, as well as the church.

"I read in the *Telegraph* that it required the passage of two private member's bills, the defiance of several preservation orders, the bribery of officials in thirteen different government departments and the black-mailing of a cabinet minister just to annex a third of the cemetery and knock down the chapel and almshouses," Begg said.

Meanwhile the small fry had looted the cemetery of its saleable masonry. Every monument had been chiselled. The severed heads of the angels were already being sold in the antique boutiques of Mayfair and St Germaine-des-Prés. Disappointed in their share of this loot, others had daubed swastikas and obscenities on the remaining stones.

"It's private building land now," said Begg. "They have dogs and fences. They bulldozed St Swithold's. You can't get to the Necropolis, let alone the river. Still, this is probably better than what they were going to build."

The activities of Barbican Begg and his associates, whose enterprises claimed more victims than Maxwell, have been discussed everywhere, but one of the consequences of BBIC's speculations was that bleak no man's land standing in place of Edwin Begg's familiar view. The legal problems of leases sold to and by at least nine separate companies means that while no further development has added to the Square's decline, attempts to redress the damage and activate the Council's preservation orders, which they ignored, have failed through lack of funds. The project, begun in the name of freedom and civic high-mindedness, always a mark of the scoundrel, remains a symbol and a monument to the asset-stripped 1980s. As yet only Frank Cornelius, Begg's close associate, has paid any satisfactory price for ruining so many lives.

"Barbican was born for that age." Edwin Begg drew down the blind against his ruined prospect and sat on his bed, his frail body scarcely denting the great Belgian pillows at his back. "Like a fly born to a dungheap. He could not help himself, my dear. It was his instinct to do what he did. Why are we always surprised by his kind?"

He had grown weak but eagerly asked if I would return the following Wednesday when he would tell me more about his visions and their effect upon his life. I promised to bring the ingredients of a meal. I would cook lunch. He was touched and amused by this. He thought the idea great fun.

I told him to stay where he was. It was easy to let myself out.

"You know," he called as I was leaving, "there's a legend in our family. How we protect the Grail which will one day bring a reconciliation between God and Lucifer. I have no Grail to pass on to you but I think I have its secret."

## THREE

*Astonishing Revelations of the Clapham Antichrist;*
*Claims the Creation of a New Messiah; His Visions of*
*Paradise & Surrendering His Soul for Knowledge;*
*Further Description of the Sporting Club Square*
*Madonna; Final Days of the Antichrist; His*
*Appearance In Death.*

"Perhaps the crowning irony," said the Clapham Antichrist of his unfrocking, "was how devoted a Christian I was then! I argued that we shouldn't wait for God or heroes but seek our solutions at the domestic level. Naturally, it would mean empowering everyone, because only a thoroughly enfranchised democracy ever makes the best of its people. Oh, well, you know the sort of thing. The universal idea that we all agree on and never seem to achieve. I merely suggested we take a hard look at the systems we used! They were quite evidently faulty! Not an especially revolutionary notion! But it met with considerable antagonism, as you know. Politics seems to be a war of labels, one slapped on top of another until any glimmer of truth is thoroughly obscured. It's no wonder how quickly they lose all grip on reality!"

"And that's what you told them?"

He stood in his dressing gown, staring down at a Square and gardens even BBIC had failed to conquer. The trees were full of the nests crows had built since the first farmers hedged the meadow. His study, with its books and big old-fashioned stereo, had hardly changed but had a deserted air now.

I had brought the ingredients of our lunch and stood in my street clothes with my bag expecting him to lead me to the kitchen, but he remained in his window and wanted me to stay. He pointed mysteriously towards the Duke's Elm and Gilbert's War Memorial, a fanciful drinking fountain that had never worked.

"That's what I told them, my dear. In the pulpit first. Then in the travelling shows. Then on the street. I was arrested for obstruction in 1937, refused to recognize the court and refused to pay the fine. This was my first brief prison sentence. Eventually I got myself in solitary.

"When I left prison I saw a London even more wretched than before. Beggars were everywhere. Vagrants were not in those days tolerated in the West

End, but were still permitted in the doorways of Soho and Somers Town. The squalor was as bad as anything Mayhew reported. I thought my anger had been brought under control in prison but I was wrong. The obscene exploitation of the weak by the strong was everywhere displayed. I did whatever I could. I stood on a box at Speaker's Corner. I wrote and printed pamphlets. I sent letters and circulars to everyone, to the newspapers, to the BBC. Nobody took me very seriously. In the main I was ignored. When I was not ignored I was insulted. Eventually, holding a sign in Oxford Street, I was again arrested but this time there was a scuffle with the arresting policeman. I went into Wormwood Scrubs until the outbreak of the Blitz when I was released to volunteer for the ambulance service. Well, I wasn't prepared to return to prison after the War and in fact my ideas had gained a certain currency. Do you remember what Londoners were like then, my dear? After we learned how to look after ourselves rather better than our leaders could? Our morale was never higher. London's last war was a war the people won in spite of the authorities. But somewhere along the line we gave our achievements over to the politicians, the power addicts. The result is that we now live in rookeries and slum courts almost as miserable as our nineteenth-century ancestors', or exist in blanketed luxury as divorced from common experience as a Russian Tsar. I'm not entirely sure about the quality of that progress, are you? These days the lowest common denominators are sought for as if they were principles."

"You're still an example to us," I said, thinking to console him.

He was grateful but shook his head, still looking

down at the old elm as if he hoped to see someone there. "I'll never be sure if I did any good. For a while, you know, I was quite a celebrity until they realized I wasn't offering an anti-Christian message and then they mostly lost interest. I couldn't get on with those Jesuits they all cultivated. But I spoke to the Fabians twice and met Wells, Shaw, Priestley and the rest. I was very cheerful. It appeared that I was spreading my message. I didn't understand that I was merely a vogue. I was quite a favourite with Bloomsbury and there was talk of putting me on Radio Luxembourg. But gradually doors were closed to me and I was rather humiliated on a couple of occasions. I hadn't started all this for fame or approval, so as soon as I realized what was happening I retired to the travelling shows and seaside fairgrounds that proliferated in England in the days before television.

"Eventually I began to doubt the value of my own pronouncements, since my audiences were dwindling and an evil force was progressing unchecked across Europe. We faced a future dominated by a few cruel dictatorships. Some kind of awful war was inevitable. During my final spell in clink I made up my mind to keep my thoughts to myself and consider better ways of getting them across. I saw nothing wrong with the message, but assumed myself to be a bad medium. In my free time I went out into the Square as much as I could. It was still easy to think there, even during the War."

He took a step towards the window, almost as if he had seen someone he recognized and then he shrugged, turning his head away sharply and pretending to take an interest in one of his Sickerts. "I found her there first, as you know, in 1933. And that one sight of her inspired a whole series of sermons. I came back week after week, but it always seemed as if I had just missed her. You could say I was in love with her. I wanted desperately for her to be real. Well, I had seen her again the evening I was 'unfrocked'. Of course I was in a pretty terrible state. I was praying. Since a boy I've always found it easy to pray in the Square. I identified God with the Duke's Elm – or at least I visualized God as a powerful old tree. I never understood why we placed such peculiar prohibitions on how we represented God. That's what they mean by 'pagan'. It has nothing to do with one's intellectual sophistication. I was praying when she appeared for the second time. First there was that strong scent of roses. When I looked up I saw her framed against the great trunk and it seemed a rose drew all her branches, leaves and blooms together and took human form!"

His face had a slight flush as he spoke. "It seemed to me I'd been given a companion to help me make the best use of my life. She had that vibrancy, that uncommon beauty; she was a sentient flower.

"Various Church examiners to whom I explained the vision understood my Rose either as an expression of my own unstable mind or as a manifestation of the devil. It was impossible for me to see her as either.

"She stepped forward and held out her hand to me. I had difficulty distinguishing her exact colours. They were many and subtle – an unbroken haze of pink and green and pale gold – all the shades of the rose. Her figure was slim but it wasn't easy to tell where her clothes met her body or even which was which. Her eyes changed in the light from deep emerald to violet. In spite of her extraordinary aura of power, her manner was almost hesitant. I think I was weeping as I went to her. I probably asked her what I should do. I know I decided to continue with my work. It was years before I saw her again, after I'd come out of prison for the last time."

"But you did see her again?"

"Very often. Especially during the Blitz. But I'd learned my lesson. I kept all that to myself."

"You were afraid of prison?"

"If you like. But I think it was probably more positive. God granted me a dream of the universe and her ever-expanding realities and I helped in the procreation of the new messiah!"

I waited for him to continue but he turned from the window with a broad smile. He was exhausted, tottering a little as he came with me to the kitchen and sat down in my place while I began to cook. He chatted amiably about the price of garlic and I prepared the dishes as he had taught me years before. This time, however, I was determined to encourage him to talk about himself.

He took a second glass of wine, his cheeks a little pinker than usual, his hair already beginning to rise about his head in a pure white fog.

"I suppose I needed her most during the War. There wasn't much time for talk, but I still came out to the Duke's Elm to pray. We began to meet frequently, always in the evening before dark, and would walk together, comparing experience. She was from a quite different world – although her world sort of included ours. Eventually we became lovers."

"Did she have a name?"

"I think so. I called her the Rose. I travelled with her. She took me to paradise, my dear, nowhere less! She showed me the whole of Creation! And so after a while my enthusiasm returned. Again, I wanted to share my vision but I had become far more cautious. I had a suspicion that I made a mistake the first time and almost lost my Rose as a result. When my nephew, who was in BBC Talks, offered me a new pulpit I was pretty much ready for it. This time I was determined to keep the reality to myself and just apply what I had experienced to ordinary, daily life. The public could not accept the intensity and implications of my pure vision. I cultivated an avuncularity that probably shocked those who knew me well. I became quite the jolly Englishman! I was offered speaking engagements in America. I was such a show-off. I spent less and less time in the Square and eventually months passed before I realized that I had lost contact with my Rose and our child! I felt such an utter fool, my dear. As soon as I understood what was happening I gave everything up. But it was too late."

"You haven't seen her since?"

"Only in dreams."

"What do you believe she was? The spirit of the tree?" I did my best to seem matter-of-fact, but he knew what I was up to and laughed, pouring himself more wine.

"She is her own spirit, my dear, make no mistake."

And then the first course was ready, a *pâté de foie gras* made by my friend Loris Murrail in Paris. Begg agreed that it was as good as his own. For our main course we had Quantock veal in saffron. He ate it with appreciative relish. He had not been able to cook much

98

lately, he said, and his appetite was reduced, but he enjoyed every bite. I was touched by his enthusiasm and made a private decision to come regularly again. Cooking him lunch would be my way of giving him something back. My spirits rose at the prospect and it was only then that I realized how much I had missed his company.

"Perhaps," he said, "she was sent to me to sustain me only when I most needed her. I had thought it a mistake to try to share her with the world. I never spoke of her again after I had told the bishop about her and was accused of militant paganism, primitive nature-worship. I saw his point of view but I always worshipped God in all his manifestations. The bishop seemed to argue that paganism was indistinguishable from common experience and therefore could not be considered a religion at all!"

"You worshipped her?"

"In a sense, my dear. As a man worships his wife."

I had made him a *tiesen sinamon* and he took his time with the meringue, lifting it up to his lips on the delicate silver fork that Begg's Cotswold benches had produced for Liberty in 1903. "I don't know if it's better or worse, dear, but the world is changing profoundly, you know. Our methods of making it safe just aren't really working any more. The danger of the simple answer is always with us and is inclined to lead to some sort of Final Solution. We are affected by turbulence as a leaf in the wind, but still we insist that the best way of dealing with the fact is to deny it or ignore it. And so we go on, hopelessly attempting to contain the thunder and the lightning and creating only further confusion! We're always caught by surprise! Yet it would require so little, surely, in the way of courage and imagination to find a way out, especially with today's wonderful computers?"

I had been depressed by the level and the outcome of the recent British election and was not optimistic. He agreed. "How we love to cling to the wrecks that took us on to the rocks in the first place. In our panic we don't even see the empty lifeboats within easy swimming distance."

He did not have the demeanour of a disappointed prophet. He remained lively and humorous. There was no sense of defeat about him, rather of quiet victory, of conquered pain. He did not at first seem disposed to tell me any more but when we were having coffee a casual remark set him off on a train of thought that led naturally back to that most significant event of his life. "We aren't flawed," he said, "just as God isn't flawed. What we perceive as flaws are a reflection of our own failure to see the whole." He spoke of a richly populated multiverse which was both within us and outside us. "We're all reflections and echoes, one of another, and our originals, dear, are lost, probably for ever. That was what I understood from my vision. I wrote it in my journal. Perhaps, very rarely, we're granted a glimpse of God's entire plan? Perhaps only when our need is desperate. I have no doubt that God sent me my Rose."

I am still of a secular disposition. "Or perhaps," I suggested, "as God you sent yourself a vision?"

He did not find this blasphemous but neither did he think it worth pursuing. "It's much of a muchness, that," he said.

He was content in his beliefs. He had questioned them once but now he was convinced. "God sent me a vision and I followed her. She was made flesh. A miracle. I went with her to where she lived, in the fields of colour, in the far ether. We were married. We gave birth to a new human creature, neither male nor female but self-reproducing, a new messiah, and it set us free at last to dwell on that vast multiplicity of the heavens, to contemplate a quasi-infinity of versions of ourselves, our histories, our experience. That was what God granted me, my dear, when he sent me my Rose. Perhaps I was the Antichrist, after all, or at least its parent."

"In your vision did you see what became of the child?"

He spoke with lighthearted familiarity, not recalling some distant dream but describing an immediate reality. "Oh, yes. It grew to lead the world upon a new stage in our evolution. I'm not sure you'd believe the details, my dear, or find them very palatable."

I smiled at this, but for the first time in my life felt a hint of profound terror and I suppressed a sudden urge to shout at him, to tell him how ridiculous I considered his visions, a bizarre blend of popular prophecy and alchemical mumbo-jumbo that even a New Age traveller would take with a pinch of E. My anger overwhelmed me. Though I regained control of it he recognized it. He continued to speak but with growing reluctance and perhaps melancholy. "I saw a peculiar inevitability to the process. What, after all, do most of us live for? Ourselves? And what use is that? What value? What profit?"

With a great sigh he put down his fork. "That was delicious." His satisfaction felt to me like an accolade.

"You're only describing human nature." I took his plate.

101

"Is that what keeps us on a level with the amoeba, my dear, and makes us worth about as much individual affection? Come now! We allow ourselves to be ruled by every brutish, greedy instinct, not by what is significantly human in our nature! Our imagination is our greatest gift. It gives us our moral sensibility." He looked away through the dining room window at the glittering domes of Gautier House and in the light the lines of his face were suddenly emphasized.

I had no wish ever to quarrel with him again. The previous argument, we were agreed, had cost us both too much. But I had to say what I thought. "I was once told the moment I mentioned morality was the moment I'd crossed the line into lunacy," I said. "I suppose we must agree to understand things differently."

For once he had forgotten his usual courtesy. I don't think he heard me. "Wasn't all this damage avoidable?" he murmured. "Weren't there ways in which cities could have grown up as we grew up, century adding to century, style to style, wisdom to wisdom? Isn't there something seriously wrong with the cycle we're in? Isn't there some way out?"

I made to reply but he shook his head, his hands on the table. "I saw her again, you know, several times after the birth. How beautiful she was! How much beauty she showed me! It's like an amplification, my dear, of every sense! A discovery of new senses. An understanding that we don't need to discard anything as long as we continue to learn from it. It isn't frightening, what she showed me. It's perfectly familiar once you begin to see. It's like looking at the quintessential versions of our ordinary realities. Trees,

102

animals – they're there, in essence. You begin to discover all that. The fundamental geometry's identified. Well, you've seen this new math, haven't you?"

He seemed so vulnerable at that moment that for once I wasn't frank. I was unconvinced by what I judged as hippy physics made possible only by the new creative powers of computers. I didn't offer him an argument.

"You can't help but hope that it's what death is like," he said. "You become an angel."

He got up and returned slowly to his dusty study, beckoning me to look out with him into the twilight gathering around the trees where crows croaked their mutual reassurances through the darkening air. He glanced only once towards the old elm, then turned his head away sharply. "You'll think this unlikely, I know, but we first came together physically at midnight under a full moon as bright and thin and yellow as honesty in a dark blue sky. I looked at the moon through those strong black branches the moment before we touched. The joy of our union was indescribable. It was a confirmation of my faith. I made a mistake going back into public life. What good did it do for anyone, my dear?"

"We all made too many easy assumptions," I said. "It wasn't your fault."

"I discovered sentimental solutions and comforted myself with them. Those comforts I turned to material profit. They became lies. And I lost her, my dear." He made a small, anguished gesture. "I'm still waiting for her to come back."

He was scarcely aware of me. I felt I had intruded upon a private moment and suggested that I had tired him and should leave. Looking at me in surprise but without dispute he came towards me, remarking in particular on the saffron sauce. "I can't tell you how much it meant to me, my dear, in every way."

I promised to return the following Wednesday and cook. He licked his pink lips in comic anticipation and seemed genuinely delighted by the prospect. "Yum, yum." He embraced me suddenly with his frail body, his sweet face staring blindly into mine.

I had found his last revelations disturbing and my tendency was to dismiss them, perhaps as an early sign of his senility. I even considered putting off my promised visit, but was already planning the next lunch when three days later I took a call from Mrs Arthur Begg who kept an eye on him and had my number. The Clapham Antichrist had died in his sleep. She had found him at noon with his head raised upon his massive pillows, the light from the open window falling on his face. She enthused over his wonderful expression in death.

*In memoriam, Horst Grimm*

# LONDON BONE

*For Ronnie Scott*

## 1.

My name is Raymond Gold and I'm a well-known dealer. I was born too many years ago in Upper Street, Islington. Everybody reckons me in the London markets and I have a good reputation in Manchester and the provinces. I have bought and sold, been the middleman, an agent, an art representative, a professional mentor, a tour guide, a spiritual bridge-builder. These days I call myself a cultural speculator.

But, you won't like it, the more familiar word for my profession, as I practised it until recently, is *scalper*. This kind of language is just another way of isolating the small businessman and making what he does seem sleazy while the stockbroker dealing in millions is supposed to be legitimate. But I don't need to convince anyone today that there's no sodding justice.

'Scalping' is risky. What you do is invest in tickets on spec and hope to make a timely sale when the market for them hits zenith. Any kind of ticket, really, but mostly shows. I've never seen anything offensive about getting the maximum possible profit out of an American matron with more money than sense who's anxious to report home with the right items ticked off the *been-to* list. We've all seen them rushing about in their overpriced limos and minibuses, pretending to be individuals: **Thursday:** Changing-of-the-Guard, Harrods, Planet Hollywood, Royal Academy, Tea-At-the-Ritz, *Cats*. It's a sort of tribal dance they are compelled to perform. If they don't perform it, they feel inadequate. **Saturday:** Tower of London, Bucket of Blood, Jack-the-Ripper talk, Sherlock Holmes Pub, Sherlock Holmes tour, Madame Tussaud's, Covent Garden Cream Tea, *Dogs*. These are people so traumatized by contact with strangers that their only security lies in these rituals, these well-blazed trails and familiar chants. It's my job to smooth their paths, to make them exclaim how pretty and wonderful and elegant and *magical* it all is. The street people aren't a problem. They're just so many charming Dick Van Dykes.

Americans need bullshit the way koala bears need eucalyptus leaves. They've become totally addicted to it. They get so much of it back home that they can't survive without it. It's your duty to help them get their regular fixes while they travel. And when they make it back after three weeks on alien shores, their friends, of

106

course, are always glad of some foreign bullshit for a change.

Even if you sell a show ticket to a real enthusiast, who has already been forty-nine times and is so familiar to the cast they see him in the street and think he's a relative, who are you hurting? Andros Loud Website, Lady Hatchet's loyal laureate, who achieved rank and wealth by celebrating the lighter side of the moral vacuum? He would surely applaud my enterprise in the buccaneering spirit of the free market. Venture capitalism at its bravest. Well, he'd applaud me if he had time these days from his railings against fate, his horrible understanding of the true nature of his coming obscurity. But that's partly what my story's about.

I have to say in my own favour that I'm not merely a speculator or, if you like, exploiter. I'm also a patron. For many years, not just recently, a Niagara of dosh has flowed out of my pocket and into the real arts faster than a cat up a Frenchman. Whole orchestras and famous soloists have been brought to the Wigmore Hall on the money they get from me. But I couldn't have afforded this if it wasn't for the definitely iffy *Miss Saigon* (a triumph of well-oiled machinery over dodgy morality) or the unbelievably decrepit *Good Rockin' Tonite* (in which the living dead jive in the aisles), nor, of course, that first great theatrical triumph of the new millennium, *Schindler: The Musical*. Make 'em weep, Uncle Walt!

So who is helping most to support the arts? You, me, the lottery?

I had another reputation, of course, which some saw as a second profession. I was one of the last great London characters. I was always on late-night telly, lit from below, and Iain Sinclair couldn't write a paragraph without dropping my name at least once. I'm a quintessential Londoner, I am. I'm a Cockney gentleman.

I read Israel Zangwill and Gerald Kersh and Alexander Barron. I can tell you the best books of Pett Ridge and Arthur Morrison. I know Pratface Charlie, Driff and Martin Stone, Bernie Michaud and the even more legendary Gerry and Pat Goldstein. They're all historians, archaeologists, revenants. There isn't another culture-dealer in London, oldster or child, who doesn't at some time come to me for an opinion. Even now, when I'm as popular as a pig at a Putney wedding and people hold their noses and dive into traffic rather than have to say hello to me, they still need me for that.

I've known all the famous Londoners or known someone else who did. I can tell stories of long-dead gangsters who made the Krays seem like Amnesty International. Bare-knuckle boxing. Fighting the fascists in the East End. Gun-battles with the police all over Stepney in the 1900s. The terrifying girl gangsters of Whitechapel. Barricading the Old Bill in his own barracks down in Notting Dale.

I can tell you where all the music halls were and what was sung in them. And why. I can tell Marie Lloyd stories and Max Miller stories that are fresh and sharp and bawdy as the day they happened, because their wit and experience came out of the market streets of London. The same streets. The same markets. The same family names. London *is* markets. Markets are London.

I'm a Londoner through and through. I know Mr Gog personally. I know Ma Gog even more personally. During the day I can walk anywhere from Bow to

Bayswater faster than any taxi. I love the markets. Brick
Lane. Church Street. Portobello. You won't find me on
a bike with my bum in the air on a winter's afternoon.
I walk or drive. Nothing in between. I wear a camel-
hair in winter and a Barraclough's in summer. You
know what would happen to a coat like that on a bike.

I love the theatre. I like modern dance, very good
movies and ambitious international contemporary
music. I like poetry, prose, painting and the decorative
arts. I like the lot, the very best that London's got, the
whole bloody casserole. I gobble it all up and bang on
my bowl for more. Let timid greenbelters creep in at
weekends and sink themselves in the West End's
familiar deodorized shit if they want to. That's not my
city. That's a tourist set. It's what I live off. What all of
us show-people live off. It's the old, familiar circus. The
big rotate.

We're selling what everybody recognizes. What
makes them feel safe and certain and sure of every
single moment in the city. Nothing to worry about in
jolly old London. We sell charm and colour by the yard.
Whole word factories turn out new rhyming slang and
saucy street characters are trained on council grants.
Don't frighten the horses. Licensed pearlies pause for a
photo opportunity in the dockside Secure Zones.
Without all that cheap scenery, without our myths and
magical skills, without our whorish good cheer and
instincts for trade – any kind of trade – we probably
wouldn't have a living city.

As it is, the real city I live in has more creative energy
per square inch at work at any given moment than
anywhere else on the planet. But you'd never know it
from a stroll up the Strand. It's almost all in those lively

little side streets the English-speaking tourists can't help feeling a bit nervous about and that the French adore.

If you use music for comfortable escape you'd probably find more satisfying and cheaper relief in a massage parlour than at the umpteenth revival of *The Sound of Music*. I'd tell that to any hesitant punter who's not too sure. Check out the phone boxes for the ladies, I'd say, or you can go to the half-price ticket-booth in Leicester Square and pick up a ticket that'll deliver real value – Ibsen or Shakespeare, Shaw or Churchill. Certainly you can fork out three hundred sheets for a fifty-sheet ticket that in a justly ordered world wouldn't be worth two pee and have your ears salved and your cradle rocked for two hours. Don't worry, I'd tell them, I make no judgements. Some hard-working whore profits, whatever you decide. So who's the cynic?

I went on one of those tours when my friends Dave and Di from Bury came up for the *Festival of London* in 2001 and it's amazing, the crap they tell people. They put sex, violence and money into every story. They know fuck-all. They soup everything up. It's *Sun*-reader history. Even the Beefeaters at the Tower. Poppinsland. All that old English duff.

It makes you glad to get back to Soho.

Not so long ago you would usually find me in the Princess Louise, Berwick Street, at lunchtime, a few doors down from the Chinese chippy and just across from Mrs White's trim stall in Berwick Market. It's only a narrow door and is fairly easy to miss. It has one bottle-glass window onto the street. This is a public house that has not altered since the 1940s when it was very popular with Dylan Thomas, Mervyn Peake,

110

Ruthven Todd, Henry Treece and a miscellaneous bunch of other Welsh adventurers who threatened for a while to take over English poetry from the Irish.

It's a shit pub, so dark and smoky you can hardly find your glass in front of your face, but the look of it keeps the tourists out. It's used by all the culture pros – from arty types with backpacks, who do specialized walking tours, to famous gallery owners and top museum management – and by the heavy-metal bikers. We all get on a treat. We are mutually dependent in our continuing resistance to invasion or change, to the preservation of the best and most vital aspects of our culture. We leave the bikers alone because they protect us from the tourists, who might recognize us and make us put on our masks in a hurry. They leave us alone because the police won't want to bother a bunch of well-connected middle-class wankers like us. It is a wonderful example of mutuality. In the back rooms, thanks to some freaky accoustics, you can talk easily above the music and hardly know it's there.

Over the years there have been some famous friendships and unions struck between the two groups. My own lady wife was known as Karla the She-Goat in an earlier incarnation and had the most exquisite and elaborate tattoos I ever saw. She was a wonderful wife and would have made a perfect mother. She died on the A1, on the other side of Watford Gap. She had just found out she was pregnant and was making her last sentimental run. It did me in for marriage for a while. And urban romance.

I first heard about London Bone in the Princess Lou when Claire Rood, that elegant old dike from the Barbican, who'd tipped me off about my new tailor, pulled my ear to her mouth and asked me in words of solid gin and garlic to look out for some for her, darling. None of the usual faces seemed to know about it. A couple of top-level museum people knew a bit, but it was soon obvious they were hoping I'd fill them in on the details. I showed them a confident length of cuff. I told them to keep in touch.

I did my Friday walk, starting in the horrible pre-dawn chill of the Portobello Road where some youth tried to sell me a bit of scrimshawed reconstitute as 'the real old Bone'. I warmed myself in the showrooms of elegant Kensington and Chelsea dealers telling out-rageous stories of deals, profits and crashes until they grew uncomfortable and wanted to talk about me and I got the message and left.

I wound up that evening in the urinal of The Dragoons in Meard Alley, swapping long-time-no-sees with my boyhood friend Bernie Michaud who begins immediately by telling me he's got a bit of business I might be interested in. And since it's Bernie Michaud telling me about it I listen. Bernie never deliberately spread a rumour in his life but he's always known how to make the best of one. This is kosher, he thinks. It has a bit of a glow. It smells like a winner. A long-distance runner. He is telling me out of friendship, but I'm not really interested. I'm trying to find out about London Bone.

"I'm not talking drugs, Ray, you know that. And it's not bent." Bernie's little pale face is serious. He takes a thoughtful sip of his whisky. "It is, admittedly, a commodity."

I wasn't interested. I hadn't dealt in goods for years. "Services only, Bernie," I said. "Remember. It's my rule. Who wants to get stuck paying rent on a warehouse full of yesterday's faves? I'm still trying to move those *Glenda Sings Michael Jackson* sides Pratface talked me into."

"What about investment?" he says. "This is the real business, Ray, believe me."

So I heard him out. It wouldn't be the first time Bernie had brought me back a nice profit on some deal I'd helped him bankroll and I was all right at the time. I'd just made the better part of a month's turnover on a package of theatreland's most profitable stinkers brokered for a party of filthy-rich New Muscovites who thought Chekhov was something you did with your lottery numbers.

As they absorbed the quintessence of Euro-ersatz, guaranteed to offer, as its high emotional moment, a long, relentless bowel movement, I would be converting their hard roubles back into Beluga.

It's a turning world, the world of the international free market, and everything's wonderful and cute and pretty and *magical* so long as you keep your place on the carousel. It's not good if it stops. And it's worse if you get thrown off altogether. Pray to Mammon that you never have to seek the help of an organization that calls you a 'client'. That puts you outside the fairground for ever. No more rides. No more fun. No more life.

Bernie only did quality art, so I knew I could trust that side of his judgement, but what was it? A new batch of Raphaels turned up in a Willesden attic? Andy Warhol's lost landscapes found at the Pheasantry?

"There's American collectors frenzied for this stuff," murmurs Bernie through a haze of Sons of the Wind, Motorchair and Montecristo fumes. "And if it's

113

decorated they go through the roof. All the big Swiss guys are looking for it. Freddy K in Cairo has a Saudi buyer who tops any price. Rose Sarkissian in Agadir represents three French collectors. It's never catalogued. It's all word of mouth. And it's already turning over millions. There's one inferior piece in New York and none at all in Paris. The pieces in Zurich are probably all fakes."

This made me feel that I was losing touch. I still didn't know what he was getting at.

"Listen," I say, "before we go any further, let's talk about this London Bone."

"You're a fly one, Ray," he says. "How did you suss it?"

"Tell me what you know," I say. "And then I'll fill you in."

We went out of the pub, bought some fish and chips at the Chinese and then walked up Berwick Street and round to his little club in D'Arblay Street where we sat down in his office and closed the door. The place stank of cat-pee. He doted on his Persians. They were all out in the club at the moment, being petted by the patrons.

"First," he says, "I don't have to tell you, Ray, that this is strictly double-schtum and I will kill you if a syllable gets out."

"Naturally," I said.

"Have you ever seen any of this Bone?" he asked. He went to his cupboard and found some vinegar and salt. "Or better still handled it?"

"No," I said. "Not unless it's fake scrimshaw."

"This stuff's got a depth to it you've never dreamed about. A lustre. You can tell it's the real thing as soon as you see it. Not just the shapes or the decoration, but

114

the quality of it. It's like it's got a soul. You could come close, but you could never fake it. Like amber, for instance. That's why the big collectors are after it. It's authentic, it's newly discovered and it's rare."

"What bone is it?"

"Mastodon. Some people still call it mammoth ivory, but I haven't seen any actual ivory. It could be dinosaur. I don't know. Anyway, this bone is *better* than ivory. It's in weird shapes, probably fragments off some really big animal."

"And where's it coming from?"

"The heavy clay of good old London," says Bernie. "A fortune at our feet, Ray. And my people know where to dig."

## 2.

I had to be straight with Bernie. Until I saw a piece of the stuff in my own hand and got an idea about it for myself, I couldn't do anything. The only time in my life I'd gone for a gold brick I'd bought it out of respect for the genius running the scam. He deserved what I gave him. Which was a bit less than he was hoping for. Rather than be conned, I would rather *throw* the money away. I'm like that with everything.

I had my instincts, I told Bernie. I had to go with them. He understood completely and we parted on good terms.

If the famous Lloyd Webber meltdown of '03 had happened a few months earlier or later I would never have thought again about going into the Bone business, but I was done in by one of those sudden changes of

public taste that made the George M. Cohan crash of
'31 seem like a run of *The Mousetrap*.

Sentimental fascism went out the window. Liberal-
humanist contemporary relevance, artistic aspiration,
intellectual and moral substance and all that stuff was
somehow in demand. It was *better* than the Sixties. It
was one of those splendid moments when the public
pulls itself together and tries to grow up. Jones's *Rhyme
of the Flying Bomb* song-cycle made a glorious come-
back. *American Angels* returned with even more punch.

And Sondheim became a quality brand name. If it
wasn't by Sondheim or based on a tune Sondheim used
to hum in the shower, the punters didn't want to know.
Overnight, the public's product loyalty had changed.
And I must admit it had changed for the better. But my
investments were in *Cats*, and *Dogs* (Lord Webber's
last desperate attempt to squeeze from Thurber what
he'd sucked from Eliot), *Duce!* and *Starlight Excess,* all
of which were now taking a walk down *Sunset
Boulevard*. I couldn't even get a regular-price ticket for
myself at *Sunday in the Park*, *Assassins* or *Follies. Into
The Woods* was solid for eighteen months ahead. I saw
*Passion* from the wings and *Sweeney Todd* from the
gods. *Five Guys Named Mo* crumbled to dust.
*Phantom* closed. Its author claimed sabotage.

"Quality will out, Ray," says Bernie next time I see
him at the Lou. "You've got to grant the public that.
You just have to give it time."

"Fuck the public," I said, with some feeling. "They're
just nostalgic for quality at the moment. Next year it'll
be something else. Meanwhile I'm bloody ruined. You
couldn't drum a couple of oncers on my entire stock.
Even my ENO side-bets have died. Covent Garden's a

disaster. The weather in Milan didn't help. That's where Cecilia Bartoli caught her cold. I was lucky to be offered half-price for the Rossinis without her. And I know what I'd do if I could get a varda at bloody Simon Rattle."

"So you won't be able to come in on the Bone deal?" said Bernie, returning to his own main point of interest.

"I said I was ruined," I told him, "not wiped out."

"Well, I got something to show you now, anyway," says Bernie.

We went back to his place.

He put it in my hand as if it were a nugget of plutonium: a knuckle of dark, golden Bone, split off from a larger piece, covered with tiny pictures.

"The engravings are always on that kind of Bone," he said. "There are other kinds that don't have drawings, maybe from a later date. It's the work of the first Londoners, I suppose, when it was still a swamp. About the time your Phoenician ancestors started getting into the upriver woad-trade. I don't know the significance, of course."

The Bone itself was hard to analyse because of the mixture of chemicals that had created it and some of it had fused, suggesting prehistoric upheavals of some kind. The drawings were extremely primitive. Any bored person with a sharp object and minimum talent could have done them at any time in history. The larger, weirder-looking Bones, had no engravings.

Stick people pursued other stick people endlessly across the fragment. The work was unremarkable. The beauty really was in the tawny ivory colour of the Bone itself. It glowed with a wealth of shades and drew you hypnotically into its depths. I imagined the huge animal of which this fragment had once been an active part. I saw the bellowing trunk, the vast ears, the glinting tusks succumbing suddenly to whatever had engulfed her. I saw her body swaying, her tail lashing as she trumpeted her defiance of her inevitable death. And now men sought her remains as treasure. It was a very romantic image and of course it would become my most sincere sales pitch.

"That's six million dollars you're holding there," said Bernie. "Minimum."

Bernie had caught me at the right time and I had to admit I was convinced. Back in his office he sketched out the agreement. We would go in on a fifty-fifty basis, funding the guys who would do the actual digging, who knew where the Bone-fields were and who would tell us as soon as we showed serious interest. We would finance all the work, pay them an upfront earnest and then load by load in agreed increments. Bernie and I would split the net profit fifty-fifty. There were all kinds of clauses and provisions covering the various problems we foresaw and then we had a deal.

The archaeologists came round to my little place in Dolphin Square. They were a scruffy bunch of students from the University of Norbury who had discovered the Bone deposits on a run-of-the-mill field trip in a demolished Southwark housing estate and knew only that there might be a market for them. Recent cuts to their grants had made them desperate. Some lefty had come up with a law out of the Magna Carta or some- where saying public land couldn't be sold to private developers and so there was a court case disputing the council's right to sell the estate to Livingstone

International, which also put a stop to the planned rebuilding. So we had indefinite time to work.

The stoodies were grateful for our expertise, as well as our cash. I was happy enough with the situation. It was one I felt we could easily control. Middle-class burbnerds get greedy the same as anyone else, but they respond well to reason. I told them for a start-off that all the Bone had to come in to us. If any of it leaked onto the market by other means, we'd risk losing our prices and that would mean the scheme was over. "Terminated," I said significantly. Since we had reputations as well as investments to protect there would also be recriminations. That was all I had to say. Since those Vserials kids think we're Krays and Mad Frankie Frasers just because we like to look smart and talk properly.

We were fairly sure we weren't doing anything obviously criminal. The stuff wasn't treasure trove. It had to be cleared before proper foundations could be poured. Quite evidently LI didn't think it was worth paying security staff to shuft the site. We didn't know if digging shafts and tunnels was even trespass, but we knew we had a few weeks before someone started asking about us and by then we hoped to have the whole bloody mastodon out of the deep clay and nicely earning for us. The selling would take the real skill and that was my job. It was going to have to be played sharper than South African diamonds.

After that neither Bernie nor I had anything to do with the dig. We rented a guarded lock-up in Clapham and paid the kids every time they brought in a substantial load of Bone. It was incredible stuff. Bernie thought that chemical action, some of it relatively recent, had caused the phenomenon. "Like chalk, you know. You hardly find it anywhere. Just a few places in England, France, China and Texas." The kids reported that there was more than one kind of animal down there, but that all the Bone had the same rich appearance. They had constructed a new tunnel, with a hidden entrance, so that even if the building site was blocked to them, they could still get at the Bone. It seemed to be a huge field, but most of the Bone was at roughly the same depth. Much of it had fused and had to be chipped out. They had found no end to it so far and they had tunneled through more than half an acre of the dense, dark clay.

Meanwhile I was in Amsterdam and Rio, Paris and Vienna and New York and Sydney. I was in Tokyo and Seoul and Hong Kong. I was in Ryad, Cairo and Baghdad. I was in Kampala and New Benin, everywhere there were major punters. I racked up so many free air-miles in a couple of months that they were automatically jumping me to first class. But I achieved what I wanted. Nobody bought London Bone without checking with me. I was the acknowledged expert. The prime source, the best in the business. If you want Bone, said the art world, you want Gold.

The Serious Fraud Squad became interested in Bone for a while, but they had been assuming we were faking it and gave up when it was obviously not rubbish.

Neither Bernie nor I expected it to last any longer than it did. By the time our first phase of selling was over we were turning over so much dough it was silly and the kids were getting tired and were worrying about exploring some of their wildest dreams. There was almost nothing left, they said. So we closed down the operation, moved our warehouses a couple of times and then let the Bone sit there to make us some money while everyone wondered why it had dried up.

And at that moment, inevitably, and late as ever, the newspapers caught on to the story. There was a brief late-night TV piece. A few supplements talked about it in their arts pages. This led to some news stories and eventually it went to the tabloids and the Bone became anything you liked, from the remains of Martians to a new kind of nuclear waste. Anyone who saw the real stuff was convinced but everyone had a theory about it. The real exclusive market was finished. We kept schtum. We were gearing up for the second phase. We got as far away from our stash as possible.

Of course, a few faces tracked me down, but I denied any knowledge of the Bone. I was a middleman, I said. I just had good contacts. Half a dozen people claimed to know where the Bone came from. Of course they talked to the papers. I sat back in satisfied security, watching the mud swirl over our tracks. Another couple of months and we'd be even safer than the house I'd bought in Hampstead overlooking the Heath. It had a rather forlorn garden the size of Kilburn, which needed a lot of nurturing. That suited me. I was ready to retire to the country and a big indoor swimming pool.

By the time a close version of the true story came out, from one of the stoodies, who'd lost all his share in a lottery syndicate, it was just one of many. It sounded too dull. I told newspaper reporters that while I would love to have been involved in such a lucrative scheme, my money came from theatre tickets. Meanwhile, Bernie and I thought of our warehouse and said nothing.

Now the stuff was getting into the culture. It was chic. *Puncher* used it in their ads. It was called Mammoth Bone by the media. There was a common story about how a herd had wandered into the swampy river and drowned in the mud. Lots of pictures dusted off from the Natural History Museum. Experts explained the colour, the depths, the markings, the beauty. Models sported a Bone motif.

Our second phase was to put a fair number of inferior fragments on the market and see how the public responded. That would help us find our popular price – the most a customer would pay. We were looking for a few good millionaires.

Frankly, as I told my partner, I was more than ready to get rid of the lot. But Bernie counselled me to patience. We had a plan and it made sense to stick to it.

The trade continued to run well for a while. As the sole source of the stuff, we could pretty much control everything. Then one Sunday lunchtime I met Bernie at The Six Jolly Dragoons in Meard Alley, Soho. He had something to show me, he said. He didn't even glance around. He put it on the bar in plain daylight. A small piece of Bone with the remains of decorations still on it.

"What about it?" I said.

"It's not ours," he said.

My first thought was that the stoodies had opened up the field again. That they had lied to us when they said it had run out.

"No," said Bernie, "it's not even the same colour. It's the same stuff – but different shades. Gerry Goldstein lent it to me."

"Where did he get it?"

"He was offered it," Bernie said.

We didn't bother to speculate where it had come from. But we did have rather a lot of our Bone to shift quickly. Against my will, I made another world tour and sold mostly to other dealers this time. It was a standard second-wave operation but run rather faster than was wise. We definitely missed the crest.

However, before deliveries were in and cheques were cashed, Jack Merrywidow, the fighting MP for Brook-gate and East Holborn, gets up in the House of Commons on telly one afternoon and asks if Prime Minister Bland or any of his dope-dazed Cabinet under-stand that human remains, taken from the hallowed burial grounds of London, are being sold by the piece in the international market place? Mr Bland makes a plummy joke enjoyed at Mr Merrywidow's expense and sits down. But Jack won't give up. They're suddenly on telly. It's *The Struggle of Parliament* time. Jack's had the Bone examined by experts. It's human. Undoubtedly human. The strange shapes are caused by limbs melting together in soil heavy with lime. Chemical reactions, he says. We have – he raises his eyes to the camera – been mining mass graves.

A shock to all those who still long for the years of common decency. Someone, says Jack, is selling more than our heritage. Hasn't free-market capitalism got a little bit out of touch when we start selling the arms, legs and skulls of our forebears? The torsos and shoulder-blades of our honourable dead? What did we used to call people who did that? When was the government going to stop this trade in corpses?

It's denied.

It's proved.

It looks like trade is about to slump.

123

I think of framing the cheques as a reminder of the vagaries of fate and give up any idea of popping the question to my old muse Little Trudi, who is back on the market, having been dumped by her corporate suit in a fit, he's told her, of self-disgust after seeing *The Tolstoy Investment* with Eddie Izzard. Bernie, I tell my partner, the Bone business is down the drain. We might as well bin the stuff we've stockpiled.

Then, two days, later the TV news reports a vast public interest in London Bone. Some lordly old queen with four names comes on the evening news to say how by owning a piece of Bone, you own London's true history. You become a curator of some ancient ancestor. He's clearly got a vested interest in the stuff. It's the hottest tourist item since Jack the Ripper razors and OJ gloves. More people want to buy it than ever.

The only trouble is, I don't deal in dead people. It is, in fact, where I have always drawn the line. Even Pratface Charlie wouldn't sell his great-great-grand-mother's elbow to some overweight Jap in a deerstalker and a kilt. I'm faced with a genuine moral dilemma.

I make a decision. I make a promise to myself. I can't go back on that. I go down to the Italian chippy in Fortess Road, stoke up on nourishing ritual grease (cod, roe, chips and mushy peas, bread and butter and tea, syrup pudding), then heave my out-of-shape, but mentally prepared, body up onto Parliament Hill to roll myself a big wacky-baccy fag and let my subconscious think the problem through.

When I emerge from my reverie, I have looked out over the whole misty London panorama and considered the city's complex history. I have thought about the number of dead buried there since, say, the time of

Boudicca, and what they mean to the soil we build on, the food we still grow here and the air we breathe. We are recycling our ancestors all the time, one way or another. We are sucking them in and shitting them out. We're eating them. We're drinking them. We're coughing them up. The dead don't rest. Bits of them are permanently at work. So what am I doing wrong?

This thought is comforting until my moral sense, sharpening itself up after a long rest, kicks in with *But what's different here is you're flogging the stuff to people who take it home with them.* Back to Wisconsin and California and Peking. You take it out of circulation. You're dissipating the deep fabric of the city. You're unravelling something. Like, the real infrastructure, the spiritual and physical bones of an ancient city . . .

On Kite Hill I suddenly realize that those bones are in some way the deep life-stuff of London.

It grows dark over the towers and roofs of the metropolis. I sit on my bench and roll myself a further joint. I watch the silver rising from the river, the deep golden glow of the distant lights, the plush of the foliage, and as I watch it seems to shred before my eyes, like a rotten curtain. Even the traffic noise grows fainter. Is the city sick? Is she expiring? Somehow it seems there's a little less breath in the old girl. I blame myself. And Bernie. And those kids.

There and then, on the spot, I renounce all further interest in the Bone trade. If nobody else will take the relics back, then I will.

There's no resolve purer than the determination you draw from a really good reefer.

## 3.

So now there isn't a tourist in any London market or antique arcade who isn't searching out Bone. They know it isn't cheap. They know they have to pay. And pay they do. Through the nose. And half of what they buy is crap or fakes. This is a question of status, not authenticity. As long as we say it's good, they can say it's good. We give it a provenance, a story, something to colour the tale to the folks back home. We're honest dealers. We sell only the authentic stuff. Still they get conned. But still they look. Still they buy.

Jealous Mancunians and Brummies long for a history old enough to provide them with Bone. A few of the early settlements, like Chester and York, start turning up something like it, but it's not the same. Jim Morrison's remains disappear from Père La Chaise. They might be someone else's bones, anyway. Rumour is they were KFC bones. The Revolutionary death-pits fail to deliver the goods. The French are furious. They accuse the British of gross materialism and poor taste. Oscar Wilde disappears. George Eliot. Winston Churchill. You name them. For a few months there is a grotesque trade in the remains of the famous. But the fashion has no intrinsic substance and fizzles out. Anyone could have seen it wouldn't run.

Bone has the image, because Bone really is beautiful.

Too many people are yearning for that Bone. The real stuff. It genuinely hurts me to disappoint them. Circumstances alter cases. Against my better judgement I continue in the business. I bend my principles, just for the duration. We have as much turnover as we had selling to the Swiss gnomes. It's the latest item on the *been-to* list. 'You *have* to bring me back some London Bone, Ethel, or I'll never forgive you!' It starts to appear in the American luxury catalogues.

But by now there are ratsniffers everywhere – from Trade and Industry, from the National Trust, from the Heritage Corp, from half a dozen South London councils, from the Special Branch, from the CID, the Inland Revenue and both the Funny and the Serious Fraud Squads.

Any busybody who ever wanted to put his head under someone else's bed is having a wonderful time. Having failed dramatically with the STOP THIS DISGUSTING TRADE approach, the tabloids switch to offering bits of Bone as prizes in circulation boosters. I sell a newspaper consortium a Tesco's plastic bagful for two and a half mill via a go-between. Bernie and I are getting almost frighteningly rich. I open some bank accounts offshore and I became an important anonymous shareholder in the Queen Elizabeth Hall when it's privatized.

It doesn't take long for the experts to come up with an analysis. Most of the Bone has been down there since the seventeenth century and earlier. They are the sites of the old plague pits where, legend had it, still-living people were thrown in with the dead. For a while it must have seemed like Auschwitz-on-Thames. The chemical action of lime, partial burning, London clay and decaying flesh, together with the broadening spread of the London water-table, thanks to various engineering works over the last century, letting untreated sewage into the mix, had created our unique London Bone. As for the decorations, that, it was opined, was the work of the pit guards, working on

127

earlier bones found on the same site.

"Blood, shit and bone," says Bernie. "It's what makes the world go round. That and money, of course."

"And love," I add. I'm doing all right these days. It's true what they say about a Roller. Little Trudi has enthusiastically rediscovered my attractions. She has her eye on a ring. I raise my glass. "And love, Bernie."

"Fuck that," says Bernie. "Not in my experience." He's buying Paul McCartney's old place in Wamering and having it converted for Persians. He has, it is true, also bought his wife her dream house. She doesn't seem to mind it's on the island of Las Cascadas about six miles off the coast of Morocco. She's at last agreed to divorce him. Apart from his mother, she's the only woman he ever had anything to do with and he isn't, he says, planning to try another. The only females he wants in his house in future come with a pedigree a mile long, have all their shots and can be bought at Harrods.

4.

I expect you heard what happened. The private Bonefields, which contractors were discovering all over South and West London, actually contained public bones. They were part of our national inheritance. They had living relatives. And stones, some of them. So it became a political and a moral issue. The Church got involved. The airwaves were crowded with concerned clergy. There was the problem of the self-named bone-miners. Kids, inspired by our leaders' rhetoric and aspiring to imitate those great captains of free enterprise they had been taught to admire, were turning over ordinary graveyards, which they'd already stripped of their saleable masonry, and digging up somewhat fresher stiffs than was seemly.

A bit too fresh. It was pointless. The Bone took centuries to get seasoned and so far nobody had been able to fake the process. A few of the older graveyards had small deposits of Bone in them. Brompton Cemetery had a surprising amount, for instance, and so did Highgate. This attracted prospectors. They used shovels mainly, but sometimes low explosives. The area around Karl Marx's monument looked like they'd refought the Russian Civil War over it. The barbed wire put in after the event hadn't helped. And, as usual, the public paid to clean up after private enterprise. Nobody in their right mind got buried any more. Cremation became very popular. The borough councils and their financial managers were happy because more valuable real estate wasn't being occupied by a non-consumer.

It didn't matter how many security guards were posted or, by one extreme authority, landmines, the teenies left no grave unturned. Bone was still a profitable item, even though the market had settled down since we started. They dug up Bernie's mother. They dug up my cousin Leonard. There wasn't a Londoner who didn't have some intimate unexpectedly back above ground. Every night you saw it on telly.

It had caught the public imagination. The media had never made much of the desecrated graveyards, the chiselled-off angel's heads and the uprooted headstones on sale in King's Road and the Boulevard St Michel since the nineteen-seventies. These had been the targets of first-generation grave-robbers. Then there had seemed nothing left to steal. Even they had baulked at doing the corpses. Besides, there wasn't a market. This second generation was making up for lost time, turning over the soil faster than an earthworm on E.

The news shots became clichés. The heaped earth, the headstone, the smashed coffin, the hint of the contents, the leader of the Opposition coming on to say how all this has happened since his mirror image got elected. The councils argued that they should be given the authority to deal with the problem. They owned the graveyards. And also, they reasoned, the Bonefields. The profits from those fields should rightly go into the public purse. They could help pay for the Health Service. "Let the dead," went their favourite slogan, "pay for the living for a change."

What the local politicians actually meant was that they hoped to claim the land in the name of the public and then make the usual profits privatizing it. There was a principle at stake. They had to ensure their friends and not outsiders got the benefit.

The High Court eventually gave the judgement to the public, which really meant turning it over to some of the most rapacious borough councils in our history. A decade or so earlier, that Charlie Peace of elected bodies, the Westminster City Council, had tried to sell their old graveyards to new developers. This current judgement allowed all councils at last to maximize their assets from what was, after all, dead land, completely unable to pay for itself, and therefore a natural target for privatization. The feeding frenzy began. It was the closest thing to mass cannibalism I've ever seen.

We had opened a fronter in Old Sweden Street and had a couple of halfway presentable slags from Bernie's club taking the calls and answering enquiries. We were straight up about it. We called it *The City Bone Exchange*. The bloke who decorated it and did the sign specialized in giving offices that long-established look. He'd created most of those old-fashioned West End hotels you'd never heard of until 1999. "If it's got a Scottish name," he used to say, "it's one of mine. Americans love the skirl of the pipes, but they trust a bit of brass and varnish best."

Our place was almost all brass and varnish. And it worked a treat. The Ritz and the Savoy sent us their best potential buyers. Incredibly exclusive private hotels gave us taxi-loads of bland-faced American boy-men, reeking of health and beauty products, bellowing their credentials to the wind, rich matrons eager for anyone's approval, massive Germans with aggressive cackles, stern orientals glaring at us, daring us to cheat them. They bought. And they bought. And they bought.

The snoopers kept on snooping but there wasn't really much to find out. Livingstone International took an aggressive interest in us for a while, but what could they do? We weren't up to anything illegal just selling the stuff and nobody could identify what – if anything – had been nicked anyway. I still had my misgivings. They weren't anything but superstitions, really. It did seem sometimes that for every layer of false antiquity, for every act of Disneyfication, an inch or two of our real foundations crumbled. You knew what happened when you did that to a house. Sooner or later you got trouble. Sooner or later you had no house.

We had more than our share of private detectives for a while. They always pretended to be customers and they always looked wrong, even to our girls.

Livingstone International had definitely made a connection. I think they'd found our mine and guessed
what a windfall they'd lost. They didn't seem at one
with themselves over the matter. They even made veiled
threats. There was some swagger came in to talk about
violence but they were spotties who'd got all their
language off old Nineties TV shows. So we sweated it
out and the girls took most of the heat. Those girls
really didn't know anything. They were magnificently
ignorant. They had tellies with chips that switch
channels as soon as they detect a news or information
programme.

I've always had a rule. If you're caught by the same
wave twice, get out of the water.

While I didn't blame myself for not anticipating the
Great Andrew Lloyd Webber Slump, I think I should
have guessed what would happen next. The tolerance
of the public for bullshit had become decidedly and
aggressively negative. It was like the Bone had set new
standards of public aspiration as well as beauty. My
dad used to say that about the Blitz. Classical music
enjoyed a huge success during the Second World War.
Everybody grew up at once. The Bone had made it
happen again. It was a bit frightening to those of us
who had always relied on a nice, passive, gullible,
greedy punter for an income.

The bitter fights that had developed over graveyard
and Bonefield rights and boundaries, the eagerness with
which some borough councils exploited their new
resource, the unseemly trade in what was, after all,
human remains, the corporate involvement, the incredible profits, the hypocrisies and politics around the Bone
brought us the outspoken disgust of Europe. We were

132

used to that. In fact, we tended to cultivate it. But that wasn't the problem.

The problem was that our *own* public had had enough.

When the elections came round, the voters systematically booted out anyone who had supported the Bone trade. It was like the sudden rise of the anti-slavery vote in Lincoln's America. They demanded an end to the commerce in London Bone. They got the Boneshops closed down. They got work on the Bonefields stopped. They got their graveyards and monuments protected and cleaned up. They got a city that started cultivating peace and security as if it was a cash crop. Which maybe it was. But it hurt me.

It was the end of my easy money, of course. I'll admit I was glad it was stopping. It felt like they were slowing entropy, restoring the past. The quality of life improved. I began to think about letting a few rooms for company.

The mood of the country swung so far into disapproval of the Bone trade that I almost began to fear for my life. Road and anti-abortion activists switched their attention to Bone merchants. Hampstead was full of screaming lefties convinced they owned the moral highground just because they'd paid off their enormous mortgages. Trudi, after three months, applied for a divorce, arguing that she had not known my business when she married me. She said she was disgusted. She said I'd been living on blood-money. The courts awarded her more than half of what I'd made, but it didn't matter any more. My investments were such that I couldn't stop earning. Economically, I was a small oil-producing nation. I had my own international dialling code. It was horrible in a way. Unless I tried very hard, it looked like I could never be ruined again. There was no justice.

I met Bernie in The King Lyar in Old Sweden Street, a few doors down from our burned-out office. I told him what I planned to do and he shrugged.

"We both knew it was dodgy," he told me. "It was dodgy all along, even when we thought it was mastodons. What it feels like to me, Ray, is – it feels like a sort of a massive transformation of the *zeitgeist* – you know, like Virginia Woolf said about the day human nature changed – something happens slowly and you're not aware of it. Everything seems normal. Then you wake up one morning and – bingo! – it's Nazi Germany or Bolshevik Russia or Thatcherite England or the Golden Age – and all the rules have changed."

"Maybe it was the Bone that did it," I said. "Maybe it was a symbol everyone needed to rally round. You know. A focus."

"Maybe," he said. "Let me know when you're doing it. I'll give you a hand."

About a week later we got the van backed up to the warehouse loading bay. It was three o'clock in the morning and I was chilled to the marrow. Working in silence we transferred every scrap of Bone to the van. Then we drove back to Hampstead through a freezing rain.

I don't know why we did it the way we did it. There would have been easier solutions, I suppose. But behind the high walls of my big back garden, under the old trees and etiolated rhododendrons, we dug a pit and filled it with the glowing remains of the ancient dead.

The stuff was almost phosphorescent as we chucked

the big lumps of clay back on to it. It glowed a rich amber and that faint rosemary smell came off it. I can still smell it to this day when I go in there. My soft fruit is out of this world. The whole garden's doing wonderfully now.

In fact London's doing wonderfully. We seem to be back on form. There's still a bit of a Bone trade, of course, but it's marginal.

Every so often I'm tempted to take a spade and turn over the earth again, to look at the fortune I'm hiding there. To look at the beauty of it. The strange amber glow never fades and sometimes I think the decoration on the Bone is an important message I should perhaps try to decipher.

I'm still a very rich man. Not justly so, but there it is. And, of course, I'm about as popular with the public as Percy the Paedophile. Gold the Bone King? I might as well be Gold the Graverobber. I don't go down to Soho much. When I do make it to a show or something I try to disguise myself a bit. I don't see anything of Bernie any more and I heard two of the stoodies topped themselves.

I do my best to make amends. I'm circulating my profits as fast as I can. Talent's flooding into London from everywhere, making a powerful mix. They say they haven't known a buzz like it since 1967. I'm a reliable investor in great new shows. Every year I back the Iggy Pop Awards, the most prestigious in the business. But not everybody will take my money. I am regularly reviled. That's why some organizations receive anonymous donations. They would refuse them if they knew they were from me.

I've had the extremes of good and bad luck riding

this particular switch in the *zeitgeist* and the only time I'm happy is when I wake up in the morning and I've forgotten who I am. It seems I share a common disgust for myself.

A few dubious customers, however, think I owe them something.

Another bloke, who used to be very rich before he made some frenetic investments after his career went down the drain, called me the other day. He knew of my interest in the theatre, that I had invested in several West End hits. He thought I'd be interested in his idea. He wanted to revive his first success, *Rebecca's Incredibly Far Out Well* or something, which he described as a powerful religious rock opera guaranteed to capture the new nostalgia market. The times, he told me, they were a-changin'. His show, he continued, was full of raw old-fashioned R&B energy. Just the sort of authentic sound to attract the new no-nonsense youngsters. Wasn't it cool that Madonna wanted to do the title role? And Bob Geldof would play the Spirit of the Well. *Rock and roll, man! It's all in the staging, man! Remember the boat in* Phantom? *I can make it look better than real. On stage, man, that well is W.E.T. WET! Rock and roll!* I could see that little wizened fist punching the air in a parody of the vitality he craved and whose source had always eluded him.

I had to tell him it was a non-starter. I'd turned over a new leaf, I said. I was taking my ethics seriously.

These days I only deal in living talent.

# THE CAIRENE PURSE

*For Robert Nye*

### 1: Her First Fond Hope Of Eden Blighted

On the edge of the Nile's fertile shadow, pyramids merged with the desert and from the air seemed almost two-dimensional in the steady light of late morning. Spreading now beyond the town of Giza, Cairo's forty million people threatened to engulf, with their old automobiles, discarded electronics and every dusty non-degradable of the modern world, the grandiose tombs of their ancestors.

Though Cairo, like Calcutta, was a monument to the enduring survival of our race, I was glad to leave. I had spent only as much time as I needed, seeking information about my archaeologist sister and discovering that everyone in the academic community thought she had returned to England at least a year ago. The noise had begun to seem as tangible as the haze of sand that hung

137

over the crowded motorways, now a mass of moving
flesh, of camels, donkeys, horses, mules and humans
hauling every variety of vehicle and cargo, with the
occasional official electric car or, even rarer, petrol-
driven truck.

I suppose it had been a tribute to my imagined status
that I had been given a place on a plane, rather than
having to take the river or the weekly train to Aswan.
Through the porthole of the little VW8 everything but
the Nile and its verdant borders were the colours of
sand, each shade and texture of which still held
meaning for the nomad Arab, the Bedouin who had
conquered the First Kingdom and would conquer
several others down the millennia. In the past only the
Ptolemies, turning their backs on the Nile and the
Sahara, ever truly lost the sources of Egypt's power.

My main reason for accepting the assignment was
personal rather than professional. My sister had not
written for some months and her letters before that had
been disconnected, hinting at some sort of emotional
disturbance, perhaps in connection with the dig on
which I knew she had been working. An employee of
UNEC, I had limited authority in Egypt and did not
expect to discover any great mysteries at Lake Nasser,
which continued to be the cause of unusual weather.
The dam's builders somewhat typically had refused to
anticipate this. They had also been warned by our
people in the 1950s that the New High Dam would
eventually so poison the river with bilharzia that
anyone using its water would die. The rain, some of it
acid, had had predictable effects, flooding quarries and
washing away towns. The local Nubians had long since
been evicted from their valleys to make way for the

lake. Their new settlements, traditionally built, had not withstood the altered environment, so the government had thrown up concrete shells for them. The road to Aswan from the airport was lined with bleak, half-built structures of rusted metal girders and cinder blocks. Today's Egyptians paid a high price for regulated water.

From the airport my horse-drawn taxi crossed the old English dam with its sluices and gigantic gauges, a Victorian engineer's dream of mechanical efficiency, and began the last lap of the journey into town. Aswan, wretched as much of it is, has a magic few Nile settlements now possess, rising from the East Bank to dominate the coppery blue waters and glinting granite islands of the wide river where white-sailed feluccas cruise gracefully back and forth, ferrying tourists and townspeople between the two sides. The heights, massive grey boulders, are commanded by a beautiful park full of old eucalyptus, poplars and monkey-puzzle trees. Above this, the stately Edwardian glory of Cook's Cataract Hotel is a marvellous example of balconied and shuttered rococo British orientalism at its finest.

The further up river one goes the poorer Aswan becomes, though even here the clapboard and corrugated iron, the asbestos sheeting and crumbling mud walls are dominated by a splendid hilltop mosque in the grand Turkish style. I had asked to be billeted at a modest hotel in the middle of town, near the Souk. From the outside, the Hotel Osiris, with its pale pink and green pseudo-neon, reminded me of those back-street Marseilles hotels where once you could take your partner for a few francs an hour. It had the same romantic attraction, the same impossible promises. I

139

found that, once within its tiny fly-thick lobby –
actually the communal hallway leading directly to the
courtyard – I was as lost to its appeal as any pop to his
lid. I had discovered a temporary spiritual home.

The Osiris, though scarcely more than a bed-and-
breakfast place by London standards, boasted four or
five porters, all of them eager to take my bag to the
rooms assigned me by a Hindu lady at the desk. I let one
carry my canvas grip up two flights of dirty stairs to a
little tiled, run-down apartment looking into the
building's central well where two exhausted dogs, still
coupled, panted on their sides in the heat. Giving him a
five-pound note, I asked my porter on the off chance if
he had heard of an Englishwoman called Noone or von
Bek living in Aswan. My sister had used the *poste
restante* and, when I had last been here, there were few
Europeans permanently living in town. He regretted
that he could not help. He would ask his brother, who
had been in Aswan several months. Evidently, now that
I had as it were paid for the information in advance he
felt obliged to me. The *bakshish* custom is usually
neither one of bribery nor begging in any European
sense, but has a fair amount to do with smooth social
intercourse. There is always, with legitimate *bakshish*,
an exchange. Some measure of mutual respect is also
usual. Most Arabs place considerable emphasis on
good manners and are not always tolerant of European
coarseness.

I had last been in Egypt long before the great
economic convulsion following that chain reaction of
destruction or near-exhaustion of so many resources.
Then Aswan had been the final port of call for the
millions of tourists who cruised the Nile from dawn to

dusk, the sound of their dance music, the smell of their barbecues, drifting over fields and mud villages which had remained unchanged for five thousand years.

In the 1980s and 1990s Aswan had possessed, among others, a Hilton, a Sheraton, a Ritz-Carlton and a Holiday Inn, but now the luckiest local families had requisitioned the hotels and only the State-owned Cataract remained, a place of pilgrimage for every wealthy enthusiast of 1930s detective stories or auto-biographies of the twentieth-century famous. Here, during wartime, secret meetings had been held and mysterious bargains struck between unlikely partici-pants. Today, on the water below the terrace, some tourists still sailed, the Israelis and the Saudis on their own elegant schooners, while other boats carried mix-tures of Americans, Italians and Germans, French, English, Swedes, Spaniards, Japanese and Hungarians, their women dressed and painted like pagan temp-tresses of the local soap operas, displaying their bodies naked on the sun decks of vast slow-moving windliners the size of an earlier era's ocean-going ships, serving to remind every decent Muslim exactly what the road to Hell looked like. No eighteenth-century English satirist could have provided a better image.

As an officer of the UN's Conservation and Preservation Department I knew all too well how little of Egypt's monuments were still visible, how few existed in any recognizable state. Human erosion, the dam raising the water-table, the volume of garbage casually dumped in the river, the activities of archaeologists and others, of tourists encouraged in their millions to visit the great sites and bring their hard currency, the two-year Arabian war, all had created a situation where those monuments still existing were banned to everyone but the desperate restorers. Meanwhile replicas had been made by the Disney Corporation and located in distant desert settlements surrounded by vacation towns, artificial trees and vast swimming pools, built by French and German experts and named "Rameses City", "Land of the Gods" or "Tutankhamen World". I was sure that this was why my sister had been secretive about her team's discoveries, why it was important to try to avoid the circumstances that now made Abu Simbel little more than a memory of two great engineering miracles.

When I had washed and changed I left the Osiris and strolled through busy evening alleys in the direction of the corniche, the restored Victorian riverfront promenade that reminded me more than anywhere of the old ocean boulevard at Yalta. Without her earlier weight of tourists, Aswan had developed a lazy, decayed glamour. The foodstalls, the fake antiquities, the flimsy headdresses and *gelabeas* sold as traditional costume, the souvenir shops and postcard stands, the "cafetrias" offering "Creme Teas" and "Mix Grile", were still patronized by a few plump Poles and tomato-coloured English who had been replaced in the main by smaller numbers of blond East Africans, Swedes and Nigerians affecting the styles and mannerisms of thirty or forty years earlier and drawn here, I had heard, by a Holy Man on the outskirts of Aswan who taught a peculiar mixture of orthodox Sunni Islam and his own brand of mysticism, which accepted the creeds of Jews and Christians as well as the existence of other planetary populations and spoke of a "pure" form of Islam practised in other parts of the galaxy.

Aswan's latter-day hippies, wearing the fashions of my own youthful parents, gave me a queer feeling at first, for although Egypt offers several experiences akin to time travel, these images of recent history, perhaps of a happier period altogether, were somehow more incongruous than a broken-down VW, for instance, being dragged behind a disgusted camel. There was a greater preponderance of charm-sellers and fortune-tellers than I remembered, together with blank-eyed European men and women, some of them with babies or young children, who begged me for drug-money on the street. With the rise of Islamic-Humanism, the so-called Arab Enlightenment, coupled to the increasing power of North Africa and the Middle East in world politics, the drug laws, introduced originally to placate foreign tour operators and their governments, had been relaxed or formally abolished. Aswan, I had heard, was now some kind of Mecca for privileged youngsters and visionary artists, much as Haight Ashbury or Ladbroke Grove had been in the 1960s. Romanticism of that heady, exaggerated, rather mystical variety was once again loose in the world and the comforts it offered seemed to me almost like devilish temptations. But I was of that puritanical, judgemental generation that had rejected the abstractions of its parents in favour of more realistic, as we saw it, attitudes. A good many of us had virtually rejected the entire Western Enlighten-ment itself and retreated into a kind of liberal medievalism not incompatible with large parts of the Arab world. In my own circles I was considered some-thing of a radical.

I had to admit, however, that I found these new Aswanians attractive. In many ways I envied them.

143

They had never known a time when Arabia had not been a major power. They came here as equals with everyone and were accepted cheerfully by the Nubians who treated them with the respect due to richer pilgrims and potential converts to the divine revelation of Islam.

Again in common with my generation, I was of a secular disposition and saw only damaging, enslaving darkness in any religion. We had even rejected the received wisdoms of Freud, Jung, Marx and their followers and embraced instead a political creed that had as its basis the eminent likelihood of ecological disaster and the slight possibility of an economic miracle. They called us the Anaemic Generation now: a decade or more that was out of step with the progress of history as it was presently interpreted. It suited me to know that I was an anachronism; it afforded me a special kind of security. Very few people took me seriously.

An Egyptian army officer marched past me as I crossed to the river side of the corniche to look down at the half-completed stairways, the crumbling, poorly mixed concrete and the piles of rat-infested rubble that the Korean engineers, who had put in the lowest tender for the work, had still neither repaired nor cleared. The officer glanced at me as if he recognized me but then went past, looking, with his neatly trimmed moustache and rigid shoulders, the perfect image of a World War Two English Guards captain. Even his uniform was in the English style. I suppose Romans coming to fifth-century Britain after some lapse of time would have been equally impressed to see a Celt striding through the streets of Londinium, impeccable in a slightly antiquated centurion's kit. The whole casual story of the human race seemed to be represented in the town as I paused to look at the hulks of converted pleasure boats, home to swarms of Nubian families impoverished by the altered climate and the shift of tourism towards the Total Egypt Experience found in the comfort of Fort Sadat and New Memphis. Despite the piles of filthy garbage along the shore, Aswan had acquired the pleasant, nostalgic qualities of unfashionable British resorts like Morecombe or Yarmouth, a local population careless of most strangers save sometimes for the money they brought.

About halfway along the corniche I stopped at a little café and sat down on a cane chair, ordering mint tea from a proprietor whose ancient tarboosh might have escaped from the costume department of a touring production of *Death on the Nile*. He addressed me as "*effendi*" and his chosen brand of English seemed developed from old British war movies. Like me, I thought, he was out of step with the times. When he brought the tea I told him to keep the change from a pound and, again on the off chance, asked after my sister. I was surprised by the enthusiasm of his response. He knew the name von Bek and was approving when I told him of our relationship. "She is very good," he said. "A tip-top gentlewoman. But now, I think, she is unwell. It is hard to see the justice of it."

Pleased and a little alarmed, I asked if he knew where she lived.

"She lived in *Sharri al Sahahaldeen*, just off the *Sharri al Souk*." He pointed with his thumb back into town. "But that was more than a year ago. Oh, she is very well known here in Aswan. The poor people like her

145

immensely. They call her *Saidneh Duukturah*."

"Doctor?" My sister had only rudimentary medical training. Her doctorate had been in archaeology. "She treats the sick?"

"Well, not so much any more. Now only if the hospitals refuse help. The Bisharim, in particular, love her. You know those nomads. They trust your sister only. But she moved from Sahahaldeen Street after some trouble. I heard she went to the English House over on the West Bank, but I'm not so sure. Perhaps you should ask the Bisharim." He raised his hand in welcome to a small man in a dark blue *gelabea* who walked briskly into the darkness of the shop's interior. "A customer." From his pocket he took a cut-throat razor. "*Naharak sa'id*," he called and, adopting the swagger of the expert barber, waved farewell to me and entered his shop.

"*Fi amani 'llah*." Picking up my hat, I crossed to a rank where the usual two or three ill-used horses stood between the shafts of battered broughams, still the commonest form of taxi in Aswan. I approached the first driver, who stood flicking at flies with his ragged whip while he smoked a cigarette and chatted with his fellows. He wore an American sailor's hat, a faded T-shirt advertising some Russian artpopper, a pair of traditional baggy trousers exposing ulcerated calves and, on his feet, pink and black Roos. From the state of his legs I guess he had retained the habit, against all current warnings, of wading into the Nile to urinate. I asked him to take me first to the dam's administration office where, for courtesy's sake, I presented myself and made an appointment with my old acquaintance Georges Abidos, the Chief Press Officer, who had been

called out to the northern end of the lake. His secretary
said he was looking forward to seeing me tomorrow
and handed me a welcoming note. I then asked the
calash-driver if he knew the Bisharim camp on the
outskirts of town. I had heard that in recent years the
tribe had returned to its traditional sites. He was
contemptuous. "Oh, yes. The barbarians are still with
us!" I told him I would give him another ten pounds to
take me there and return. He made to bargain but then
accepted, shrugging and gesturing for me to get in his
carriage. I guessed he was maintaining some sort of face
for himself. In my travels I had grown used to all kinds
of mysterious body-language, frequently far harder to
interpret than any spoken tongue.

We trotted back to town and jogged beside a river
strewn with old plastic water-bottles, with all the
miscellaneous filth from the boats that no legislation
appeared able to limit, past flaking quasi-French
façades still bearing the crests of Farouk and his
ancestors and each now occupied by twenty or thirty
families whose washing hung over the elaborate iron
balconies and carved stone sphinxes like bunting celebrating some joyous national holiday. We passed
convents and churches, mosques and graveyards,
shanties, monuments, little clumps of palm trees
sheltering donkeys and boys from a sun that as noon
approached grew steadily more intense.

We went by the English holiday villas where hippies
nowadays congregated; we passed the burned-out
shells of warehouses and store-rooms, victims of some
forgotten riot, the stained walls sprayed with the
emerald-coloured ankh of the Green Jihad, and eventually, turning inland again, reached the old Muslim

147

necropolis, almost a mile long and half a mile across, surrounded by a low, mud wall and filled with every shape and size of stone or sarcophagus. Beyond this, further up the hill, I made out clumps of palms and the dark woollen tents of the Bisharim.

My driver reined in his horse some distance from the camp, beside a gate into the graveyard. "I will wait for you here," he said significantly.

## 2: Ah, Whence, and Whither Flown Again, Who Knows?

The nomad camp, showing so few outward signs of Western influence, had the kind of self-contained dignity that city Arabs frequently manage to recreate in their homes and yet which is not immediately noticed by those visitors merely disgusted by, for instance, Cairo's squalor.

Sheikh Khamet ben Achmet was the patriarch of this particular clan. They had come in a month ago, he said, from the Sudan, to trade horses and camels. They all knew my sister but she had disappeared. He employed a slow, classical Arabic which was easy for me to understand and in which I could easily respond. "God has perhaps directed thy sister towards another vocation," he suggested gently. "It was only a short time since she would visit us whenever we put down our tents here. She had a particularly efficient cure for infections of the eye, but it was the women who went to her, chiefly." He looked at me with quiet amusement. "The best type of Englishwoman, as we say. Sometimes God sends us His beneficence in strange forms."

"Thou hast no knowledge of her present dwelling?"
I sipped the coffee a servant brought us. I was glad to
be in the cool tent. Outside it was now at least thirty-
five degrees. There was little danger of freak rain today.
He looked up at me with his ironic grey eyes. "No," he
said. "She always visits us. When we needed her we
would send messages to the Copt's house. You know,
the carpenter who lives on the street leading from the
great mosque to the souk."

I did not know him, I said.

"He is as gold-haired as thou. They nickname him
The German, but I know he is a Copt from Alexandria.
I think he is called Iskander. I know that he is easily
found."

"Thou knowest my sister was an archaeologist?" I
was a little hesitant.

"Indeed, I do! We discussed all manner of ancient
things together and she had the courtesy to say that I
was at least as informative as the great Egyptian
Museum in Cairo!" He was amused by what he
perceived as elegant flattery. My sister, if I still knew
her, had done no more than to state her direct opinion.

It would have been ill-mannered of me to have left as
soon as I had the information I sought, so I spent two
further hours answering the Sheikh's questions about
current American and European politics. I was not
surprised that he was well-informed. I had seen his
digital radio (doubtless full of *piles noires*) standing on
the ivory-inlaid chest on the far side of the tent. I was
also unsurprised by his interpretations of what he had
learned. They were neither cynical nor unintelligent,
but they were characteristic of certain desert Arabs who
see everything in terms of power and opportunity and

149

patronage. They simply cannot grasp the reverence for political institutions that we have in the West. For a few minutes I foolishly tried to re-educate him until it became clear I must give offence. Recalling my old rules, I accepted his terms. As a result we parted friends. Any Irish apologist for apartheid could not have been more approving of my good manners.

When I got up to leave, the old man took my arm and wished me God's grace and help in finding my sister. "She was associated with Jews." He spoke significantly. "Those who did not like her said that she was a witch. And it is true that two of my women saw her consorting with the spell-seller from the Souk. The one called Lallah Zenobia. The black woman. Thou and I art men of the world and understand that it is superstitious folly. But thou knowest how women are. And they are often," he added in an even lower tone, "susceptible to Yehudim flattery and lies."

It was by no means the first time I had to accept such sentiments from the mouth of one who was otherwise hospitality, tolerance and kindness personified. To persuade a desert Arab that Jews are not in direct and regular touch with Satan and all His minions is still no easier than persuading a Dixie Baptist that the doors of a Catholic Church are not necessarily a direct gateway to Hell. One is dealing with powerful survival myths that only direct experience will disprove. In such circumstances I never mention my mother's family. I said I would visit Iskander the Carpenter. At this point a braying, bellowing and snorting chorus grew so loud I could barely hear his elaborate goodbyes. The stock was being beaten back from the water. As I emerged from the tent I saw my driver in the distance. He was sitting on the wall of the cemetery feinting with his whip at the boys and girls who flowed like a tide around him, daring one another to run within his range.

### 3: Crystal to the Wizard Eye

I had no difficulty in discovering Iskander the Carpenter. He was a slight man wearing a pair of faded denim overalls. Sanding off a barley-sugar chairleg, he sat just inside his workshop, which was open to the street and displayed an entire suite of baroque bedroom and living-room furniture he had almost completed. He chose to speak in French. "It is for a couple getting married this weekend. At least they are spending their money on furniture rather than the wedding itself!" He put down his chairleg and shook my hand. He was fair-skinned and blond, as Sheikh Achmet had said, though I could not have taken him for anything but Egyptian. His features could have come straight from the Egyptian Museum's clay statue displays of ancient tradespeople. He might have been a foreman on a Middle Kingdom site. He turned up a chair, which still had to have the upholstery done over its horsehair seat, indicated that I should sit and sent his son to get us a couple of bottles of Pyramid beer.

"Of course I know Saidneh Duukturah. She was my friend. That one," he pointed to his disappearing boy, "owes his life to her. He was poisoned. She treated him. He is well. It is true I knew where she lived and would get messages to her. But for a year or more she went away from us. Until recently she was staying at the

English House. There are many rumours. Most of them are simply stupid. She is no witch. She was a woman blessed by God with the healing touch. The other woman, now, is undoubtably a witch. My wife heard that your sister fell in love and went to the Somalin, Zenobia, for a philtre. Certainly, by chance, my wife saw her handing Zenobia a heavy purse. A Cairene purse, she was sure."

"I do not know what that is." I moved further into the shade. Outside, Aswan had fallen into a doze as the population closed its shutters until mid-afternoon. The yellow walls of the houses were now almost blistering to the touch.

"A purse of money, that's all. It used to mean a bag of gold. About twenty sovereigns. That is what a witch demands for a very powerful spell. Something very valuable, my friend."

"My sister was buying a charm from a spell-seller?"

"A powerful one, yes. That negress has been involved with the police more than once. She was suspected of killing a rival suitor at the behest of another, of being responsible for the death of a man who was owed over a thousand pounds by another man. Now, if your sister was disposed to witchcraft, why would she go to a witch and pay her a healthy sum for a job she could as readily do herself?"

I agreed it was unlikely my sister was a witch. I asked how the matter had come to official attention.

"The police went to see her, I think. My wife's friend – friend no more – gossiped. They arrested Zenobia, then let your sister go. You should visit the *mamur* at the *markaz*, the police department. The *mamur* here is a very just man. He never accepts money unless he can do whatever it is he promises. His name is Inspector el-Bayoumi. If anyone knows where your sister is living in Aswan he probably will."

By the time I had discussed the affairs of the day and thanked the carpenter for the beer, it was already cooler and I walked down to the *Sharri el Souk* which was beginning to open for business again, filling with women in black lacy *milayum* that barely revealed the vivid colours of their house dresses beneath, clutching bright plastic shopping bags and going about their weekend buying. Because it was Friday afternoon the butchers were displaying the calves' heads and bullocks' tails, their sheeps' hearts and heads, their divided carcasses, all protected from an unforgiving sun by the thick coating of black flies that also covered the fish and offal on other stalls. Sellers of turkeys, pigeons and chickens took water in their mouths to force between the beaks of their wares so that they would not dehydrate before they were sold, and seemed to be kissing, tenderly, each one. Cheerful greengrocers called out the virtues of their squash, mangoes, potatoes or green beans. Gas lorries, electroscoots, bicycles and a few official cars moved in slow competition with rickshaws, donkeys, mules or camels through alleys where, every so often, a bright sign would advertise in English the virtues of unobtainable Panasonic televisions or Braun refrigerators and others would, almost pathetically, alert the passer-by to the Color Xerox machine or Your Local Fax Office. Like every similar souk in the Arab world, the tools and artefacts of the centuries were crowded side by side and functioning in perfect compatibility. Aswan had adapted, far more readily and more cheerfully, to modern energy restraints than had London, for instance, where it had taken an Act of Parliament to reintroduce the public horse trough.

I made my way to the northern end of the street where the police station, the *markaz*, resembling an old British garrison, was guarded by two boys in khaki serge who were armed with the Lee Enfield 303s with which Lawrence had armed his men for the Desert War and which had, then, been an Arab's most prized possession. Now it was unlikely any reliable ammunition existed for these antiques. I understood only the crack militia was allowed to sport the old Kalashnikovs or M16s issued to regular infantry. With the end of international arms trading, almost any well-made gun was valuable, if only as status.

I had no appointment and was informed by the bright young civilian woman on the duty desk that Inspector el-Bayoumi would be back from New Town, the concrete development near the airport, in about an hour. I gave my name, my business, and said I would be back at about five-thirty. Courteously she assured me that the Inspector would await me.

### 4: Her Heart All Ears and Eyes, Lips Catching the Avalanche Of the Golden Ghost

I had forgotten how much time one had to spend on enquiries of this kind. I returned to my apartment to find an envelope pushed under my door. It was not, as I had hoped, from my sister, but a letter welcoming me to Aswan, a short personal note from my friend

Georges, a list of appointments with various engineers and officials, some misleading publicity about the dam, consisting mainly of impressive photographs, a variety of press releases stressing the plans for "an even better dam" and so on. I went out again having glanced at them. I was obsessed with all the mysteries with which I had been presented in a single day. How had my sister metamorphosed from a dedicated archaeologist to some kind of local Mother Teresa?

Disturbed by my own speculations I forced myself to think about the next day's work when I would be discussing methods of reducing pollution in all its varieties and rebuilding the dam to allow silt down to the arable areas. The signs of serious "redesertization", as ugly official jargon termed it, were now found everywhere in the Nile valley. In other words, the Aswan Dam was now seriously contributing to ecological damage as well as helping to wipe out our most important links with the remote past. I could not believe how intelligent scientists, who were not those industrial developers motivated only by greed, failed to accept the dreadful psychic damage being done to people whose whole identities were bound up with a particular and very specific landscape. My own identity, for instance, was profoundly linked to a small Oxfordshire village that had remained unchanged for hundreds of years after successfully resisting developers wanting to surround it with high-quality modern properties instead of its existing beeches and oaks.

Few Egyptians were in such comfortable circumstances or could make any choice but the one promising the most immediate benefit, yet they had the same understanding of their tribal homes and what values

155

they represented, and still resisted all attempts to force them to lose their traditional clothes, language and attitudes and make them modern citizens of their semi-democratic society. Unfortunately, this attitude also extended to a dam now much older than many of its staff and never at any time an engineering miracle. UNEC had plans for a replacement. Currently they and the Rajhidi government were arguing over the amounts each would contribute. Happily, that was not my problem.

With a slightly clearer head, I walked to the Post Office on the corner of Abdel el Taheer street. Though almost fifty years had passed since the First Revolution, the building still bore the outlines of earlier royal insignia. The elaborate cast-ironwork on doors and windows was of that "Oriental" pattern exported from the foundries of Birmingham to adorn official buildings throughout the Empire east of Gibraltar. Even by the 1970s the stuff was still available from stock, during the brief period after the death of Britain's imperial age and before the birth of that now much-despised and admittedly reckless Thatcher period known ironically as "the Second Empire", the period that had shaped my own expectations of life as well as those of uncounted millions of my fellows, the period in which my uncle had died, a soldier in the Falklands cause.

I entered the main door's cool archway and walked through dusty shafts of light to a tiled counter where I asked to speak to the Post Master. After a moment's wait I was shown into his little gloomy mahogany office, its massive fan stirring piles of documents that moved like a perpetually unsettled flight of doves. A small, handsome Arab entered and closed the door carefully behind him. His neat Abraham Lincoln beard suggested religious devotion. I told him that my name was von Bek and I was expecting mail. I handed him an envelope I had already prepared. On the outside was my name and occupation. Inside was the conventional "purse" – actually another envelope containing a few pounds. I said I would appreciate his personal interest in my mail and hoped he could ensure it was available to me the moment it arrived. Absently, he took the envelope and put it in his trouser pocket. He had brightened at the sound of my name. "Are you related to that woman of virtue whom we know here in Aswan?" He spoke measured, cultured Arabic with the soft accents of Upper Egypt.

"My sister." I was trying to locate her, I said. Perhaps her mail was delivered here?

"It has not been collected, Si von Bek, for several months. Yet she has been seen in Aswan recently. There was a small scandal. I understand that El Haj Sheikh Ibrahim Abu Halil intervened. Have you asked him about your sister?"

"Is he the governor?"

He laughed. Clearly the idea of the governor intervening on behalf of an ordinary member of the public amused him. "No. Sheikh Abu Halil is the gentleman so many come to Aswan to see these days. He is the great Sufi now. We are blessed in this. God sends us everything that is good, even the rain. So much more grows and blooms. People journey to us from all over the world. Here, God has chosen to reveal a glimpse of Paradise."

I was impressed by his optimism. I told him I would go to see Sheikh Abu Halil as soon as possible.

157

Meanwhile I had an appointment with the police chief. At this his face grew a little uncertain, but his only response was some conventional greeting concerning Allah's good offices.

Police Inspector el-Bayoumi was one of those suave career officers produced by the new academies. His manners were perfect, his hospitality generous and discreet, and when I had replied to his questions, telling him where I had been born in England, he confessed affectionate familiarity with another nearby Cotswold village. Together, we deplored the damage tourism had done to the environment and confessed it to be a major problem in both our countries, which depended considerably on the very visitors who contributed to the erosion. He sighed. "I think the human race has rather foolishly cancelled many of its options."

Since he preferred to speak it, I replied in English. "Perhaps our imaginative resources are becoming as scarce as our physical ones?"

"There has been a kind of psychic withering," he agreed. "And its worst symptom, in my view, Mr von Bek, is found in the religious and political fundamentalism to which so many subscribe. As if, by some sort of sympathetic magic, the old, simpler days will return. We live in complicated times with complicated problems. It's a sad fact that they require sophisticated solutions."

I admitted I had been schooled in many of those fundamentalist notions and sometimes found them difficult to resist. We chatted about this for a while. Coffee was brought, together with a selection of delicious *gurrahiya* pastries, whose secret the Egyptians inherited from the Turks, and we talked for another half-hour, during which time we took each other's measure and agreed the world would be a better place if civilized people like ourselves were allowed a greater voice. Whereupon, in that sometimes abrupt change of tone Arabs have, which can mislead Europeans into thinking they have somehow given offence, Inspector el-Bayoumi asked what he could do for me.

"I'm looking for my sister. She's an economic archaeologist who came here two and a half years ago with the Burbank College Project. It was an international team. Only about half were from California and those returned the next year, after the big earthquake. Most of them, of course, had lost relatives. My sister stayed on with the remaining members." I did not mention her talk of a wonderful discovery out in the Western Sahara. Their sonavids had picked up a New Kingdom temple complex almost perfectly preserved but buried some hundred feet under the sand. My sister had been very excited about it. It was at least on a par with the discovery of the Tutankhamen treasures and probably of far greater historical importance. She and the team kept the discovery quiet, of course, especially since so many known monuments had suffered. Naturally, there were some conflicts of interest. There was little she could tell me in a letter and most of that was a bit vague, making reference to personal or childhood incidents whose relevance escaped me. I added delicately, "You know about the discovery, naturally."

He smiled as he shook his handsome head. "No, Mr von Bek, I don't. I think an elaborate dig would not escape my notice." He paused, asking me if he might smoke. I told him I was allergic to cigarette smoke and he put his case away. Regretfully, he said: "I should tell

159

you that your sister is a little disturbed. She was arrested by us about a year ago. There was something we had to follow up. An outbreak of black magic amongst the local people. We don't take such things very seriously until it's possible to detect a cult growing. Then we have to move to break it up as best we can. Such things are not a serious problem in London, but for a policeman in Aswan they are fairly important. We arrested a known witch, a Somali woman they call Madame Zenobia, and with her an Englishwoman, also rumoured to be practising. That was your sister, Mr von Bek. She was deranged and had to be given a sedative. Eventually, we decided against charging her and released her into the custody of Lady Roper."

"The Consul's wife?"

"He's the Honorary Consul here in Aswan now. They have a large house on the West Bank, not far from the Ali Khan's tomb. You can't see it from this side. It is our miracle. Locally, it's called the English House. More recently they've called it the Rose House. You'll find no mysteries there!"

"That's where my sister's staying?"

"No longer. She left Aswan for a while. When she came back she joined the community around Sheikh Abu Halil and I understand her to be living in the old holiday villas on the Edfu road, near the race course. I'll gladly put a man to work on the matter. We tend not to pursue people too much in Aswan. Your sister is a good woman. An honest woman. I hope she has recovered herself."

Thanking him, I said I hoped my search would not involve the time of a hard-working police officer. I got up to leave. "And what happened to Madame Zenobia?"

"Oh, the courts were pretty lenient. She got a year, doing quarry work for the Restoration Department in Cairo. She was a fit woman. She'll be even fitter now. Hard labour is a wonderful cure for neurosis! And far more socially useful than concocting love potions or aborting cattle."

He sounded like my old headmaster. As an afterthought, I said, "I gather Sheikh Abu Halil took an interest in my sister's case."

He flashed me a look of intelligent humour. "Yes, he did. He is much respected here. Your sister is a healer. The Sufi is a healer. He sometimes makes an accurate prophecy. He has a following all over the world, I believe."

I appreciated his attempt at a neutral tone, given his evident distaste for matters psychic and mystical. We shared, I think, a similar outlook.

I found myself asking him another question. "What was the evidence against my sister, Inspector?"

He had hoped I would not raise the matter, but was prepared for it. "Well," he began slowly, "for instance, we had a witness who saw her passing a large bag of money to the woman. The assumption was that she was paying for a spell. A powerful one. A love philtre, possibly, but it was also said that she wanted a man dead. He was the only other member of her team who had remained behind. There was some suggestion, Mr von Bek," he paused again, "that he made her pregnant. But this was all the wildest gossip. He did in fact die of a heart attack shortly after the reported incident. Sometimes we must treat such cases as murder. But we only had circumstantial evidence. The man was a drug addict and apparently had tried to force your sister to give him money. There was just a hint of blackmail involved in the case, you see. These are all, of course, the interpretations of a policeman. Maybe the man had been an ex-lover, no more. Maybe she wanted him to love her again?"

"It wasn't Noone, was it?"

"It was not her estranged husband. He is, I believe, still in New Zealand."

"You really think she got tangled up in black magic?"

"When confused, men turn to war and women to magic. She was not, as the Marrakshim say, with the caravan." He was just a little sardonic now. "But she was adamant that she did not wish to go home."

"What did she tell you?"

"She denied employing the witch. She claimed the Somali woman was her only friend. Otherwise she said little. But her manner was all the time distracted, as if she imagined herself to be surrounded by invisible witnesses. We were not unsympathetic. The psychiatrist from the German hospital came to see her. Your sister is a saintly woman who helped the poor and the sick and asked for no reward. She enriched us. We were trying to help her, you know."

He had lost his insouciance altogether now and spoke with controlled passion. "It could be that your sister had an ordinary breakdown. Too much excitement in her work, too much sun. Caring too much for the hardships of others. She tried to cure the whole town's ills and that task is impossible for any individual. Her burden was too heavy. You could see it written in every line of her face, every movement of her body. We wanted her to recover. Some suspected she was in the witch's power, but in my own view she carried a personal weight of guilt, perhaps. Probably pointlessly, too. You know how women are. They are kinder, more feeling creatures than men."

### 5: The Seasons of Home –
### Aye, Now They Are Remembered!

That evening, while there was still light, I took the felucca across the Nile, to the West Bank. The ferryman, clambering down from his high mast where he had been reefing his sail, directed me through the village to a dirt road winding up the hillside a hundred yards or so from the almost austere resting place of the Ali Khan. "You will see it," he assured me. "But get a boy."

There were a couple of dozen children waiting for me on the quay. I selected a bright-looking lad of about ten. He wore a ragged Japanese T-shirt with the inscription I LOVE SEX WAX, a pair of cut-off jeans and Adidas trainers. In spite of the firmness with which I singled him out, we were followed by the rest of the children all the way to the edge of the village. I had a couple of packs of old electronic watches that I distributed, to a pantomime of disappointment from the older children. Watches had ceased to be fashionable currency since I had last been in Aswan. Now, from their requests, I learned it was "real" fountain pens. They showed me a couple of Sheaffers some tourist had already exchanged for their services as guides and companions of the road.

I had no fountain pen for the boy who took me to the

163

top of the hill and pointed down into the little valley where, amongst the sand and the rocks, had been erected a large two-storey house, as solidly Edwardian as any early-twentieth-century vicarage. Astonishingly, it was planted with cedars, firs and other hardy trees shading a garden to rival anything I had ever seen in Oxfordshire. There were dozens of varieties of roses, of every possible shade, as well as hollyhocks, snap-dragons, foxgloves, marigolds and all the flowers one might find in an English July garden. A peculiar wall about a metre high surrounded the entire mirage and I guessed that it disguised some kind of extraordinarily expensive watering and sheltering apparatus that had allowed the owners to do the impossible and bring a little bit of rural England to Upper Egypt. The grounds covered several acres. I saw some stables, a garage, and a woman on the front lawn. She was seated in a faded deckchair watching a reader or a video that she rested in her left hand. With her right hand she took a glorious drink from the little table beside her and sipped through the straw. As I drew nearer, my vision was obscured by the trees and the wall, but I guessed she was about sixty-five, dressed in a thoroughly unfashionable Marks and Ashley smock, a man's trilby hat and a pair of rubber-tyre sandals. She looked up as I reached the gate and called "Good afternoon". Happy with cash, my boy departed.

"Lady Roper?"

She had a quick, intelligent, swarthy face, her curls all grey beneath the hat, her long hands expressive even when still. "I'm Diana Roper."

"My name's Paul von Bek. I'm Beatrice's brother."

"The engineer!" She was full of welcome. "My

goodness, you know, I think Bea could foretell the future. She *said* you'd be turning up here about now."

"I wrote and told her!" I was laughing as the woman unlocked the gate and let me in. "I knew about this job months ago."

"You're here on business."

"I'm going through the rituals of sorting out a better dam and trying to do something about the climatic changes. I got sent because I know a couple of people here – and because I asked to come. But there's little real point to my being here."

"You don't sound very hopeful, Mr von Bek." She led me towards the back of the house, to a white wrought-iron conservatory which was a relatively recent addition to the place and must have been erected by some forgotten imperial dignitary of the last century.

"I'm always hopeful that people will see reason, Lady Roper."

We went into the sweet-smelling ante-room, whose glass had been treated so that it could admit only a certain amount of light, or indeed reflect all the light to perform some needed function elsewhere. Despite its ancient appearance, I guessed the house to be using up-to-date EE technologies and to be completely self-sufficient. "What an extraordinary garden," I said.

"Imported Kent clay." She offered me a white basket chair. "With a fair bit of Kenyan topsoil, I understand. We didn't have it done. We got it all dirt cheap. It takes such a long time to travel anywhere these days, most people don't want the place. It belonged to one of the Fayeds, before they all went off to Malaysia. But have you looked carefully at our roses, Mr von Bek? They

165

have a sad air to them, a sense of someone departed, someone mourned. Each bush was planted for a dead relative, they say." Her voice grew distant. "Of course, the new rain has helped enormously. I've survived because I know the rules. Women frequently find their intuition very useful in times of social unrest. But things are better now, aren't they? We simply refuse to learn. We refuse to learn."

Grinning as if enjoying a game, a Nubian girl of about sixteen brought us a tray of English cakes and a pot of Assam tea. I wondered how I had lost the thread of Lady Roper's conversation.

"We do our best," I said, letting the girl take tongs to an éclair and with a flourish pop it on my plate. "I believe Bea lived here for a while."

"My husband took quite a fancy to her. As did I. She was a sweetie. And so bright. Is that a family trait? Yes, we shared a great deal. It was a luxury for me, you know, to have such company. Not many people have been privileged as she and I were privileged." She nodded with gentle mystery, her eyes in the past. "We were friends of your uncle. That was the funny thing we found out. All at Cambridge together in the late Sixties. We thought conservation an important subject *then*. What? Fifty years ago, almost? Such a jolly boy. He joined up for extremely complicated reasons, we felt. Did you know why?"

I had never really wondered. My picture of my mother's brother was of the kind of person who would decide on a military career, but evidently they had not been acquainted with that man at all. Finding this disturbing, I attempted to return to my subject. "I was too young to remember him. My sister was more

166

curious than I. Did she seem neurotic to you, while she was here?"

"On the contrary. She was the sanest of us all! Sound as a bell upstairs, as Bernie always said. Sharp intelligence. But, of course, she had been there, you see. And could confirm everything we had been able to piece together at this end."

"You're referring to the site they discovered?"

"That, of course, was crucial. Especially at the early stages. Yes, the site was extraordinary. We went out to see it with her, Bernie and I. What a mind-blower, Paul! Amazing experience. Even the small portion they had excavated. Four mechanical sifters just sucking the sand gradually away. It would have taken years in the old days. Unfortunately three of the operators left after the earthquake and the sifters were recalled for some crucial rescue work over in Sinai. And then, of course, everything changed."

"I'm not sure I'm . . ."

"After the ship came and took Bea."

"A ship? On the Nile?"

She frowned at me for a moment and then her tone changed to one of distant friendliness. "You'll probably want a word with Bernie. You'll find him in his playroom. Nadja will take you. And I'm here if you need to know anything."

She glanced away, through the glass walls of the conservatory and was at once lost in melancholy reflection on the roses and their guardian trees.

MICHAEL MOORCOCK

### 6: *The Smoke Along the Track*

Some antique BBC radio programme was playing as I knocked on the oak door and was admitted by a white-haired old man wearing a pair of overalls and a check shirt, with carpet slippers on his feet. His skin had the healthy sheen of a sun-baked reptile's and his blue eyes were brilliant with trust. I was shocked enough to remain where I was, even as he beckoned me in. He turned down his stereo, a replica of some even older audio contraption, and stood proudly to display a room full of books and toys. One wall was lined with glass shelves on which miniature armies battled amidst a wealth of tiny trees and buildings. "You don't look much like a potential playmate!" His eyes strayed towards the brilliant jackets of his books.

"And you're not entirely convincing as Mr Dick, sir." I stood near the books, which were all well ordered, and admired his illustrated Dickens. The temperature in the room was, I guessed, thoroughly controlled. Should the power fail for just a few hours the desert would fade and modify this room as if it had been a photograph left for an hour in the sun.

My retort seemed to please him. He grinned and came forward. "I'm Bernie Roper. While I have no immediate enemies, I enjoy in this room the bliss of endless childhood. I have my lead soldiers, my bears and rabbits, my model farm, and I read widely. *Treasure Island* is very good, as are the 'William' books, and Edgar Rice Burroughs and, as you say, Charles Dickens, though he's a bit on the scary side sometimes. E. Nesbit and H.G. Wells and Shaw. I enjoy so much. For music I have the very best of *Children's Favourites* from the

168

BBC – a mixture of comic songs, Gilbert and Sullivan, *Puff the Magic Dragon*, *The Laughing Policeman*, popular classics and light opera. Flanders and Swann, Danny Kaye, *Sparky's Magic Piano*, *Peter and the Wolf* and *Song of the South*. Do you know any of those? But I'm a silly chap! You're far too young. They'd even scrapped *Children's Hour* before you were born. Oh, dear. Never to enjoy *Larry the Lamb* or Norman and Henry Bones, the Boy Detectives! Oh!" he exclaimed with a knowing grin, "Calamity!" Then he returned his attention to his toys for a moment. "You think I should carry more responsibility?"

"No." I had always admired him as a diplomat. He deserved the kind of retirement that suited him.

"I feel sorry for the children," he said. "The pleasures of childhood are denied to more and more of them as their numbers increase. Rajhid and Abu Halil are no real solution, are they? We who remember the Revolution had hoped to have turned the desert green by now. I plan to die here, Mr—?"

"My name's von Bek. I'm Bea's brother."

"My boy! Thank goodness I offered an explanation. I'm not nearly as eccentric as I look! 'Because I could not stop for Death, He kindly stopped for me. We shared a carriage, just we two, and Immortality.' Emily Dickinson, I believe. But I could also be misremembering. 'The child is Father to the Man,' you know. And the lost childhood of Judas. Did you read all those poems at school?"

"I was probably too young again," I said. "We didn't do poetry as such."

"I'm so sorry. All computer studies nowadays, I suppose."

"Not all, sir." The old-fashioned courtesy surprised us both. Sir Bernard acted as one cheated and I almost apologized. Yet it was probably the first time I had used the form of address without irony. I had, I realized, wanted to show respect. Sir Bernard had come to the same understanding. "Oh, well. You're a kind boy. But you'll forgive me, I hope, if I return to my preferred world."

"I'm looking for my sister, Sir Bernard. Actually, I'm pretty worried about her."

Without irritation, he sighed. "She was a sweet woman. It was terrible. And nobody believing her."

"Believing what, Sir Bernard?"

"About the spaceship, you know. But that's Di's field, really. Not my area of enthusiasm at all. I like to make time stand still. We each have a different way of dealing with the fact of our own mortality, don't we?" He strolled to one of his displays and picked up a charging 17th Lancer. "Into the Valley of Death rode the six hundred."

"Thank you for seeing me, Sir Bernard."

"Not at all, Paul. She talked about you. I liked her. I think you'll find her either attending Abu Halil's peculiar gymnasium or at the holiday homes. Where those Kenyan girls and boys are now living."

"Thank you. Goodbye, sir."

"Bye, bye!" Humming some stirring air, the former Director General of the United Nations hovered, contented, over his miniature Death or Glory Boys.

## 7: Another Relay in the Chain of Fire

Lady Roper had remained in her conservatory. She rose as I entered. "Was Bernie able to help?"

"I could be narrowing things down." I was anxious to get back to the East Bank before dark. "Thank you for your kindness. I tried to find a phone number for you."

"We're not on the phone, lovie. We don't need one."

"Sir Bernard mentioned a spaceship." I was not looking forward to her reply.

"Oh, dear, yes," she said. "The flying-saucer people. I think one day they will bring us peace, don't you? I mean one way or another. This is better than death for me, at any rate, Paul. But perhaps they have a purpose for us. Perhaps an unpleasant one. I don't think anybody would rule that out. What could we do if that were the case? Introduce a spy? That has not proved a successful strategy. We know that much, sadly. It's as if all that's left of Time is here. A few shreds from a few ages."

Again I was completely nonplussed and said nothing.

"I think you share Sir B's streak of pessimism. Or realism is it?"

"Well, we're rather different, actually . . ." I began to feel foolish.

"He was happier as Ambassador, you know. Before the UN. And then we were both content to retire here. We'd always loved it. The Fayeds had us out here lots of times, for those odd parties. We were much younger. You probably think we're both barking mad." When I produced an awkward reply she was sympathetic. "There *is* something happening here. It's a *centre*. You can feel it everywhere. It's an ideal place. Possibly we shall be the ones left to witness the birth of the New Age."

At that moment all I wished to do was save my sister from that atmosphere of half-baked mysticism and desperate faith, to get her back to the relative reality of London and a doctor who would know what was wrong with her and be able to treat it.

"Bea was never happier than when she was in Aswan, you know," said Lady Roper.

"She wrote and told me as much."

"Perhaps she risked a bit more than was wise. We all admire her for it. What I don't understand is why she was so thick with Lallah Zenobia. The woman's psychic, of course, but very unsophisticated."

"You heard about the witness? About the purse?"

"Naturally."

"And you, too, are sure it was a purse?"

"I suppose so. It's Cairo slang, isn't it, for a lot of money? The way the Greeks always say 'seven years' when they mean a long time has passed. Bernie's actually ill, you realize? He's coherent much of the time. A form of PD, we were told. From the water when we were in Washington. He's determined to make the best of it. He's sweet, isn't he?"

"He's an impressive man. You don't miss England?"

She offered me her hand. "Not a bit. You're always welcome to stay if you are bored over there. Or the carping materialism of the Old Country gets to you. Simplicity's the keynote at the Rose House. Bernie says the British have been sulking for years, like the Lost Boys deprived of their right to go a-hunting and a-pirating at will. I'm afraid, Paul, that we don't think very much of home any more."

172

## 8: And All These in
## Their Helpless Days . . .

The great Egyptian sun was dropping away to the horizon as, in the company of some forty blue-cowled Islamic schoolgirls and a bird-catcher, I sailed back to the East. Reflected in the Nile the sky was the colour of blood and saffron against every tone of dusty blue; the rocks, houses and palms dark violet silhouettes, sparkling here and there as lamps were lit, signalling the start of Aswan's somewhat orderly nightlife. Near the landing stage I ate some *mulakhiya*, rice and an antique salad at Mahommeds' Cafetria, drank some mint tea and went back to the Osiris, half expecting to find that my sister had left word, but the Hindu woman had no messages and handed me my key with a quick smile of encouragement.

I slept poorly, kept awake by the constant cracking of a chemical "equalizer" in the basement and the creak of the all-but-useless wind-generator on the roof. It was ironic that Aswan, so close to the source of enormous quantities of electricity, was as cruelly rationed as everyone.

I refused to believe that my sister, who was as sane as I was and twice as intelligent, had become entangled with a black-magic flying-saucer cult. Her only purpose for associating with such people would be curiosity, perhaps in pursuit of some anthropological research connected with her work. I was, however, puzzled by her secrecy. Clearly, she was deliberately hiding her whereabouts. I hoped that, when I returned the next day, I would know where she was.

My meetings were predictably amiable and

inconsequential. I had arrived a little late, having failed to anticipate the levels of security at the dam. There were police, militia and security people everywhere, both on the dam itself and in all the offices and operations areas. I had to show my pass to eleven different people. The dam was under increased threat from at least three organizations, the chief being Green Jihad. Our main meetings were held in a large, glass-walled room overlooking the lake. I was glad to meet so many staff, though we all knew that any decisions about the dam would not be made by us but by whoever triumphed in the Geneva negotiations. It was also good to discover that earlier attitudes towards the dam were changing slightly and new thinking was being done. Breakfasted and lunched, I next found myself guest of honour at a full-scale Egyptian dinner that must have taken everyone's rations for a month, involved several entertainments and lastly a good deal of noisy toasting, in cokes and grape juice, of our various unadmired leaders.

At the Hotel Osiris, when I got back that night, there was no note for me so I decided next day to visit the old vacation villas before lunching as arranged at the Cataract with Georges Abidos, who had told me that he was retiring as Public Relations officer for the dam. I had a hunch that my sister was probably living with the neo-hippies. The following morning I ordered a calash to pick me up and sat on the board beside the skinny, cheerful driver as his equally thin horse picked her way slowly through busy Saturday streets until we were on the long, cracked concrete road with the railway yards on one side and the river on the other, flanked by dusty palms, that led past the five-storey Moorish-style vacation complex, a tumble of typical tourist architecture of the kind once found all around the Mediterranean, Adriatic and parts of the Black and Red Seas. The white stucco was patchy and the turquoise trim on window-frames and doors was peeling, but the new inhabitants, who had occupied it when the Swedish owners finally abandoned it, had put their stamp on it. Originally the place had been designed for Club Med, but had never sustained the required turnover, even with its special energy dispensations, and had been sold several times over the past ten years. Now garishly dressed young squatters from the wealthy African countries, from the Australias, North and South America, as well as Europe and the Far East, had covered the old complex with their sometimes impressive murals and decorative graffiti. I read a variety of slogans. LET THE BLOOD CONSUME THE FIRE, said one. THE TYGERS OF THE MIND RULE THE JUNGLE OF THE HEART, said another. I had no relish for such undisciplined nonsense and did not look forward to meeting the occupants of this bizarre New New Age fortress. Psychedelia, even in its historical context, had never attracted me.

As I dismounted from the calash I was greeted by a young woman energetically cleaning the old Club Med brass plate at the gate. She had those startling green eyes in a dark olive skin that one frequently comes across everywhere in Egypt and are commonly believed to be another inheritance from the Pharaonic past. Her reddish hair was braided with multicoloured ribbons and she wore a long green silk smock that complemented her eyes.

"Hi!" Her manner was promiscuously friendly. "I'm

175

Lips. Which is short for Eclipse, to answer your question. Don't get the wrong idea. You're here to find a relative, right?" Her accent was Canadian with a trace of something else, possibly Ukrainian. "What's your name?"

"Paul," I said. "My sister's called Bea. Are the only people who visit you trying to find a relative?"

"I just made an assumption from the way you look. I'm pretty good at sussing people out." Then she made a noise of approving excitement. "Becky Beak, is it? She's famous here. She's a healer and an oracle. She's special."

"Could you take me to her apartment?" I did my best not to show impatience with the girl's nonsense.

"Lips" answered me with a baffled smile. "No. I mean, sure I could take you to one of her rooms. But she's not here now."

"Do you know where she went?"

The girl was vaguely apologetic. "Mercury? Wherever the ship goes."

My irritation grew more intense. But I controlled myself. "You've no idea when the ship gets back?"

"Now? Yesterday? There's so much time-bending involved. No. You just have to hope."

I walked past her into the complex.


## 9: Fast Closing Toward The Undelighted Night . . .

By the time I had spoken to a dozen or so *enfants des fleurs* I had found myself a guide who introduced himself as Magic Mungo and wore brilliant face paint

176

beneath his straw hat. He had on an old pair of glitter-
jeans that whispered and flashed as he walked. His
jacket announced in calligraphic Arabic phonetic
English: THE NAME IS THE GAME. He was probably
no older than thirteen. He asked me what I did and
when I told him he said he, too, planned to become an
engineer "and bring back the power." This amused me
and restored my temper. "And what will you do about
the weather?" I asked.

"It's not the weather," he told me, "not Nature – it's
the ships. And it's not the dam, or the lake, that's
causing the storms and stuff. It's the Reens."

I misheard him. I thought he was blaming the Greens.
Then I realized, belatedly, that he was expressing a
notion popular amongst the New New Agers, which by
the time I had heard it several times more had actually
begun to improve my mood. The Reens, the flying-
saucer people, were used by the hippies as an explanation for everything they couldn't understand. In
rejecting Science, they had substituted only a banal
myth. Essentially, I was being told that the Gods had
taken my sister. In other words, they did not know
where she was. At last, after several further short but
keen conversations, in various rug-strewn galleries and
cushion-heavy chambers smelling strongly of kif,
incense and patchouli, I met a somewhat older woman,
with grey streaks in her long black hair and a face the
colour and texture of well-preserved leather.

"This is Ayesha." Mungo gulped comically. "She-
who-must-be-obeyed!" He ran to the woman who smiled
a perfectly ordinary smile as she embraced him. "We
encourage their imaginations," she said. "They read
books here and everything. Are you looking for Beck?"

Warily expecting more Reen talk, I admitted that I was trying to find my sister.

"She went back to Aswan. I think she was at the medrassah for a bit – you know, with the Sufi – but after that she returned to town. If she's not there, she's in the desert again. She goes there to meditate, I'm told. If she's not there, she's not anywhere. Around here, I mean."

I was relieved by the straightforward nature of her answer. "I'm greatly obliged. I thought you, too, were going to tell me she was taken into space by aliens!"

Ayesha joined in my amusement. "Oh, no, of course not. That was more than a year ago!"

## 10: Thoughts of Too Old a Colour Nurse My Brain

I decided to have a note delivered to the Sufi, El Haj Ibrahim Abu Halil, telling him that I planned to visit him next day. Then, with a little time to spare before my appointment, I strolled up the corniche, past the boat-ghetto at the upper end, and along the more fashionable stretches where some sporadic attempt was made to give the railings fresh coats of white paint and where a kiosk, closed since my first time here, advertised in bleached Latin type the *Daily Telegraph*, *Le Monde* and the *New York Herald-Tribune*. A few thin strands of white smoke rose from the villages on Elephantine Island, and from *Gazirat-al-Bustan*, Plantation Island, whose botanical gardens, begun by Lord Kitchener, had long since mutated into marvellously exotic jungle, came the laughter of the children and teenagers who habitually spent their free days there.

Outside the kiosk stood an old man holding a bunch of faded and ragged international newspapers under one arm and *El Misr* under the other. "All today!" he called vigorously in English, much as a London coster shouted "All fresh!" A professional cry rather than any sort of promise. I bought an *El Misr*, only a day old, and glanced at the headlines as I walked up to the park. There seemed nothing unusually alarming in the paper. Even the EC rate had not risen in the last month. As I tried to open the sheet a gust came off the river and the yellow-grey paper began to shred in my hands. It was low-density recyke, unbulked by the sophisticated methods of the West. Before I gave up and dumped the crumpled mess into the nearest reclamation bin I had glimpsed references to the UNEC conference in Madagascar and something about examples of mass hysteria in Old Paris and Bombay, where a group called *Reincarnation* was claiming its leader to be a newly born John Lennon. There were now about as many reincarnated Lennons abroad as there had been freshly risen Christs in the early Middle Ages.

I stopped in the park to watch the gardeners carefully tending the unsweet soil of the flower beds, coaxing marigolds and nasturtiums to bloom at least for a few days in the winter, when the sun would not burn them immediately they emerged. The little municipal café was unchanged since British days and still served only ice creams, tea, coffee or soft drinks, all of them made with non-rationed ingredients and all equally tasteless. Pigeons wandered hopelessly amongst the debris left by customers, occasionally pecking at a piece of wrapping or a sliver of *Sustenance* left behind by some poor devil who had been unable to force his stomach to accept the high-concentrate nutrients we had developed at UNEC for his benefit.

The Cataract's entrance was between pillars that, once stately, Egyptianate and unquestionably European, were now a little the worse for wear, though the gardens on both sides of the drive were heavy with freshly planted GM flowers. Bougainvilleas of every brilliant variety covered walls behind avenues of palms leading to a main building the colour of Nile clay, its shutters and ironwork a dark, dignified green, the kind of colour Thomas Cook himself would have picked to represent the security and solid good service that established him as one of the Empire's noblest champions.

I walked into the great lobby cooled by massive carved mahogany punkahs worked on hidden ropes by screened boys. Egypt had had little trouble implementing many of the UN's mandatory energy saving regulations. She had either carried on as always or had returned, perhaps even with relief, to the days before electricity and gas had become the necessities rather than the luxuries of life.

I crossed the lobby to the wooden verandah where we were to lunch. Georges Abidos was already at our table by the rail looking directly over the empty swimming pool and, beyond that, to the river itself. He was drinking a cup of Lipton's tea and I remarked on it, pointing to the label on the string dangling from his tiny metal pot. "Indeed!" he said. "At ten pounds the pot why shouldn't the Cataract offer us Lipton's, at least!" He dropped his voice. "Though my guess is the tea bag has seen more than one customer through the day's heat. Would you like a cup?"

I refused. He hadn't, I said, exactly sold me on the idea. He laughed. He was a small, attractively ugly Greek from Alexandria. Since the flooding, he had been driven, like so many of his fellow citizens, to seek work inland. At least half the city had not been thought worth saving as the sea level had steadily risen to cover it.

"Can't you," he asked, "get your American friends to do something about this new embargo? One misses the cigarettes and I could dearly use a new John B." He indicated his stained Planter's straw and then picked it up to show me the label on the mottled sweatband so that I might verify it was a genuine product of the Stetson Hat Co. of New Jersey. "Size seven and a quarter. But don't get anything here. The Cairo fakes are very close. Very good. But they can't fake the finish, you see."

"I'll remember," I promised. I would send him a Stetson next time I was in the USA.

I felt we had actually conducted our main business before we sat down. The rest of the lunch would be a social affair with someone I had known both professionally and as a close personal acquaintance for many years.

As our mixed *hors d'oeuvres* arrived, Georges Abidos looked, with a despairing movement of his mouth, out towards the river. "Well, Paul, have you solved any of our problems?"

"I doubt it," I said. "That's all going on in Majunga now. I'm wondering if my function isn't some kind of minor smokescreen."

"I thought you'd volunteered."

"Only when they'd decided that one of us had to come. It was a good chance, I thought, to see how my sister was. I had spare relative allowance and lots of energy and travel owing, so I got her a flight out with me. It took forever! But I grew rather worried. The last note I had from her was three months ago and very disjointed. It didn't tell me anything. I'd guessed that her husband had turned up. It was something she said. That's about all I know that would frighten her that much. My mistake, it's emerged. Then I wondered if she wasn't pregnant. I couldn't make head or tail of her letters. They weren't like her at all."

"Women are a trial," said Georges Abidos. "My own sister has divorced, I heard. But then," as if to explain it, "they moved to Kuwait." He turned his eyes back to the river, which seemed almost to obsess him. "Look at the Nile. An open sewer running through a desert. What has Egypt done to deserve rescue? She gave the world the ancestors who first offered Nature a serious challenge. Should we be grateful for that? From Lake Nasser to Alexandria the river remains undrinkable and frequently unusable. She once replenished the Earth. Now, what with their fertilizers and sprays, she helps poison it." It was as if all the doubts he had kept to himself as a publicity officer were now being allowed to emerge. "I listen to Blue Danube Radio from Vienna. The English station. It's so much more reliable than the World Service. We are still doing less than we could, they say, here in Egypt."

The tables around us had begun to fill with Saudis and wealthy French people in fashionable silk shifts, and the noise level rose so that it was hard for me to hear my acquaintance's soft tones.

We discussed the changing nature of Aswan. He said he would be glad to get back to Cairo where he had a new job with the Antiquities Department raising money for specific restoration or reconstruction projects.

We had met at the reopening of the Cairo Opera House in 1989, which had featured the Houston Opera Company's *Porgy and Bess*, but had never become more than casual friends, though we shared many musical tastes and he had an extraordinary knowledge of modern fiction in English. His enthusiasm was for the older writers like Gilchrist or DeLillo, who had been amongst my own favourites at college.

We were brought some wonderfully tasty Grönburgers and I remarked that the cuisine had improved since I was last here. "French management," he told me. "They have one of the best teams outside of Paris. They all came from Nice after the troubles. Lucky for us. I might almost be tempted to stay! Oh, no! I could not. Even for that! Nubian music is an abomination!"

I told him about my sister, how I was unable to find her and how I was beginning to fear the worst. "The police suggested she was mad."

Georges was dismissive of this. "A dangerous assumption at any time, Paul, but especially these days. And very difficult for us to define here, in Egypt, just as justice is at once a more brutal and a subtler instrument in our interpretations. We never accepted, thank God, the conventional wisdoms of psychiatry. And madness here, as elsewhere, is defined by the people in power, usually calling themselves the State. Tomorrow those power holders could be overthrown by a fresh dynasty, and what was yesterday simple common sense today becomes irresponsible folly. So I do not like to make

183

hasty judgements or pronounce readily on others' moral or mental conditions – lest, indeed, we inadvertently condemn ourselves." He paused. "They say this was not so under the British, that it was fairer, more predictable. Only real troublemakers and criminals went to jail. Now it isn't as bad as it was when I was a lad. Then anyone was liable to arrest. If it was better under the British, then that is our shame." And he lowered his lips to his wineglass.

We had slipped, almost automatically, into discussing the old, familiar topics. "It's sometimes argued," I said, "that the liberal democracies actually stopped the flow of history. A few hundred years earlier, as feudal states, we would have forcibly Christianized the whole of Islam and changed the entire nature of the planet's power struggle. Indeed, all the more childish struggles might have been well and truly over by now!"

"Or it might have gone the other way," Georges suggested dryly, "if the Moors had reconquered France and Northern Europe. After all, Islam did not bring the world to near-ruin. What has the European way achieved except the threat of death for all?"

I could not accept an argument that had already led to massive conversions to Islam amongst the youth of Europe, America and Democratic Africa, representing a sizeable proportion of the vote. This phenomenon had, admittedly, improved the tenor of world politics, but I still deplored it.

"Oh, you're so thoroughly out of step, my friend." Georges Abidos smiled and patted my arm. "The world's changing!"

"It'll die if we start resorting to mystical Islamic solutions."

"Possibly." He seemed unconcerned. I think he believed us unsavable.

A little drunk, I let him take me back to the Osiris in a calash. He talked affectionately of our good times, of concerts and plays we had seen in the world's capitals before civilian flight had become so impossibly expensive, of the Gilbert and Sullivan season we had attended in Bangkok, of Wagner in Bayreuth and Britten in Glyndebourne. We hummed a snatch from *Iolanthe* before we parted.

When I got up to my room all the shutters had been drawn back to give the apartment the best of the light. I recognized the subtle perfume even as my sister came out of the bathroom to laugh aloud at my astonishment.

## 11 : Saw Life to Be
## A Sea-Green Dream

Beatrice had cut her auburn hair short and her skin was paler than I remembered. While her blue eyes and red lips remained striking, she had gained an extra beauty. I was overjoyed. This was the opposite of what I had feared to find.

As if she read my mind, she smiled. "Were you expecting the Mad Woman of Aswan?" She wore a light blue cotton skirt and a darker blue shirt.

"You've never looked better." I spoke the honest truth.

She took both my hands in hers and kissed me. "I'm sorry I didn't write. It began to seem such a sham. I *couldn't* write for a while. I got your letters today,

185

when I went to the post office. What a coincidence, I thought – my first sally into the real world and here comes good old Paul to help me. If anyone understands reality, you do."

I was flattered and grinned in the way I had always responded to her half-mocking praise. "Well, I'm here to take you back to it, if you want to go. I've got a pass for you on the Cairo plane in four days' time, and from there we can go to Geneva or London or anywhere in the Community."

"That's marvellous," she said. She looked about my shabby sitting room with its cracked foam cushions, its stained tiles. "Is this the best you get at your rank?"

"This is the best for any rank, these days. Most of us don't travel at all and certainly not by plane."

"The schoomers are still going out of Alex, are they?"

"Oh, yes. To Genoa, some of them. Who has the time?"

"That's what I'd thought of, for me. But here you are! What a bit of luck!"

I was immensely relieved. "Oh, Bea. I thought you might be dead – you know, or worse."

"I was selfish not to keep you in touch, but for a while, of course, I couldn't. Then I was out there for so long . . ."

"At your dig, you mean?"

She seemed momentarily surprised, as if she had not expected me to know about the dig. "Yes, where the dig was. That's right. I can't remember what I said in my letters."

"That you'd made a terrific discovery and that I must come out the first chance I got. Well, I did. This really was the first chance. Am I too late? Have they closed down the project completely? Are you out of funds?"

"Yes," she smiled. "You're too late, Paul. I'm awfully worried. You must think I've brought you on a wild goose chase."

"Nonsense. That wasn't why I really came. Good Lord, Bea, I care a lot for you!" I stopped, a little ashamed. She was probably in a more delicate condition than she permitted me to see. "And, anyway, I had some perks coming. It's lovely here, still, isn't it? If you ignore the rubbish tips. You know, and the sewage. And the Nile!" We laughed together. "And the rain and the air," she said. "And the sunlight! Oh, Paul! What if this really is the future?"

## 12 : A Man In the Night
## Flaking Tombstones

She asked if I would like to take a drive with her beside the evening river and I agreed at once. I was her senior by a year but she had always been the leader, the initiator and I admired her as much as ever.

We went up past the ruins of the Best Western and the Ramada Inn, the only casualties of a shelling attack in '02, when the Green Jihad had attempted to hole the dam and six women had died. We stopped near the abandoned museum and bought a drink from the ice-stall. As I turned, looking out at the river, I saw the new moon, huge and orange, in the cloudless night. A few desultory mosquitoes hung around our heads and were easily fanned away as we continued up the corniche, looking out at the lights from the boats, the flares on

187

the far side, the palms waving in the soft breeze from the North.

"I'm quitting my job," she said. "I resigned, in fact, months ago. I had a few things to clear up."

"What will you do? Get something in London?"

"Well, I've my money. That was invested very sensibly by Jack before our problems started. Before we split up. And I can do freelance work." Clearly, she was unwilling to discuss the details. "I could go on living here."

"Do you want to?"

"No," she said. "I hate it now. But is the rest of the world any better, Paul?"

"Oh, life's still a bit easier in England. And Italy's all right. And Scandinavia, of course, but that's closed off, as far as residency's concerned. The population's dropping quite nicely in Western Europe. Not everything's awful. The winters are easier."

She nodded slowly as if she were carefully noting each observation. "Well," she said, "anyway, I don't know about Aswan. I'm not sure there's much point in my leaving Egypt. I have a permanent visa, you know."

"Why stay, Bea?"

"Oh, well," she said. "I suppose it feels like home. How's Daddy? Is everything all right in Marrakesh?"

"Couldn't be better, I gather. He's having a wonderful time. You know how happy he always was there. And with the new government! Well, you can imagine."

"And mother?"

"Still in London. She has a house to herself in West Hampstead. Don't ask me how. She's installed the latest EE generators and energy storers. She's got a TV set, a pet option and a gas licence. You know mother.

She's always had the right contacts. She'll be glad to know you're OK."

"Yes. That's good, too. I've been guilty of some awfully selfish behaviour, haven't I? Well, I'm putting all that behind me and getting on with my life."

"You sound as if you've seen someone. About whatever it was. Have you been ill, Bea?"

"Oh, no. Not really." She turned to reassure me with a quick smile and a hand out to mine, just as always. I nearly sang with relief. "Emotional trouble, you know."

"A boyfriend?"

"Well, yes, I suppose so. Anyway, it's over."

"All the hippies told me you'd been abducted by a flying saucer!"

"Did they?"

I recognized her brave smile. "What's wrong? I hadn't meant to be tactless."

"You weren't. There are so many strange things happening around here. You can't blame people for getting superstitious, can you? After all, we say we've identified the causes, yet can do virtually nothing to find a cure."

"Well, I must admit there's some truth in that. But there are still things we can do."

"Of course there are. I didn't mean to be pessimistic, old Paul." She punched me on the arm and told the driver to let his horse trot for a bit, to get us some air on our faces, since the wind had dropped so suddenly.

She told me she would come to see me at the same time tomorrow and perhaps after that we might go to her new flat. It was only a temporary place while she made up her mind. Why didn't I just go to her there? I said. Because, she said, it was in a maze. You couldn't get a calash through and even the schoolboys would sometimes mislead you by accident. Write it down, I suggested, but she refused with an even broader smile. "You'll see I'm right. I'll take you there tomorrow. There's no mystery. Nothing deliberate."

I went back into the damp, semi-darkness of the Osiris and climbed through black archways to my room.

## 13: You'll Find No Mirrors
## In That Cold Abode

I had meant to ask Beatrice about her experience with the Somali woman and the police, but her mood had swung so radically I had decided to keep the rest of the conversation as casual as possible. I went to bed at once more hopeful and more baffled than I had been before I left Cairo.

In the morning I took a cab to the religious academy, or *madrassah*, of the famous Sufi, El Haj Sheik Ibrahim Abu Halil, not because I now needed his help in finding my sister, but because I felt it would have been rude to cancel my visit without explanation. The *madrassah* was out near the old obelisk quarries. Characteristically Muslim, with a tower and a domed mosque, it was reached, on foot or by donkey, up a winding, artificial track that had been there for at least two thousand years. I climbed to the top, feeling a little dizzy as I avoided looking directly down into the ancient quarry and saw that the place was built as a series of stone colonnades around a great courtyard with a fountain in it. The fountain, in accordance with the law, was silent.

The place was larger than I had expected and far more casual. People, many obviously drugged, of every age and race sat in groups or strolled around the cloisters. I asked a pale young woman in an Islamic *burqa* where I might find Sheikh Abu Halil. She told me to go to the office and led me as far as a glass door through which I saw an ordinary business layout of pens and paper, mechanical typewriters, acoustic calculators and, impressively, an EMARGY console. I felt as if I were prying. My first job, from which I had resigned, was as an Energy Officer. Essentially the work involved too much peeping-Tomism and too little real progress.

A young black man in flared Mouwes and an Afghan jerkin signalled for me to enter. I told him my business and he said, "No problem, man." He asked me to wait in a little room furnished like something still found in any South London dentist's. Even the magazines looked familiar and I did not intend to waste my battery ration plugging in to one. A few minutes later the young man returned and I was escorted through antiseptic corridors to the Sufi's inner sanctum.

I had expected some rather austere sort of Holy Roller's Executive Suite, and was a trifle shocked by the actuality, which resembled a scene from *The Arabian Nights*. The Sufi was clearly not celibate, and was an epicurean rather than an aescetic. He was also younger than I had expected. I guessed he was no more than forty-five. Dressed in red silks of a dozen shades, with a massive scarlet turban on his head, he lay on cushions smoking from a silver-and-brass hookah while behind him, on rich, spangled divans, lolled half a dozen young

191

women, all of them veiled, all looking at me with frank, if discreet, interest. I felt as if I should apologize for intruding on someone's private sexual fantasy, but the Sufi grinned, beckoned me in, then fell to laughing aloud as he stared into my face. All this, of course, only increased my discomfort. I could see no reason for his amusement.

"You think this a banal piece of play-acting?" He at once became solicitous. "Pardon me, *Herr Doktor*. I misunderstood your expression for a moment. I thought you were an old friend." Now he was almost grave. "How can I help you?"

"Originally," I said, "I was looking for my sister Beatrice. I believe you know her." Was this my sister's secret? Had she involved herself with a charismatic charlatan to whom even I felt drawn? But the banality of it all! True madness, like true evil, I had been informed once, was always characterized by its banality.

"That's it, of course. Becky Bakka was the name the young ones used. She is a very good friend of mine. Are you looking for her no longer, Dr Bakka?"

I pointed out that 'von Bek' was the family name. The hippies had not made an enormously imaginative leap.

"Oh, the children! Don't they love to play? They are blessed. Think how few of us in the world are allowed by God to play."

"Thou art most tolerant indeed, sidhi." I used my best classical Arabic, at which he gave me a look of considerable approval and addressed me in the same way.

"Doth God not teach us to tolerate, but not to imitate, all the ways of mankind? Are we to judge God, my compatriot?" He had done me the honour, in his own eyes, of addressing me as a co-religionist. When he smiled again his expression was one of benign happiness. "Would you care for some coffee?" he asked in educated English. "Some cakes and so on? Yes, of course." And he clapped his hands, whispering instructions to the nearest woman who rose and left. I was so thoroughly discomforted by this outrageously old-fashioned sexism – which, whatever their private practices, few sophisticated modern Arabs were willing to admit to – that I remained silent.

"And I trust that you in turn will tolerate my stupid self-indulgence," he said. "It is a whim of mine – and of these young women – to lead the life of Haroun-el-Raschid, eh? Or the great chiefs who ruled in the days before the Prophet. We are all nostalgic for that, in Egypt. The past, you know, is our only escape. You don't begrudge it us, do you?"

I shook my head, although by training and temperament I could find no merit in his argument. "These are changing times," I said. "Your past is crumbling away. It's difficult to tell good from evil or right from wrong, let alone shades of intellectual preference."

"But I can tell you really do still think there are mechanical solutions to our ills."

"Don't you, sidhi?"

"I do. I doubt, though, that they're much like a medical man's."

"I'm an engineer, not a doctor of medicine."

"Pardon me. It's my day for gaffes, eh? But we're all guilty of making the wrong assumptions sometimes. Let us open the shutters and enjoy some fresh air." Another of the women went to fold back the tall wooden blinds

193

and let shafts of sudden sunlight down upon the maroons, burgundies, dark pinks, bottle-greens and royal blues of that luxurious room. The women sank into the shadows and only Sheik Abu Halil remained with half his face in light, the other in shade, puffing on his pipe, his silks rippling as he moved a lazy hand. "We are blessed with a marvellous view."

From where we sat it was possible to see the Nile, with its white sails and flanking palms, on the far side of an expanse of glaring granite.

"My sister—" I began.

"A remarkable woman. A saint, without doubt. We have tried to help her, you know."

"I believe you're responsible for getting her out of police custody, sidhi."

"God has chosen her and has blessed her with unusual gifts. Dr von Bek, we are merely God's instruments. She has brought a little relief to the sick, a little consolation to the despairing."

"She's coming home with me. In three days."

"A great loss for Aswan. But perhaps she's more needed out there. Such sadness, you know. Such deep sadness." I was not sure if he described my sister or the whole world. "In Islam, you see," an ironic twitch of the lip, "we share our despair. It is a democracy of misery." And he chuckled. "This is blasphemy, I know, in the West. Especially in America."

"Well, in parts of the North maybe." I smiled. My father was from Mississippi and settled first in Morocco, then in England after he came out of the service. He said he missed the old, bitter-sweet character of the US South. The New South, optimistic and, in his view, Yankified, no longer felt like home. He

194

was more in his element in pre-Thatcher Britain. When she, too, began a programme of "Yankification" of her own he retreated into fantasy, leaving my mother and going to live in a working-class street in a run-down north-eastern town where he joined the Communist Party and demonstrated against closures in the mining, fishing and steel industries. My mother hated it when his name appeared in the papers or, worse in her view, when he wrote intemperate letters to the weekly journals or the heavy dailies. But "Jim Beck" was a contributor to *Marxism Today* and, later, *Red is Green* during his brief flirtation with Trotskyist Conservationism. He gave that up for anarcho-socialism and disappeared completely into the world of the abstract. He now wrote me letters describing the "Moroccan experiment" as the greatest example of genuinely radical politics in action. I had never completely escaped the tyranny of his impossible ideals. This came back to me, there and then, perhaps because in some strange way I found this sufi as charming as I had once found my father. "We say that misery loves company. Is that the same thing?" I felt I was in some kind of awful contest. "Is that why she wanted to stay with you?"

"I knew her slightly before it all changed for her. Afterwards, I knew her better. She seemed very delicate. She came back to Aswan, then went out to the dig a couple more times, then back here. She was possessed of a terrible restlessness she would allow nobody here to address and which she consistently denied. She carried a burden, Dr von Bek." He echoed the words of Inspector el-Bayoumi. "But, perhaps we, even we, shall never know what it was."

## 14 : On Every Hand –
## The Red Collusive Stain

She arrived at the Osiris only a minute or two late. She wore a one-piece worksuit and a kind of bush-hat with a veil. She also carried a briefcase, which she displayed in some embarrassment. "Habit, I suppose. I don't need the maps or the notes. I'm taking you into the desert, Paul. Is that OK?"

"We're not going to your place?"

"Not now."

I changed into more suitable clothes and followed her down to the street. She had a calash waiting that carried us to the edge of town, to a camel camp where, much to my dismay, we transferred to grumbling dromedaries. I had not ridden a camel for ten years, but mine proved fairly tractable once we were moving out over the sand.

I had forgotten the peace and the wonderful smell of the desert and it was not long before I had ceased to pay attention to the heat or the motion and had begun to enjoy a mesmeric panorama of dunes and old rock. My sister occasionally used a compass to keep course but sat her high saddle with the confidence of a seasoned drover. We picked up speed until the heat became too intense and we rested under an outcrop of red stone that offered the only shade. It was almost impossible to predict where one would find shade in the desert. A year ago this rock might have been completely invisible beneath the sand; in a few months it might be invisible again.

"The silence is seductive," I said after a while.

My sister smiled. "Well, it whispers to me, these days. But it is wonderful, isn't it? Here you have nothing but yourself, a chance to discover how much of your identity is your own and how much is actually society's. And the ego drifts away. One becomes a virgin beast."

"Indeed!" I found this a little too fanciful for me. "I'm just glad to be away from all that . . ."

"You're not nervous?"

"Of the desert?"

"Of getting lost. Nothing comes out here, ever, now. Nomads don't pass by and it's been years since a motor vehicle or plane was allowed to waste its ER on mere curiosity. If we died, we'd probably never be found."

"This is a bit morbid, isn't it, Bea? It's only a few hours from Aswan, and the camels are healthy."

"Yes." She rose to put our food and water back into their saddle-bags, causing a murmuring and an irritable shifting of the camels. We slept for a couple of hours. Bea wanted to be able to travel at night, when we would make better time under the almost full moon.

The desert at night will usually fill with the noises of the creatures who waken as soon as the sun is down, but the region we next entered seemed as lifeless as the Bical flats, though without their aching mood of desolation. The sand still rose around our camels' feet in silvery gasps and I wrapped myself in the other heavy woollen *gelabea* Beatrice had brought. We slept again, for two or three hours, before continuing on until it was almost dawn and the moon faint and fading in the sky.

"We used to have a gramophone and everything," she said. "We played those French songs mainly. The old ones. And a lot of classic Rai. It was a local collection someone had brought with the machine. You wouldn't believe the mood of camaraderie that was

197

here, Paul. Like Woodstock must have been. We had quite a few young people with us – Egyptian and European, mostly – and they all said the same. We felt privileged."

"When did you start treating the sick?" I asked her.

"Treating? Scarcely that! I just helped out with my first-aid kit and whatever I could scrounge from a pharmacy. Most of the problems were easily treated, but not priorities as far as the hospitals are concerned. I did what I could whenever I was in Aswan. But the kits gradually got used and nothing more was sent. After the quake, things began to run down. The Burbank Foundation needed its resources for rebuilding at home."

"But you still do it. Sometimes. You're a legend back there. Ben Achmet told me."

"When I can, I help these nomads cure themselves, that's all. I was coming out here a lot. Then there was some trouble with the police."

"They stopped you? Because of the Somali woman?"

"That didn't stop me." She raised herself in her saddle suddenly. "Look. Can you see the roof there? And the pillars?"

They lay in a shallow valley between two rocky cliffs and they looked in the half-light as if they had been built that very morning. The decorated columns and the massive flat roof were touched a pinkish gold by the rising sun and I could make out hieroglyphics, the blues and ochres of the Egyptian artist. The building, or series of buildings, covered a vast area. "It's a city," I said. I was still disbelieving. "Or a huge temple. My God, Bea! No wonder you were knocked out by this!"

"It's not a city or a temple, in any sense *we* mean."

Though she must have seen it a hundred times, she was still admiring of the beautiful stones. "There's nothing like it surviving anywhere else. No record of another. Even this is only briefly mentioned and, as always with Egyptians, dismissively as the work of earlier, less exalted leaders, in this case a monotheistic cult that attempted to set up its own God-king and, in failing, was thoroughly destroyed. Pragmatically, the winners in that contest rededicated the place to Sekhmet and then, for whatever reason – probably economic – abandoned it altogether. There are none of the usual signs of later uses. By the end of Nyusere's reign no more was heard of it at all. Indeed, not much more was heard of Nubia for a long time. This region was never exactly the centre of Egyptian life."

"It was a temple to Ra?"

"Ra, or a sun deity very much like him. The priest here was represented as a servant of the sun. We call the place Onu'us, after him."

"Four thousand years ago? Are you sure this isn't one of those new Dutch repros?" My joke sounded flat, even to me.

"Now you can see why we kept it dark, Paul. It was an observatory, a scientific centre, a laboratory, a library. A sort of university, really. Even the hieroglyphics are different. They tell all kinds of things about the people and the place. And it had a couple of other functions." Her enthusiasm died and she stopped, dismounting from her camel and shaking sand from her hat. Together we watched the dawn come up over the glittering roof. The pillars, shadowed now, stood only a few feet out of the sand, yet the brilliance of the colour was almost unbelievable. Here was the classic

199

MICHAEL MOORCOCK

language of the Fifth Dynasty, spare, accurate, clean.
And it was obvious that the whole place had only
recently been refilled. Elsewhere churned, powdery
earth and overturned rock spoke of vigorous activity by
the discovering team; there was also, on the plain which
stretched away from the Southern ridge, a considerable
area of fused sand. But even this was now covered by
that desert tide which would soon bury and again
preserve this uncanny relic.

"You tried to put the sand back?" I felt stupid and
smiled at myself.

"It was all we could think of in the circumstances.
Now it's far less visible than it was a month ago."

"You sound very proprietorial." I was amused that
the mystery should prove to have so obvious a solution.
My sister had simply become absorbed in her work. It
was understandable that she should.

"I'm sorry," she said. "I must admit . . ."

For a moment, lost in the profound beauty of the
vision, I did not realize she was crying. Just as I had as a
little boy, I moved to comfort her, having no notion at all
of the cause of her grief, but assuming, I suppose, that
she was mourning the death of an important piece of
research, the loss of her colleagues, the sheer disappointment at this unlucky end to a wonderful adventure. It
was plain, too, that she was completely exhausted.

She drew toward me, smiling an apology. "I want to
tell you everything, Paul. And only you. When I have,
that'll be it. I'll never mention it again. I'll get on with
some sort of life. I'm sick of myself at the moment."

"Bea. You're very tired. Let's go home to Europe
where I can coddle you for a bit."

"Perhaps," she said. She paused as the swiftly risen

200

sun outlined sunken buildings and revealed more of a structure lying just below the surface, some dormant juggernaut.

"It's monstrous," I said. "It's the size of the large complex at Luxor. But this is different. All the curved walls, all the circles. Is that to do with sun worship?"

"Astronomy, anyway. We speculated, of course. When we first mapped it on the sonavids. This is the discovery to launch a thousand theories, most of them crackpot. You have to be careful. But it felt to us to be almost a contrary development to what was happening at roughly the same time around Abu Ghurab, although of course there were sun cults there, too. But in Lower Egypt the gratification and celebration of the Self had reached terrible proportions. All those grandiose pyramids. This place had a mood to it. The more we sifted it out the more we felt it. Wandering amongst those light columns, those open courtyards, was marvellous. All the turquoises and reds and bright yellows. This had to be the centre of some ancient Enlightenment. Far better preserved than Philae, too. And no graffiti carved anywhere, no Christian or Muslim disfigurement. We all worked like maniacs. Chamber after chamber was opened. Gradually, of course, it dawned on us! You could have filled this place with academic people and it would have been a functioning settlement again, just as it was before some petty Pharaoh or local governor decided to destroy it. We felt we were taking over from them after a gap of millennia. It gave some of us a weird sense of responsibility. We talked about it. They knew so much, Paul."

"And so little," I murmured. "They only had limited information to work with, Bea . . ."

"Oh, I think we'd be grateful for their knowledge today." Her manner was controlled, as if she desperately tried to remember how she had once talked and behaved. "Anyway, this is where it all happened. We thought at first we had an advantage. Nobody was bothering to come out to what was considered a very minor find and everyone involved was anxious not to let any government start interfering. It was a sort of sacred trust, if you like. We kept clearing. We weren't likely to be found. Unless we used the emergency radio nobody would waste an energy unit on coming out. Oddly, we found no monumental statuary at all, though the engineering was on a scale with anything from the Nineteenth Dynasty – not quite as sophisticated, maybe, but again far in advance of its own time."

"How long did it take you to uncover it all?"

"We never did. We all swore to reveal nothing until a proper international preservation order could be obtained. This government is as desperate for cruise-schoomer dollars as anyone . . ."

I found myself interrupting her. "This was all covered by hand, Bea?"

"No, no." Again she was amused. "No, the ship did that, mostly. When it brought me back."

A sudden depression filled me. "You mean a space-ship, do you?"

"Yes," she said. "A lot of people here know about them. And I told Di Roper, as well as some of the kids, and the Sufi. But nobody ever believes us – nobody from the real world, I mean. And that's why I wanted to tell you. You're still a real person, aren't you?"

"Bea – you could let me know everything in London.

202

Once we're back in a more familiar environment. Can't we just enjoy this place for what it is? Enjoy the world for what it is?"

"It's not enjoyable for me, Paul."

I moved away from her. "I don't believe in space-ships."

"You don't believe in much, do you?" Her tone was unusually cool.

I regretted offending her, yet I could not help but respond. "The nuts and bolts of keeping this ram-shackle planet running somehow. That's what I believe in, Bea. I'm like that chap in the first version of *The African Queen*, only all he had to worry about was a World War and a little beam-engine. Bea, you were here alone and horribly over-tired. Surely . . . ?"

"Let me talk, Paul." There was a note of aching despair in her voice which immediately silenced me and made me lower my head in assent.

We stood there, looking at the sunrise pouring light over that dusty red and brown landscape with its drowned architecture, and I listened to her recount the most disturbing and unlikely story I was ever to hear.

The remains of the team had gone into Aswan for various reasons and Bea was left alone with only a young Arab boy for company. Ali worked as a general servant and was as much part of the team as anyone else, with as much enthusiasm. "He, too, understood the reasons for saying little about our work. Phil Springfield had already left to speak to some people in Washington and Professor al-Bayumi, no close relative of the inspector, was doing what he could in Cairo though you can imagine the delicacy of his position. Well, one morning, when I was cleaning the dishes and

Ali had put a record on the gramophone, this freak storm blew up. It caused a bit of panic, of course, though it was over in a minute or two. And when the sand settled again there was the ship – there, on that bluff. You can see where it came and went."

The spaceship, she said, had been a bit like a flying saucer in that it was circular, with deep sides and glowing horizontal bands at regular intervals. "It was more drum-shaped, though there were discs – I don't know, they weren't metal, but seemed like visible electricity, sort of protruding from it, half on the inside, half on the outside. Much of that moved from a kind of hazy gold into a kind of silver. There were other colours, too. And, I think, sounds. It looked a bit like a kid's tambourine – opaque, sparkling surfaces top and bottom – like the vellum on a drum. And the sides went dark sometimes. Polished oak. The discs, the flange things, went scarlet. They were its main information sensors."

"It was organic?"

"It was a bit. You'd really have to see it for yourself. Anyway, it stood there for a few minutes and then these figures came out. I thought they were test pilots from that experimental field in Libya and they'd made an emergency landing. I was going to offer them a cup of tea when I realized they weren't human. They had dark bodies that weren't suits exactly but an extra body you wear over your own. Well, you've seen something like it. We all have. It's Akhenaten and Nefertiti. Those strange abdomens and elongated heads, their herma-phroditic quality. They spoke a form of very old-fashioned English. They apologized. They said they had had an instrument malfunction and had not expected to find anyone here. They were prepared to take us with them, if we wished to go. I gathered that these were standard procedures for them. We were both completely captivated by their beauty and the wonder of the event. I don't think Ali hesitated any more than I. I left a note for whoever returned, saying I'd had to leave in a hurry and didn't know when I'd be back. Then we went with them."

"You didn't wonder about their motives?"

"Motives? Yes, Paul, I suppose hallucinations have motives. We weren't the only Earth-people ever to go. Anyway, I never regretted the decision. On the dark side of the Moon the main ship was waiting. That's shaped like a gigantic dung-beetle. You'll laugh when I tell you why. I still find it funny. They're furious because their bosses won't pay for less antiquated vessels. Earth's not a very important project. The ship was designed after one of the first organisms they brought back from Earth, to fit in with what they thought was a familiar form. Apparently their own planet has fewer species but many more different sizes of the same creature. They haven't used the main ship to visit Earth since we began to develop sensitive detection equipment. Their time is different, anyway, and they still find our ways of measuring and recording it very hard to understand."

"They took you to their planet?" I wanted her story to be over. I had heard enough to convince me that she was in need of immediate psychiatric help.

"Oh, no. They've never been there. Not the people I know. Others have been back, but we never communicated with them. They have an artificial environment on Mercury." She paused, noticing my distress.

"Paul, you know me. I hated that von Daniken stuff. It was patently rubbish. Yet this was, well, horribly like it. Don't think I wasn't seriously considering I might have gone barmy. When people go mad, you know, they get such ordinary delusions. I suppose they reflect our current myths and apocrypha. I felt foolish at first. Then, of course, the reality grew so vivid, so absorbing, I forgot everything. I could not have run away, Paul. I just walked into it all and they let me. I'm not sure why, except they know things – even circumstances, if you follow me – and must have felt it was better to let me. They hadn't wanted to go underwater and they'd returned to an old location in the Sahara. They'd hoped to find some spares, I think. I know it sounds ridiculously prosaic.

"Well, they took us with them to their base. If I try to pronounce their language it somehow sounds so ugly. Yet it's beautiful. I think in their atmosphere it works. I can speak it, Paul. They can speak our languages, too. But there's no need for them. Their home planet's many light years beyond the Solar System which is actually very different to Earth, except for some colours and smells, of course. Oh, it's so lovely there, at their base. Yet they complain all the time about how primitive it is and long for the comforts of home. You can imagine what it must be like.

"I became friends with a Reen. He was exquisitely beautiful. He wasn't really a he, either, but an androgyne or something similar. There's more than one type of fertilization, involving several people, but not always. I was completely taken up with him. Maybe he wasn't so lovely to some human eyes, but he was to mine. He was golden-pale and looked rather negroid, I suppose, like one of those beautiful Masai carvings you see in Kenya, and his shape wasn't altogether manlike, either. His abdomen was permanently rounded – most of them are like that, though in the intermediary sex I think there's a special function. My lover was of that sex, yet he found it impossible to make me understand how he was different. Otherwise they have a biology not dissimilar to ours, with similar organs and so on. It was not hard for me to adapt. Their food is delicious, though they moan about that, too. It's sent from home. Where they can grow it properly. And they have extra-ordinary music. They have recordings of English TV and radio – and other kinds of recordings, too. Earth's an entire department, you see. Paul," she paused as if regretting the return of the memory, "they have recordings of events. Like battles and ceremonies and architectural stuff. He – my lover – found me an open-air concert at which Mozart was playing. It was too much for me. An archaeologist, and I hadn't the nerve to look at the past as it actually was. I might have got round to it. I meant to. I'd planned to force myself, you know, when I settled down there."

"Bea, don't you know how misanthropic and nuts that sounds?"

"They haven't been 'helping' us or anything like that. It's an observation team. We're not the only planet they're keeping an eye on. They're academics and scientists like us." She seemed to be making an effort to convince me and to repeat the litany of her own faith, whatever it was that she believed kept her sane. Yet the creatures she described, I was still convinced, were merely the inventions of an overtaxed, isolated mind. Perhaps she had been trapped somewhere underground?

"I could have worked there, you see. But I broke the rules."

"You tried to escape?" Reluctantly I humoured her.

"Oh, no!" Her mind had turned backward again and I realized then that it was not any far-off interstellar world but her own planet that had taken her reason. I was suddenly full of sorrow.

"A flying saucer, Bea!" I hoped that my incredulity would bring her back to normality. She had been so ordinary, so matter-of-fact, when we had first met.

"Not really," she said. "The hippies call them Reens. They don't know very much about them, but they've made a cult of the whole thing. They've changed it. Fictionalized it. I can see why that would disturb you. They've turned it into a story for their own purposes. And Sheikh Abu Halil's done the same, really. We've had arguments. I can't stand the exploitation, Paul."

"That's in the nature of a myth." I spoke gently, feeling foolish and puny as I stood looking down on that marvellous construction. I wanted to leave, to return to Aswan, to get us back to Cairo and from there to the relative sanity of rural Oxfordshire, to the village where we had lived with our aunt during our happiest years. She nodded her head. "That's why I stopped saying anything.

"You can't imagine how hurt I was at first, how urgent it seemed to talk about it. I still thought I was only being taught a lesson and they'd return for me. It must be how Eve felt when she realized God wasn't joking." She smiled bitterly at her own naivety, her eyes full of old pain. "I was there for a long time, I thought, though when I got back it had only been a month or two and it emerged that nobody had ever returned here from Aswan. There had been that Green Jihad trouble and everyone was suddenly packed off back to Cairo and from there, after a while, to their respective homes. People assumed the same had happened to me. If only it had! But really, Paul, I wouldn't change it."

I shook my head. "I think you were born in the wrong age, Bea. You should have been a priestess of Amon, maybe. Blessed by the Gods."

"We asked them in to breakfast, Ali and me." Shading her eyes against the sun, she raised her arm to point. "Over there. We had a big tent we were using for everything while the others were away. Our visitors didn't think much of our C-Ral and offered us some of their own rations, which were far tastier. It was just a scout, that ship. I met my lover later. He had a wonderful sense of irony. As he should, after a thousand years on the same shift."

I could bear no more of this familiar modern apocrypha. "Bea. Don't you think you just imagined it? After nobody returned, weren't you anxious? Weren't you disturbed?"

"They weren't away long enough. I didn't know they weren't coming back, Paul. I fell in love. That wasn't imagination. Gradually, we found ourselves unable to resist the mutual attraction. I suppose I regret that." She offered me a sidelong glance I might have thought cunning in someone else. "I don't blame you for not believing it. How can I prove I'm sane? Or that I was sane then?"

I was anxious to assure her of my continuing sympathy. "You're not a liar, Bea. You never were."

"But you think I'm crazy." All at once her voice became more urgent. "You know how terribly dull madness can be. How conventional most delusions are. You never think you could go mad like that. Then maybe it happens. The flying saucers come down and take you off to Venus, or paradise, where war and disease and atmospheric disintegration are long forgotten. You fall in love with a Venusian. Sexual intercourse is forbidden. You break the law. You're cast out of Paradise. You can't have a more familiar myth than that, can you, Paul?" Her tone was disturbing. I made a movement with my hand, perhaps to silence her.

"I loved him," she said. "And then I watched the future wither and fade before my eyes. I would have paid the price, done anything, to get back."

That afternoon, as we returned to Aswan, I was full of desperate, bewildered concern for a sister I knew to be in immediate need of professional help. "We'll sort all this out," I reassured her, "maybe when we get to Geneva. We'll see Frank."

"I'm sorry, Paul." She spoke calmly. "I'm not going back with you. I realized it earlier, when we were out at the site. I'll stay in Aswan, after all."

I resisted the urge to turn away from her, and for a while I could not speak.


### 15: Whereat Serene And Undevoured He Lay . . .

The flight was leaving in two days and there would be no other ticket for her. After she went off, filthy and withered from the heat, I rather selfishly used my whole outstanding water allowance and bathed for several hours as I tried to separate the truth from the fantasy. I thought how ripe the world was for Bea's revelation, how dangerous it might be. I was glad she planned to tell no one else, but would she keep to that decision? My impulse was to leave, to flee from the whole mess before Bea started telling me how she had become involved in black magic. I felt deeply sorry for her and I felt angry with her for not being the strong leader I had looked up to all my life. I knew it was my duty to get her back to Europe for expert attention.

"I'm not interested in proving what's true or false, Paul," she had said after agreeing to meet me at the Osiris next morning. "I just want you to *know*. Do you understand?"

Anxious not to upset her further, I had said that I did.

That same evening I went to find Inspector el-Bayoumi in his office. He put out his cigarette as I came in, shook hands and, his manner both affable and relaxed, offered me a comfortable leather chair. "You've found your sister, Mr von Bek. That's excellent news."

I handed him a "purse" I had brought and told him, in the convoluted manner such occasions demanded, that my sister was refusing to leave, that I had a ticket for her on a flight and that it was unlikely I would have a chance to return to Aswan in the near future. If he could find some reason to hold her and put her on the plane, I would be grateful.

With a sigh of regret – at my folly, perhaps – he handed back the envelope. "I couldn't do it, Mr von Bek, without risking the peace of Aswan, which I have kept pretty successfully for some years. We have a lot of trouble with Green Jihad, you know. I am very short-staffed as a result. You must convince her, my dear sir, or you must leave her here. I assure you, she is much

211

loved and respected. She is a woman of considerable substance and will make her own decisions. I promise, however, to keep you informed."

"By the mail packet? I thought you wanted me to get her out of here!"

"I had hoped you might *persuade* her, Mr von Bek."

I apologized for my rudeness. "I appreciate your concern, Inspector." I put the money back in my pocket and went out to the corniche, catching the first felucca across to the West Bank where this time I paid off my guides before I reached the English House.

The roses were still blooming around the great brick manor and Lady Roper was cutting some of them, laying them carefully in her bucket. "Really, Paul, I don't think you must worry, especially if she doesn't want to talk about her experiences. *We* all know she's telling the truth. Why don't you have a man-to-man with Bernie? There he is, in the kitchen."

Through the window, Sir Bernard waved with his cocoa cup before making a hasty and rather obvious retreat.

## 16: Your Funeral Bores Them With Its Brilliant Doom

Awaking at dawn the next morning I found it impossible to return to sleep. I got up and tried to make some notes but writing down what my sister had told me somehow made it even more difficult to understand. I gave up. Putting on a cotton *gelabea* and some slippers I went down to the almost empty street and walked to the nearest corner café where I ordered tea and a couple of rolls. All the other little round tables were occupied and from the interior came the sound of a scratched Oum Kal Thoum record. The woman's angelic voice, singing the praises of God and the joys of love, reminded me of my schooldays in Fez, when I had lived with my father during his brief entrepreneurial period, before he had returned to England to become a Communist. Then Oum Kal Thoum had been almost a goddess in Egypt. Now she was as popular again, like so many of the old performers who had left a legacy of 78 rpms which could be played on spring-loaded gramophones or the new clockworks which could also play a delicate LP but which few Egyptians could afford. Most of the records were re-pressed from ancient masters purchased from Athenian studios that, fifty years earlier, had mysteriously manufactured most Arabic recordings. The quality of her voice came through the surface noise as purely as it had once sounded through fractured stereos or on crude pirate tapes in the days of licence and waste. *Inte el Hob*, wistful, celebratory, thoughtful, reminded me of the little crooked streets of Fez, the stink of the dyers and tanners, the extraordinary vividness of the colours, the pungent mint bales, the old men who loved to stand and declaim on the matters of the day with anyone who would listen, the smell of fresh saffron, of lavender carried on the backs of donkeys driven by little boys crying *"Balek!"* and insulting, in the vocabulary of a professional soldier, anyone who refused to move aside for them. Life had been sweet then, with unlimited television and cheap air-travel, with any food you could afford and any drink freely available for a few dirhams, and every pleasure in the

213

reach of the common person. The years of Easy, the years of Power, the paradise from which our lazy greed and hungry egos banished us to eternal punishment, to the limbo of the Age of Penury, for which we have only ourselves to blame! But Fez was good, then, in those good, old days.

A little more at peace with myself, I walked down to the river while the muezzin called the morning prayer and I might have been back in the Ottoman Empire, leading the simple, steady life of a small landowner or a civil servant in the family of the Bey. The debris of the river, the ultimate irony of the Nile filling with all the bottles that had held the water needed because we had polluted the Nile, drew my attention. It was as if the water industry had hit upon a perfect means of charging people whatever they wanted for a drink of *eau naturelle*, while at the same time guaranteeing that the Nile could never again be a source of free water. All this further reinforced my assertion that we were not in the Golden Age those New New Aquarians so longed to recreate. We were in a present that had turned our planet into a single, squalid slum, where nothing beautiful could exist for long, unless in isolation, like Lady Roper's rose garden. We could not bring back the Golden Age. Indeed, we were now paying the price of having enjoyed one.

I turned away from the river and went back to the café to find Sheikh Abu Halil sitting in the chair I had recently occupied. "What a coincidence, Mr von Bek. How are you? How is your wonderful sister?" He spoke educated English.

I suspected for a moment that he knew more than he allowed but then I checked myself. My anxiety was turning into paranoia. This was no way to help my sister.

"I was killing time," he said, "before coming to see you. I didn't want to interrupt your beauty sleep or perhaps even your breakfast, but I guessed aright. You have the habits of Islam." He was flattering me and this in itself was a display of friendship or, at least, affection.

"I've been looking at the rubbish in the river." I shook his hand and sat down in the remaining chair. "There aren't enough police to do anything about it, I suppose."

"Always a matter of economics." He was dressed very differently today in a conservative light and dark blue *gelabea*, like an Alexandrian businessman. On his head he wore a discreet matching cap. "You take your sister back today, I understand Dr von Bek."

"If she'll come."

"She doesn't want to go?" The Sufi's eyelid twitched almost raffishly, suggesting to me that he had been awake most of the night. Had he spent that time with Bea?

"She's not sure now," I said. "She hates flying."

"Oh, yes. Flying is a very difficult and unpleasant thing. I myself hate it and would not do it if I could."

I felt he understood far more than that and I was in some way relieved. "You couldn't persuade her of the wisdom of coming with me, I suppose, Sidhi?"

"I have already told her what I think, Paul. I think she should go with you. She is unhappy here. Her burden is too much. But she would not and will not listen to me. I had hoped to congratulate you and wish you God Speed."

"You're very kind." I now believed him sincere.

"I love her, Paul." He gave a great sigh and turned to look up at the sky. "She's an angel! I think so. She will come to no harm from us."

"Well—" I was once again at a loss. "I love her too, sidhi. But does she want our love, I wonder?"

"You are wiser than I thought, Paul. Just so. Just so." He ordered coffee and sweetac for us both. "She knows only the habit of giving. She has never learned to receive. Not here, anyway. Especially from you."

"She was always my best friend." I said. "A mother, sometimes. An alter ego. I want to get her to safety, Sheikh Abu Halil."

"Safety?" At this he seemed sceptical. "It would be good for her to know the normality of family life. She has a husband."

"He's in New Zealand. They split up. He hated what he called her 'charity work'."

"If he was unsympathetic to her calling, that must be inevitable."

"You really think she has a vocation?" The coffee came and the oversweetened breakfast cakes which he ate with considerable relish. "We don't allow these at home. All those chemicals!" There was an element of self-mockery in his manner now that he was away from his *madrassah*. "Yes. We think she has been called. We have many here who believe that of themselves, but most are self-deluding. Aswan is becoming a little over-stocked with mystics and wonder-workers. Eventually, I suppose, the fashion will change, as it did in Nepal, San Francisco or Essaouira. Your sister, however, is special to us. She is so sad, these days, doctor. There is a chance she might find happiness in London. She is spending too long in the desert."

"Isn't that one of the habitual dangers of the professional mystic?" I asked him.

He responded with quiet good humour. "Perhaps of the more old-fashioned type, like me. Did she ever tell you what she passed to Lallah Zenobia that night?"

"You mean the cause of her arrest? Wasn't it money? A purse. The police thought it was."

"But if so, Paul, what was she buying?"

"Peace of mind, perhaps," I said. I asked him if he really believed in people from space, and he said that he did, for he believed that God had created and populated the whole universe as He saw fit. "By the way," he said. "Are you walking up towards the Cataract? There was some kind of riot near there an hour or so ago. The police were involved and some of the youngsters from the holiday villas. Just a peaceful demonstration, I'm sure. That would be nothing to do with your sister?"

I shook my head.

"You'll go back to England, will you, Dr von Bek?"

"Eventually," I told him. "The way I feel at the moment I might retire. I want to write a novel."

"Oh, your father was a vicar, then?"

I was thoroughly puzzled by this remark. Again he began to laugh. "I do apologize. I've always been struck by the curious fact that so much enduring English literature has sprung, as it were, from the loins of the minor clergy. I wish you luck, Dr von Bek, in whatever you choose to do. And I hope your sister decides to go with you tomorrow." He kissed me three times on my face. "You both need to discover your own peace. *Sabah el Kher.*"

"*Allah yisabbe'h Kum bil-Kher.*"

The holy man waved a dignified hand as he strolled down towards the corniche to find a calash.

By now the muezzin was calling the mid-morning prayer. I had been away from my hotel longer than planned. I went back through the crowds to the green and white entrance of the Osiris and climbed slowly to my room. It was not in my nature to force my sister to leave and I felt considerably ashamed of my attempt to persuade Inspector el-Bayoumi to extradite her. I could only pray that, in the course of the night, she had come to her senses. My impulse was to seek her out but I still did not know her address.

I spent the rest of the morning packing and making official notes until, at noon, she came through the arch-way, wearing a blue cotton dress and matching shawl. I hoped this was a sign she was preparing for the flight back to civilization. "You haven't eaten, have you?" she said.

She had booked a table on the Mut, a floating restaurant moored just below the Cataract. We boarded a thing resembling an Ottoman pleasure barge, all dark green trellises, scarlet fretwork and brass ornament, while inside it was more luxurious than the Sufi's "harem". "It's hardly used, of course, these days," Bea said. "Not enough rich people wintering in Aswan any more. But the atmosphere's nice still. You don't mind? It's not against your puritan nature, is it?"

"Only a little." I was disturbed by her apparent normality. We might never have ridden into the desert together, never have talked about aliens and spaceships and Ancient Egyptian universities. I wondered, now, if she were not seriously schizophrenic.

"You do seem troubled, though." She was

218

interrupted by a large man in a dark yellow *gelabea* smelling wildly of garlic who embraced her with affectionate delight. "Beatrice! My Beatrice!" We were introduced. Mustafa shook hands with me as he led us ecstatically to a huge, low table looking over the Nile, where the feluccas and great sailing barges full of holidaymakers came close enough to touch. We sat on massive brocaded foam cushions.

I could not overcome my depression. I was faced with a problem beyond my scope. "You've decided to stay, I take it?"

The major-domo returned with two large glasses of Campari Soda. "Compliments of the house." It was an extraordinary piece of generosity. We saluted him with our glasses, then toasted each other.

"Yes. She drew her hair over her collar and looked towards the water. "For a while, anyway. I won't get into any more trouble, Paul, I promise. And I'm not the suicide type. That I'm absolutely sure about."

"Good." I would have someone come out to her as soon as possible, a psychiatrist contact in MEDAC who could provide a professional opinion.

"You'll tell me your address?"

"I'm moving. Tomorrow. I'll stay with the Ropers if they'll have me. Any mail care of them will be forwarded. I'm not being deliberately mysterious, dear, I promise. I'm going to write. And meanwhile, I've decided to tell you the whole of it. I want you to remember it, perhaps put it into some kind of shape that I can't. It's important to me that it's recorded. Do you promise?"

I could only promise that I would make all the notes possible.

219

"Well, there's actually not much else."

I was relieved to know I would not for long have to suffer those miserably banal inventions.

"I fell in love, you see."

"Yes, you told me. With a spaceman."

"We knew it was absolutely forbidden to make love. But we couldn't help ourselves. I mean, with all his self-discipline he was as attracted to me as I was to him. It was important, Paul."

I did my best to give her my full attention while she repeated much of what she had already told me in the desert. There was a kind of Biblical rhythm to her voice. "So they threw me out. I never saw my lover again. I never saw his home again. They brought me back and left me where they had found me. Our tents were gone and everything was obviously abandoned. They let their engines blow more sand over the site. Well, I got to Aswan eventually. I found water and food and it wasn't too hard. I'm not sure why I came here. I didn't know then that I was pregnant. I don't think I knew you could get pregnant. There isn't a large literature on sexual congress with semi-males of the alien persuasion. You'd probably find him bizarre, but for me it was like making love to an angel. All the time. It was virtually our whole existence. Oh, Paul!" She pulled at her collar. She smoothed the tablecloth between her knife and fork. "Well, he was wonderful and he thought I was wonderful. Maybe that's *why* they forbid it. The way they'd forbid a powerful habit-forming stimulant. Do you know I just this second thought of that?"

"That's why you were returned here?" I was still having difficulty following her narrative.

"Didn't I say? Yes. Well, I went to stay with the

Ropers for a bit, then I stayed in the commune and then the *madrassah*, but I kept going out to the site. I was hoping they'd relent, you see. I'd have done almost anything to get taken back, Paul."

"To escape from here, you mean?"

"To be with him. That's all. I was – I am – so lonely. Nobody could describe the void."

I was silent, suddenly aware of her terrible vulnerability, still convinced she had been the victim of some terrible deception.

"You're wondering about the child," she said. She put her hand on mine where I fingered the salt. "He was born too early. He lived for eight days. I had him at Lallah Zenobia's. You see, I couldn't tell what he would look like. She was better prepared, I thought. She even blessed him when he was born so that his soul might go to heaven. He was tiny and frail and beautiful. His father's colouring and eyes. My face, I think, mostly. He would have been a *wunderkind*, I shouldn't be surprised. Paul . . ." Her voice became a whisper. "It was like giving birth to the Messiah."

With great ceremony, our meal arrived. It was a traditional Egyptian *meze* and it was more and better food than either of us had seen in years. Yet we hardly ate.

"I took him back to the site." She looked out across the water again. "I'd got everything ready. I had some hope his father would come to see him. Nobody came. Perhaps it needed that third sex to give him the strength? I waited, but there was not, as the kids say, a Reen to be seen." This attempt at humour was hideous. I took firm hold of her hands. The tears in her eyes were barely restrained.

"He died." She released her hands and looked for something in her bag. I thought for a frightening moment she was going to produce a photograph. "Eight days. He couldn't seem to get enough nourishment from what I was feeding him. He needed that – whatever it was he should have had." She took a piece of linen from her bag and wiped her hands and neck. "You're thinking I should have taken him to the hospital. But this is Egypt, Paul, where people are still arrested for witchcraft and here was clear evidence of my having had congress with an *ifrit*. Who would believe my story? I was aware of what I was doing. I'd never expected the baby to live or, when he did live, to look the way he did. The torso was sort of pear-shaped and there were several embryonic limbs. He was astonishingly lovely. I think he belonged to his father's world. I wish they had come for him. It wasn't fair that he should die."

I turned my attention to the passing boats and controlled my own urge to weep. I was hoping she would stop, for she was, by continuing, hurting herself. But, obsessively, she went on. "Yes, Paul. I could have gone to Europe as soon as I knew I was pregnant and I would have done if I'd had a hint of what was coming, but my instincts told me he would not live or, if he did live, it would be because his father returned for him. I don't think that was self-deception. Anyway, when he was dead I wasn't sure what to do. I hadn't made any plans. Lallah Zenobia was wonderful to me. She said she would dispose of the body properly and with respect. I couldn't bear to have some future archaeologist digging him up. You know, I've always hated that. Especially with children. So I went to her lean-to

in Shantytown. I had him wrapped in a shawl –
Mother's lovely old Persian shawl – and inside a
beautiful inlaid box. I put the box in a leather bag and
took it to her."

"That was the Cairene Purse? Or did you give her
money, too?"

"Money had nothing to do with it. Do the police still
think I was paying her? I offered Zenobia money but
she refused. 'Just pray for us all,' was what she said. I've
been doing it every night since. The Lord's prayer for
everyone. It's the only prayer I know. I learnt it at one
of my schools."

"Zenobia went to prison. Didn't you try to tell them
she was helping you?"

"There was no point in mentioning the baby, Paul.
That would have constituted another crime, I'm sure.
She was as good as her word. He was never found. She
made him safe somewhere. A little funeral boat on the
river late at night, away from all the witnesses, maybe.
And they would have found him if she had been
deceiving me, Paul. She got him home somehow."

Dumb with sadness, I could only reach out and
stroke her arms and hands, reach for her unhappy face.

We ate so as not to offend our host, but without
appetite. Above the river the sun was at its zenith and
Aswan experienced the familiar, unrelenting light of an
African afternoon.

She looked out at the river with its day's flow of debris,
the plastic jars, the used sanitary towels, the paper and
filth left behind by tourists and residents alike.

With a deep, uneven sigh, she shook her head, folded
her arms under her breasts and leaned back in the
engulfing foam.

All the *fhouls* and the marinated salads, the *ruqaq* and the meats lay cold before us as, from his shadows, the proprietor observed us with discreet concern.

There came a cry from outside. A boy perched high on the single mast of his boat, his white *gelabea* tangling with his sail so that he seemed all of a piece with the vessel, waved to friends on the shore and pointed into the sky. One of our last herons circled overhead for a moment and then flew steadily south, into what had been the Sudan.

My sister's slender body was moved for a moment by some small, profound anguish.

"He could not have lived here."

# FURNITURE

*For Jewell Hodges*

There's something to be said, she thought, for spending money on old-fashioned furniture. Most of this modern stuff's rubbish. Just look at the joints. Dovetailing's a forgotten art. All wire staples and hardboard. And the price! She'd had her table since she and Mo got married. Just like her mum's. *That oak's hard as iron.* Vi Corren smiled.

She'd be dead now if it wasn't for good furniture. When this bomb went off, her table had somehow been lifted across her chair, protecting her from the collapsing walls. It was pitch dark, so she knew there'd be a lot on top of her. But she didn't think she was in any immediate danger. And her chair was solid as a rock.

The suite was in perfect condition when she bought it at MacMurtry's. Hardly used. It cost a fraction of that spindly modern stuff. OK for a coffee bar, but you wouldn't want it in your home.

225

MacMurtry's furniture was *better* than new. Made by real craftsmen, like her dad. Sound as a bell. Good prices. Of course, she had everything thoroughly cleaned.

Give me what you want to spend, she'd tell Mo. And then let me go and find what I want. He'd been glad of her savings when his back went out that time.

Over the years most of her furniture came from MacMurtry's. That lovely sideboard, her cabinets. Mick MacMurtry had a big shop on the corner of Old Sweden Street. When his lease ran out they knocked the whole block down and erected some sort of insurance building. She couldn't get on with all these new featureless skyscrapers.

Her dad had been a joiner and worked for Heals. Mo's dad had been a Princelet Street tailor. "You tell me about three-piece *suits*," she'd say, "and I'll tell you about three-piece *suites*."

He'd always liked her humour. He was a couple of years younger. The only kid she had, she told people affectionately. He'd be retiring soon and she'd be glad of it. He wanted a clean break from Brookgate. He'd set his heart on Tudor Hamlets. There wouldn't be any argument from her now. She'd love a little garden.

The big armchair moved under her like a living monster.

*Oh!*

Huge stones groaning in the darkness overhead.

Then a terrible stillness.

Dust fell. Something squeaked and scraped and juddered, but the table held.

"No time for panic, Vi."

She breathed slowly and easily, the way she did at the

dentist. She refused to think of all the rubble that had to be on top of her.

Another noise. Not a shot. Guns made a simultaneous *crack, thud, bang*. This was like something snapping.

"Calm down, Vi."

Most of her childhood Brookgate was already gone. Buried under glassy concrete. Streets you didn't recognize. People you didn't know. No proper shops. Really, it would be a relief to move. Their insurance would easily cover them, though finding the furniture would be a problem. Everything decent was an antique, these days. Those old parlour drawleafs, still with their wartime utility marks, were selling to Americans for hundreds.

All their married life Mo had complained about her taste. Being a cabby, he picked up the latest trends. She'd bowed to him on decorations but she'd been firm about the furniture.

*A second-hand table saved my life in 1945.* They'd had an indoor shelter – steel sheeting and wire screens around your ordinary table. She felt so safe sleeping under it. Then the V2 hit Bacon Street. Mum at the pictures. Dad catching a few hours upstairs. The ARP dug her out. Bruised, stiff and wheezing, but unhurt. Just this permanent allergy to dust. She could feel her skin coming up now. The *Mirror* had called her The Miracle Girl. There'd been quite a few miracles in 1945. She loved to see the sun come up over St Paul's. If she had a wish it would be to enjoy one more London sunrise without all these new buildings in the way.

Mo had insisted on buying their flat. He'd seen ahead. You could ask any price you liked for a ground

floor since the boom. Business people wanting somewhere near the City. Not much of the flat left now! Just
the table, the chair and her. The basics.

She was surprised by her own spontaneous laughter.
She was almost relieved. She spoke aloud, into the
settling dust.

"I could do with a cup of tea."

Still, then she'd need to go to the toilet. So it was
probably for the best. She wondered what the time was.
She'd find out soon from the wireless. When she knew
they were searching for her, she'd turned it off to save
the battery. These new headphones were so good she
hadn't heard the loudspeakers outside. What a fool!
Everyone safe but her. Even the cat. People thought
she'd left in the first evacuation. Mistaken her for the
other Mrs Corren. Ticked her off the residents' list. The
other Mrs Corren wouldn't have said anything.

They'd double-checked. But even if you stuck your
head round the door you couldn't see a person sitting in
this big chair. So while everybody else responded to the
bomb warning, she'd been in a world of her own,
looking out of her window at the grey drizzle, the slow,
reflective concrete, listening to her tape. *Velia, O, Velia,
the witch of the wood* . . . Looking forward to Mo
bringing in their usual Friday fish and chips.

According to the news, it had been a huge explosion
centred on the bank next door. As warned, it had gone
off at exactly eight p.m. She must have blacked out
when it happened.

Terrible devastation. All the surrounding office
blocks affected. The wireless had said Mo was on his
way home when he heard the news. He usually rang her
on his mobile. A real worrier, Mo. She felt so sorry for

228

him. He hadn't had her happy childhood.

Her mum had just been glad she was alive. Aunties all over the place. So much space. So much freedom. Ruins to play in. A vast adventure playground. And something more: that rediscovery of a wise, safe, dreaming, dignified, permanent London only made visible again by Hitler's bombs.

A high price to pay, though.

She remembered when she'd run barefoot over grass, through the rosebay willowherb and dandelions and cow parsley down to St Paul's. Good old St Paul's. Thanks to the bombs you had a clear view across the city. Ludgate Circus. The Old Bailey. The way it had been centuries ago. The Tower. The Mint. Not much in the way of tourists, then. She'd known so many people. She'd loved it, running everywhere she wanted to go, cycling over footpaths trodden down to Smithfield, the river, the Customs House, Billingsgate. Wild flowers blooming. All the markets doing noisy business. In the evening, when the office workers had gone to their stations, you could sit on a ruined roof and watch the sun set over great stretches of river. Timeless security in the heart of the city.

As a girl she'd volunteered for the hardest paper round just so she could get up before dawn and stand on a pile of weed-grown rubble to watch the sun rise over St Paul's. You couldn't do that any more, now that they'd built those big, brutal barbicans.

What kind of happy childhood was it, she wondered, that made you so nostalgic for ruins? Ruins were all she'd really known. And there were so few records of them. Lots of pictures of Brookgate before the war, when all the old buildings were still standing. Lots of stuff afterwards, with the big cranes and the permanent scaffolding. By then she was working at the old cigarette factory and the big changes all went on behind hoardings. Then they closed the factory and turned it into executive offices. She got a job at Mullards, Clerkenwell, until that went, too, under that computer tower.

Her childhood had been wonderful. They never really left London. After staying in Wales for a week, they'd all come home. Mum said she'd rather die of an air raid than die of boredom. The peace and quiet got on your nerves. Made you think about things too much. Better to be in it and doing something than out of it and worrying all the time. She'd wanted to be near Dad.

Vi's hands were numb. She wished she could get up and move around. She turned on the wireless.

Radio Five. Some chat about sports, then, abruptly, the news. It was five in the morning. Rescue workers still had hopes of finding her alive. A real drama.

Her chair shook and the table overhead scraped a bit lower. She could feel its pressure on her left shoulder. Like the weight of the earth.

A long moment. It seemed like an hour.

Something fell towards her and seemed to land at her feet. There was a rushing sound, a human yell. Then a surprising gap in the darkness. Lights. Dogs barking. Distant voices. She drew a deep breath of the cool air and shouted. "Here. I'm here." Her voice was too hoarse. "Here!"

Exclamations. More scrabbling. The sound of a motor. Urgent tones. Instructions. Something moved. The table shifted again, but this time the pressure eased.

The patch of pale grey widened. It was the outside.

Shadows. Torch beams. Something flashed in her eyes.

"Are you OK, love?"

"Well, I could do with a cup of tea."

"We're just bracing all this rubbish up so we can get you out properly." The face in the torchlight was heavily bearded, wearing a turban. Was it Doctor Singh?

He smiled. "And I'll tell Tom to put the kettle on."

Suddenly she was freezing. The morning air. She was only wearing a pair of light slacks and a cotton sweater.

Another squeak and the table was off her shoulder altogether. The bearded man was crawling carefully towards her. "We're going to make it. We're going to make it, love." He seemed to be reassuring himself. She wasn't worried at all. She had faith in her furniture.

But when he reached her she almost cried, gripping his lovely warm hand.

"Now we're both under the table," she said. He smiled, checking this, feeling that.

"Nothing wrong with me, doc."

"Amazing."

He murmured rapidly and calmly into his mobile phone.

"We shan't have any trouble getting you clear. The explosion blew most of the heavy stuff away from you. This table formed a sort of shelter. You're a lucky woman, Mrs Corren."

"Oh, I know that, dear," she said. "This isn't the first time I've been stuck in a bit of rubble. Could you ring my husband and tell him I'm all right?"

"He knows by now, love, don't worry. He's out there waiting."

"It's done terrible damage, hasn't it?"

He was bleak. "You wouldn't recognize anything. All in ruins. Your chances were a million to one. Like winning the lottery."

The big steel arms were dragging the concrete back, as if a curtain lifted. Dawn light. Dawn breezes on her face. It was like being born.

"Oh!"

Suddenly she could see her rescuers, the sky, the broken landscape, the vast, shallow crater, the rubble beyond.

The light revealed more and more. Through a smoky haze she could see all the way to St Paul's.

"It's a miracle," he said. "A genuine miracle."

She watched as the sun began to rise, a radiant harmony of pale golds and reds, behind the cathedral's glittering dome.

"Yes," she said. "You can always rely on good furniture."

# THROUGH THE SHAVING MIRROR; or How We Abolished the Future

After Maurice Richardson

"Has anyone noticed," Monsignor Cornelius spoke urgently, hoping to divert Sir Perkin Float, on his third bottle of claret, from developing that familiar litany about discovering Chaos Math years before Mandelbrot, thus being cheated of his place in history and his video royalties, "how cats can turn off time? With a suitable lens, of course."

Engelbrecht, the dwarf metaphysical boxer, grew alert. Professional curiosity. A founder of the Surrealist Sporting Club, he refused to fight anything lighter than a cathedral clock. Against advice he'd challenged Big Ben to a 'no quarter' fin-de-millennium celebratory bout. Serious Soho backers. Chinese calendar promoters. That the parliamentary clock had accepted was surprising, that it lost was suspicious. Strong rumbles in the sporting fancy. Someone had slipped the monster timepiece a heavy envelope to lie down. London was

233

now on Chinese time with all serious punters refusing mah-jong bets involving politicians.

"It reminds me," said the time-battered pug, "of that night in New York I almost lost to the Union Square Clock Tower. My career would have been over if it hadn't been for some fancy photon-work."

Tactfully, the Corinthian Jesuit drew us into Engelbrecht's confidence. "Your mother discovered that time isn't a dimension of space, but a field whose properties are affected by the nature of space existing within it?"

"Space a quality of time?" Sir Perkin snorted into his wine. Glinting rubies fell to the linen. But Cornelius's clever sourcing meant outright disagreement would be dangerous.

Clearing the cloth, Engelbrecht used a carpenter's pencil and the condensed mathematical logic developed at his famous Marrakesh ashram to illuminate us. "Time alters when it interacts with space. In common with all observable nature, the universe, or multiverse, grows organically and is best imagined as a vast tree, or perhaps even a forest with common roots."

"And the soil for this tree?" Float's reckless scepticism terrified us. Expensive watches would only be the first victims of our dwarf's distemper.

The tiny slugger observed philosophically that this was the level of logic he must commonly suffer. "An analogy," he growled. "There's a theory that the multiverse is created by the common will, but as to its origins . . . ?" He cracked his knuckles. "I think, therefore I thump."

Float's timid attention returned to the claret. The merest whisper of big bangs had him reaching for his jug.

Engelbrecht scowled reminiscently. "We're familiar

234

with the disappearing neutron, we've recently learned how light can travel faster than light. Conventional method produces Heath Robinson physics turned into formulae by crazed Euclidians. At some point, as Columbus told the Pope, we have to let go of the premise that the world is flat."

"Can we see these alternative worlds?" 'Prof' Aspinall had been kicking the gong around and wasn't ready for further shocks.

Cornelius embellished smoothly. "I understand it's a question of scale and mass. Put simply, millions of subtly different versions of our reality are separated by size. Each version, though scarcely different in terms of the multiversal compass, is as invisible to us as if we were only seeing a single magnified pixel out of a complex computer image. We never see the whole. It is either too small or too large. We coexist in the same space through scale. Each alternative world has greater or lesser density and is invisible to the others."

"Proliferating to infinity. Whales, fairies," Engelbrecht paused. "Dwarves."

"Space curves," mumbled 'Prof' into his spoon. "Don't it?"

"Organically and often, as a branch curves." Cornelius smiled. "Like ourselves, space consists of spheres, but isn't itself spherical. Nature would be contradicted if it were. Certain entities somehow adjust their mass and move 'intrabranally'. For instance, few creatures are as expert at varying their size as cats. Thus their mysterious 'disappearances'. Happily the phenomenon hasn't occurred with dogs."

"Bigfoot, however . . ." 'Prof' began.

"Cats," said Cornelius hastily, "see space invisible to

us, coming and going through the multiverse pretty much at will."

"Bunkum," hiccuped Float. "We were supposed to hear about that New York match our dwarf won by a whisker. In funny circumstances."

Engelbrecht swelled. "A classy clock fighting for a consortium of Istanbul high rollers backing the Julian calendar. Twice my form and landing some tricky Byzantine jabs. By Round Sixty I'd borrowed all available time. I'm on my back looking like someone just unwrapped the Mummy.

"I've already squared the ref, of course. While shaving I've also dreamed up some insurance. Fortunately I have a prism hidden in one glove, a photon in the other. Resting on the count with my hands invisible I pull Harness's old baffled-quantum trick. On nine. Works like a charm. Time hesitates. My seconds Coleman and Benford produce the mirror, rescaling mass and size to shrink the heavy bastard enough so I can stagger up and deliver the dynamite. Gravity completes the job. Down he goes. Dead weight. Space-time readjusts. It's all over. The new reality! The Yankee Boomer's stretched full size on the canvas, his gob-smacked hands chasing themselves round his face. Cheering punters. GMT keeps the title!"

"Convincing," admitted Aspinall. "Except no way would Coleman and Benford help snatch a fix."

Engelbrecht winked. "Prof, you can't name a physicist in the multiverse who isn't in my pocket. Now, padre, your cats?"

"Oh, another time I think," said Cornelius, contentedly filling his pipe.

Float was at last profoundly asleep.

236

# LOST LONDON WRITERS

*For Iain Sinclair*

Few modern Londoners are willing to die for their city's honour like John Scott, passionate editor of *The London Magazine*, who published Leigh Hunt, Lamb, Hazlitt, Shelley, Keats and *The Opium Eater* in the 1820s. Scott was killed in a duel with a representative of his bitter Edinburgh rival, the aggressively Tory *Blackwood's*, which derided his London writers as 'Cockneys'. There wasn't a happier name for those eloquent radicals who shared London's profound sense of democracy. In 1813, Hunt got two years for describing the Prince of Wales as a libertine 'without one claim on the gratitude of his country or the respect of posterity'. In Horsemonger Road jail, Southwark, Hunt made himself defiantly at home, almost ethereal in the vast, loose-flying nightgown he always wore for work, entertaining his friends and decorating his cell.

Hunt's amiable *London Journal*, according to a contemporary, 'illumined the fog and smoke of London with a halo of glory, and peopled the streets and buildings with the life of past generations.' But it was the modern world that really fascinated the Cockneys. By 1820, when George IV ruled at last, Byron's Don Juan saw 'a mighty mass of brick, and smoke, and shipping' – a city we recognize as our own.

While Shakespeare's plays addressed Londoners with familiar references, it took the likes of Thomas Dekker (*The Shoemaker's Holiday*, *The Bel-man of London*) and Ben Jonson (*Bartholomew Fair*) to make London a subject as much as a scene and begin a literary relationship with the capital herself. In *A Journal of the Plague Year*, Defoe was perhaps the first to create London as fiction, with all his convincing tricks of invented detail. Then, somewhere between Defoe and Dickens, between the Age of Satire and the Age of Sentiment, certainly via Blake, 'the Towne' became The City. A sentient, often threatening monster, bigger than the sum of her parts.

"Blake showed Southey a perfectly mad poem called 'Jerusalem'. Oxford Street is in Jerusalem," said Crabb Robinson, a founder of London University. "Oxford-street, stony-hearted step-mother! Thou that listenest to the sighs of orphans, and drinkest the tears of children," said the Opium Eater. Hardly an ideal location for Mothercare, the Virgin Megastore, or even Waterstones.

Not all De Quincey's contemporaries shared his opinion. For them Oxford Street was mere background to tales of high society. Thackeray satirized these so-called 'Silver Fork' novelists whose doyen was the witty, readable Mrs Gore (*Modern Chivalry, Peers and Parvenus*). Serialized in *Belgravia* and *London Society*, they shared shelves at Mudie's Library with their Gothic and sometimes more questioning sisters Mrs Radcliffe, Mrs Reeve, Mrs Shelley and the lively Maria Edgeworth (*Belinda*). My own literary ancestress, Rachel Moorcock (*Gleanings from the Apocalypse, Poland, The Death of Cobden*) supported parliamentary reform and universal suffrage. A convinced dissenter, she had no time for the anti-Romish fiction written by militant Protestants like Mrs Craven (who dedicated a novel 'TO *THE ALMIGHTY!!*'), Mrs Sewell (*Hawkstone*), or Catherine Sinclair whose *London Homes* sounds so pleasantly genteel in contrast to its contents — *The Murder Hole, The Drowning Dragoon, The Priest and the Curate* &c.

Dickens was the greatest writer to turn London into a creature, but he had many imitators and rivals. Massive bestsellers in their day, they contributed to the idea of the Thames as a stinking, murky Styx, its surrounding slums the city's corrupted, fascinating heart.

Some, like Harrison Ainsworth, specialized in bloody historical melodramas that would later feed Hollywood (*The Tower of London, Old St Paul's*). Others, like the unfairly neglected Sir Walter Besant (*The Chaplain of the Fleet, St Catherine's by the Tower*), tried to paint an accurate picture of London through fact and fiction from earliest times. Steeped in Scott, often inspired by De Quincey's opium extravagances, imitated by scores of popular serial writers (*Night Rider of London Fields, Mysteries of London*) they created an authentic myth, more potent than fact.

239

The myth becomes derisory when sentimentalized by Hollywood, but easily survives assault. In that invented city Holmes and the Ripper, Jekyll and Hyde, struggle forever in a foggy Whitechapel never bombed or redeveloped and the whole stew of English class, repression and neurosis, achieves a universal symbolism.

Almost buried under that heavy myth lies the equally authentic city we recognize in Steele, Smollett, Fielding, Gay and Thackeray. It is a domestic city, a vulgar city, a cruelly snobbish and comically arrogant city, a busy, greedy, good-humoured, generous city, a trading city, a supremely articulate and democratic city. A jolly jeering fishwife rather than a leering whore.

Whether describing London society (Mrs Ritchie's excellent *Old Kensington*), barge life on the Thames (Marryat's *Jacob Faithful*, whose spontaneous-combustion scene rivals Dickens's) or the 'gay' world of London's pleasure gardens and gambling houses (Pierce Egan's *Life in London*, introducing the original Tom & Jerry) it's a place generally more familiar to us than George Gissing's Grub Street, Edgar Wallace's Limehouse or even Peter Ackroyd's haunted Spitalfields. It's frequently salacious, as in the low life tales and fake autobiographies of famous rakes and courtesans. That exemplary hack, Michael Cornelius O'Crook, saw his *London Rakehell*, *London By Night* and *Love Frolics of a Young Scamp* bought eagerly, swiftly enjoyed and as casually binned as a modern tabloid.

In the last quarter of the nineteenth century, and thanks to the reforming efforts of her writers, London changed. The worst slums were cleared, public health improved and education was made universal. Authors emerged whose literary values were often shared with

Wilde, Beerbohm and the *fin de siècle*, but whose work was driven more by social conscience. They'd taken advantage of idealistic educational ventures like the People's Palace, the Normal School of Science, University College and the Birkbeck Institute, all set up to provide people without means with a first-class education.

The impeccable Walter Besant was a founder of the Palace (suggested in his novel *All Sorts and Conditions of Men*) and his passion for social reform was their inspiration. Coming from impoverished backgrounds, they were determined to look at London's problems with unsentimental eyes. Admiring Gissing, they were temperamentally indisposed to examine his depths. Their writing shared something with the best music-hall songs, *My Old Man*, *The Houses in Between* or *The Future Mrs 'Awkins*, sung by observant wits like Marie Lloyd or Gus Elen.

After Arthur Morrison, whose *Tales of Mean Streets* remains the best portrait of East End life before the slum clearances, my own favourite is the prolific W. Pett Ridge, champion of social causes and creator of *Maude Em'ly*, who in the 1890s begins her determined career in one of South London's infamous girl gangs. Pett Ridge is an invaluable memoirist. With a score or two of highly readable novels, he left us *A Story Teller*, *Forty Years a Londoner*, and other unique reminiscences of his world. He worked with W.T. Stead, campaigning editor of *The Pall Mall Gazette*, who would go down in the *Titanic*. Soon after H.G. Wells's first sale to the *Gazette*, Pett Ridge introduced him to J.M. Barrie, then best known as a novelist. Barrie's published advice had encouraged a hopeless Wells to sell his first article to the *P.M.G.*

Featuring Conan Doyle, Grant Allen, L.T. Meade and the great urban adventure-story writers, the illustrated monthlies, *London, Strand* and *Pall Mall*, ran some other outstanding contributors – the likes of Leonard Merrick (*The Actor Manager*), Richard Whiteing (*No. 5 John Street*), E. Nesbit (*Daphne in Fitzroy Street, Harding's Luck*), W.W. Jacobs (*A Master of Craft, The Lady of the Barge*), Arthur Morrison (*A Child of the Jago, The Hole in the Wall*), Barry Pain (*De Omnibus*), Israel Zangwill (*The King of Schnorrers*), H.M. Tomlinson (*Old Junk*), and a little later Compton Mackenzie (*Our Street*) evoke a London of cobbles, fierce class divisions, sardonic humour, killing disease, vicious crime, knockers-up and blanket-funds which even then, through their efforts, was vanishing. Characteristically, these writers offered their readers an ordinary domestic mirror rather than Dickens's dark reflective river. Ordinary Londoners were seen to be sarcastic, sympathetic, quick-witted and profoundly democratic.

We've known Trollope's, Disraeli's and Gals-worthy's London, the Westminster of *Mrs Dalloway*, Shaw Desmond's sporting and night-time London, Michael Arlen's languid Mayfair, Wodehouse's fantasy clubland, Waugh's *demi-monde*. The menaced Fitzrovia of Bowen's *The Heat of the Day*, Greene's surrealistic *The Ministry of Fear* and Hamilton's *Hangover Square* merge with fog-diffused images of Allingham's convincing parables, *Tiger in the Smoke* and *Hide My Eyes*, the half-real Notting Hill of MacInnes's *City of Spades*, the crooked Soho and East End of Frank Norman's *Bang To Rights* and the shabby-genteel Kensington of Angus Wilson's *Such Darling Dodos*. As non-fiction William Kent's *London for Everyman*, Elliott's *Heartbeat London*, Raban's *Soft City* or Nicholas Shakespeare's *Londoners* perpetuate Besant's enquiring tradition. London's transformed again in the hands of so many enthusiastic modern writers, but few display the same obsessed, complicated creative relationship with the city as do Ackroyd and Sinclair.

If Ballard's symbolic suburbs could be anywhere and aren't strong on slapstick, Jack Trevor Story's suburbs and dormitory towns are rooted in comic reality. They give an ironically affectionate picture of the aspiring post-war lower middle class. Story put phrases into the language. He wrote *The Trouble With Harry* and was typically ruined when Hitchcock bought it. He wrote *Live Now, Pay Later* and *The Urban District Lover*, whose film versions sometimes re-emerge on cable. He wrote the best of Adam Faith's *Budgie*. For years he described his life and adventures in a weekly column for *The Guardian*. Women loved him. He had an innocent, knowing, honest eye. His worlds and Mike Leigh's have much in common. The Jack Trevor Story Memorial Prize, given in conjunction with Nicholas Royle's *Time Out Book of New Writers*, is awarded on condition that the money be blown in two weeks and the recipient not have a thing to show for it. His exhilarating, unguardedly autobiographical *One Last Mad Embrace* is only matched by my other lasting favourite, Gerald Kersh's *Fowler's End*.

Unspeakably depressing, Fowler's End, N.E. has a mephitic cinema. The manager's struggles with his quarrelsome punters make this perhaps the funniest of

243

MICHAEL MOORCOCK

Kersh's marvellous books. Self-invented, Kersh came from Twickenham but painted a rich, detailed picture of post-war bohemian/criminal London. He wrote chilling short stories ("The Horrible Dummy" is one) and his best work is unmatched. Reprinted recently, his moody, ambiguous *Night and the City* has been filmed twice.

London inspires wonderful poetry. Like Blake, Aidan Dunn's epic *Vale Royal* has a mystical idealism entirely focused on the city. The most moving narrative poem to emerge from the War was Mervyn Peake's *Rhyme of the Flying Bomb* – which Langdon Jones set to music – with its hallucinatory vision of the city as a living creature, tortured and ruined, but still, in the character of the sailor who finds a baby in the rubble, full of the will not merely to survive but to triumph with dignity. Peake's own drawings of Londoners are superb, reminding us how much Hogarth, Leach, Gilray, Browne, May, Topolski and so many other illustrators contributed to the city's lasting image.

A capital city is civilization's ultimate expression. What we do with it is the best test of our collective creativity and humanity. Disraeli said London is a nation, not a city. While some smugly declare that she isn't the 'real' England, London, like Washington, Tokyo or Berlin *is* the quintessence of her nation's history and aspirations. She's the best of our virtues, the worst of our vices – the true measure of our morality. Despite continuing injustices and irritations, London – thanks in large part to her writers – has always been the richest, most coherent, civilized, tolerant and inspiring cosmopolitan megapolis in the world.

With an inconstant future, a malleable past, a

questionable present, London is forever volatile, forever the same.

If you don't believe me, go to Charing Cross Road, find yourself some Thomas Dekker, Leigh Hunt, Arthur Morrison, Jack Trevor Story or Gerald Kersh, then sit in the Embankment gardens and read to the tranquil hum of traffic until it rains or the resident loony decides you're his significant other. After that, you could always try an afternoon with Pett Ridge and the *Big Issue* on the Northern Line. You'll be surprised how little's changed.

# ACKNOWLEDGEMENTS

A WINTER ADMIRAL was first published in the *Daily Telegraph* (courtesy John Coldstream) 1994*

LONDON BLOOD was first published in *The Time Out Book of London Stories* (courtesy Nicholas Royle) 2000

DOVES IN THE CIRCLE was first published in *The Time Out Book of New York Stories* (courtesy Nicholas Royle) 1997

THE CLAPHAM ANTICHRIST was first published in *Smoke Signals* (ed. London Arts Council) 1993

LONDON BONE was first published in *New Worlds* (courtesy David Garnett) 1997*

THE CAIRENE PURSE was first published in *Zenith* (courtesy David Garnett) 1990. The chapter quotes are from poems or lyrics by: 1. Hood; 2. Khayyam/Fitzgerald; 3. AE; 4. Dylan Thomas; 5. Wheldrake; 6. Yokum; 7. Aeschylus/ MacNiece; 8. Vachel Lindsay; 9. F. Thompson; 10. Peake; 11. Treece; 12. Duffy; 13. Nye; 14. C. D. Lewis; 15. E. St. V. Millay; 16. Nye.

FURNITURE was first broadcast by BBC Radio 4 on *Book at Bedtime*, 1999*

THROUGH THE SHAVING MIRROR was first published in *Nature*, 2000*

LOST LONDON WRITERS was first published in *Waterstones Magazine* (courtesy Andrew Holgate) 1999

*Exists in audio or net audio versions

Michael Moorcock was a central figure in the 'alternative' culture of the sixties and seventies, performing with his own band, The Deep Fix, and with Hawkwind. He has written many novels, won the Guardian Fiction Award for *The Condition of Muzak* and was short-listed for the Whitbread Prize for *Mother London*. In recent years he has achieved an international reputation and is recognised as a major contemporary novelist. A long-time resident of London, he now lives in Texas, USA, with his wife.